ABOUT T

Jon Gray's final school report read: 'Gray's too preoccupied with existential questions.'

True. Questions about life and love. And outer space. So he climbed on trains, planes, and bicycles and escaped to the brightest jungles in Malaysia and the darkest recesses of China. And somewhere that he never, ever wants to go to again.

Now a Post-Graduate in Conflict Resolution from the University of London and having worked with refugees from across the planet, some of the dirtiest windows on the world have opened, fuelling the imagination every writer thrives on.

Based in rural England, Gray pictures the best, fears the worst, and hopes for revelation.

We all need adventures, real and imagined…

Meet Charlie Dangerfield!

And those who were seen dancing were thought to be insane by those who could not hear the music.

Nietzsche

DEADLINE

JON GRAY

DEADLINE
by Jon Gray

Cover design: Hannah Linder Designs

ISBN: 978-1-7399234-0-2

First edition published 2021

A copy of this book has been deposited with the British Library Board.

For Daniel and Hannah

ACKNOWLEDGEMENTS

My primary thanks go to Christina Morgan for her overarching help as ideas-bouncer and editor. Also multiple thanks for the enduring support and perceptively critical inputs of Kerry Cassidy, Catherine Bowdler, Polly Stretton and Lynne Nugent.

Many thanks for the technical skills of the erudite Louis Walpole and Lesley Reynolds. And thanks to Vicky Blunden for her suggestions for crucial structural revisions and to Clare Adams and Tony Hawken for timely line-editing.

Historical thanks to Pete Curphey and Pat Griffin for being inspirational teachers at Hanley Castle.

I am eternally grateful, also, for the invaluable support from the irrepressible Ira Trattner.

I hold huge posthumous gratitude to my fellow caffeine-addict, the genius scriptwriter Troy Kennedy Martin, for our regular Saturday catch-ups in our favourite coffee shop in Portobello Market. As I wrote Chapter 51, I could hear Troy's words: 'You were only supposed to blow the bloody doors off!'

I have to give a shout-out to the cover designer, Hannah Linder, who proved wonderfully insightful.

I am also in awe of those within SIS and GCHQ who assisted but who prefer to remain anonymous. They know to whom I refer. Thank you.

Prologue

"The body lay sprawled in the undergrowth. Losing heat. Gaining moisture," Anna muttered, quietly to herself. She rolled her eyes. Every smug self-help book she'd read had triumphantly stated, 'It's the journey, not the destination.'

Well, so far, her journey had been shit.

And today's destination?

She was lying hidden in someone's back garden, her combat trousers soaking wet, and her body heat ebbing away, as it melted the frost on the foliage crushed beneath her.

She was cold, stiff and alone.

And waiting.

Waiting to photograph a woman cheating on her partner.

Private eye. Sounded exciting at first. But six months in, witnessing infidelity after infidelity, and the job was undoing the last iota of faith she had in finding love herself.

Today's client had contacted her anonymously, the email address a random set of numbers and letters. Nothing unusual there. But a couple of aspects of this job she found very odd. For starters, the target had also been kept anonymous. Hardly conducive to an investigation. An email attachment featured a single photo. A natural blonde. Late twenties. Corporate clothes. Confident smile. Clearly some seniority. Obviously a cropped screenshot from some company website.

But no name.

Weird.

The second thing she couldn't get her head around was the client's insistence on no trailing, only photos to be taken at a given list of locations. How the hell was she to catch the target *in flagrante* if she wasn't to use her investigative talents?

As she ticked off each location by taking a surreptitious photo of the target, she'd failed to catch any interactions with a potential lover. The target was always solo. Even in what was probably her regular coffee shop, unless she was having an affair with her conjoined laptop. Anna found herself rooting for the woman. There was a confidence about her, a manner she admired.

She'd never met the client, but she'd taken an instant dislike to him. She assumed it was a 'him'. By god, his email made such a song and dance about a deadline. That was a first. But she'd worked that out. Imminent court proceedings. Had to be. Divorce settlement no doubt.

His emails had been so instructional and officious that her gut reaction had been to turn the job down. But hey, business had been quiet of late. Very quiet. And he'd offered to double her normal fee for meeting his deadline.

Two pairs of socks and walking boots and her feet were still freezing. Maybe this is where I belong, she reflected, lying here on this sodden ground, cap in hand to this capitalist world… "Come on Anna, 'You Can Do This!'" she said, quoting the title of a recent book she'd skimmed through. "OK. Final location." She knew this must be where the target lived. Quiet village. Small cottage. Cute. One day… one day.

She looked away for one second to ensure a dog walker hadn't spotted her.

Sod it! Missed her… she caught the target entering her neighbour's cottage.

But not on camera.

Shit.

She zoomed in on the neighbour's window.

Twenty minutes passed. Not a cup of sugar then. Was she screwing the neighbour? Not uncommon, she was discovering. The latest book eating her down-time was called 'The Laws of Attraction'. Each chapter covered a different 'law'. Chapter one, and top of the list, was proximity.

When she'd bought the book, she'd convinced herself it was purely for research for her new career. But deep down she knew the real reason. Her brave face on singledom was beginning to slip.

Hang on… Movement!

Anna looked through her camera lens. Zoomed in slightly.

French windows. Two people. One blonde. One dark. She adjusted the zoom again.

Turn round… come on, you bastard… show us your face.

Here we go… here we go…

Fuck! It's a woman. Oh well. Good for her.

Anna took the photo.

*

Fresh out of the shower, and wrapped in her thick dressing gown, Anna emailed the client.

Dear Sir/Madam, I've attached the photos of Miss Liz Green as per your request. I can report nothing incriminating whatsoever.

She'd identified and named the target. Basic really for a private eye. She wasn't merely a photographer. She thought it might get her more work, word of mouth, whoever this guy was.

She signed off, adding a smiley face.

Attached an invoice that would never get paid.

And pressed send on the last email she would ever write.

Chapter One

At 6.00am Liz's alarm clock yanked her out of her dream, exactly at the point things were getting juicy. She quickly reached to mute the raucous sound, disappeared back under the duvet and attempted re-entry. Bollocks. Gone. Every time. She sat up in bed, sipped from last night's glass of water, pulled a face and then opened her iPad, tapping on The Guardian News icon. Its leading headline yelled at her. She re-read it in disbelief. The headline was disturbing enough, but what disturbed her most, was that she'd written it. Or thought she had. She threw herself out of bed and dressed before realising she hadn't showered.

Between Kings Cross Station and the short walk to the Guardian News Headquarters, Liz called into Starbucks. She needed five minutes to calm down and collect her thoughts before meeting with her Editor-in-Chief, Simon Smith.

Why the hell had he changed her headline? It reversed the whole emphasis of her story. And the context of her article had been altered too. Radically. Not his usual judicious tweaks here and there. He'd twisted her whole argument on its head. She wanted answers. Specifics. Not some vague palm-off about telling the reader what he wants to hear. 'Remember, Liz, our readers are our customers'. *How about the damn truth for once!*

"Hey, George." Liz's pace eased as she entered the huge glass cube of a building.

"How's my favourite reporter today?"

The reply was just what she needed. George, security guard at the Guardian since the Crimean War, beamed at her in his perfect grandad kind of way. His beloved wife of forty-three years had passed away only last autumn and yet he still glowed with warmth for humanity. This security guard's primary weapon was his charm offensive, and as fall-back he always had his trusty walking stick. He'd made the news himself recently when he'd clonked a rabid intruder unconscious with it.

"Go get him!"

Liz stopped in her tracks and stared him out, until she couldn't hold her smile back any longer. "Are you some kind of mind reader, George?"

George chuckled, nodding towards the newspaper lying on his desk.

"Just read your article. Is it really the end of the world?"

"It is for someone!" said Liz.

"George chuckled again. "I don't believe in vaccinations anyway."

"This one matters!" Liz stepped onto the escalator. Whereas normally she would allow it to control the speed of her arrival, a brief moment to reflect on the tasks ahead, today she climbed with it.

Walking the long corridor between open-plan cubicles, her reply to all greetings was kept to a brief nod, her focus on the far door to the office of Simon 'The Spinster' Smith.

Not that "The Spinster" was like an old lady. Quite the reverse. Liz had discovered Smith's memory to be perfect. Freakish, some insisted. A publishing industry legend. His memory was far more than merely an asset. It was a weapon. And one that Smith used ruthlessly in arguments. 'Merely a discussion darling,' he'd insist after crushing his victim to the point of tears. The man was an argument addict. Discussion was competition. Chit-chat the chance to belittle. As the Prime Minister, John Blake once joked during one of his Cabinet meetings on Press regulation, 'The Spinster could put a spin on a square cricket ball.'

The instant Liz stepped into Smith's office, his laconic tone slithered from his mouth.

"I know why you're—"

"God, Simon!" Liz thumped his desk with both fists so hard that his keyboard jumped.

"Hold it there." Smith gestured with his hands for silence, repeating her words back to her. "God Simon... Hmm." He smiled at her. "I like the sound of that."

Liz could feel her adrenaline surge. "You've flipped my whole report! Why?" She didn't wait for a reply, jabbing with her finger wildly, "Believe me Simon, my headline 'Worldwide Euthanasia' was bang on the money!"

"A little provocative, don't you think?" Smith quizzed, his smile still hovering.

"Simon, when the hell have you ever had a problem with provocative? Surely we want our readers' attention. And especially with such a huge story." Liz sighed loudly. "Sack me or shoot me, Simon. I don't care. But you have to re-redact my article."

"Liz, Liz, Liz. I know I've only been Editor-in-Chief for eighteen years, but 're-redact'... I don't think that such a word exists."

"Don't play games with me Simon." Liz took a deep breath as Smith stepped from behind his desk.

"I wouldn't dream of it, darling." He offered his arms in plea. "You know I'm your biggest fan. Ever since I asked you in your interview if you had any questions for the interview board."

"So why—" Liz started.

Smith guffawed, ignoring her. "Your reply… pure Lizonian. You said 'None whatsoever,' and told us that you'd done your research and probably knew more about the company than we did." Smith snorted. "So damn ballsy! And whilst the board was still reeling, you then informed us that you'd decided to take the job and would start immediately."

Liz shrugged. "So? I was keen."

"But we hadn't even offered you the job!"

Liz kept eye contact and shrugged again. "So why did you change my headline? I thought we'd gone to press."

Smith shrugged back in mockery and pointed at the ceiling.

Liz shook her head. "God told you to do it?"

"As good as. Thomasz Mann himself. He thought it a bit scaremongery… so I tweaked it."

"Tweaked it! You flipped the whole article!"

"Well, it was a bit doom and gloom. After Covid it might be seen as a little *too* provocative, don't you think?" said Smith.

"Am I hearing right? The man whose motto is 'Bad news is good news'." Liz took another deep breath, "You're the Editor-in Chief. You're supposed to have the final word."

Smith smiled. "We're all somebody's bitch, darling."

"Not all of us," said Liz under her breath, as the door sprang open behind her.

"Simon. Thomasz is trying to get hold of you. Says you're not answering your phone." The fresh face winked at Liz. "Sorry, Liz."

She quickly shook her head. "No problem."

"Thank you, Rupert. I'm on silent. Won't be long."

"Sorry, sir. But he says it's urgent."

"Vamoosh!" said Smith impatiently, gesturing for the young man to close the door behind him.

"Scaremongery?" exclaimed Liz. "My report may well be scary, but it was accurate."

Smith sighed. "We can't be delivering the immunisation programme willy nilly."

"Who's we?" Liz folded her arms. "Who precisely *is* we?"

"Oh come on, Liz, I haven't got time for this. The powers that be. The Governments of the world. Or more precisely, the World Health Organisation."

"I spoke to Dr Hendry on the phone two days ago. The W.H.O.'s most senior medical researcher, and according to him there's a ghost in the machine—"

"A ghost!" Smith snorted again. "Mann was right. That is scary."

Liz ignored him. "…a glitch in the statistics. If a brand new strain of virus goes the same way as Ebola or Corona then he insists we could all be fucked. To quote him directly, 'Any program of inoculation should not be selective'." Liz looked directly into Smith's eyes. "But then you know that, because you specifically deleted Hendry's statement from my article."

"Mann is merely advocating calm. It's simple. The last thing we want is provocative reporting on such a potentially volatile situation," said Smith.

"But Simon, our readers are our customers. Remember? Surely they'll be very interested to read why some people's lives are being judged more worthy of saving than others. Surely we're all equal when it comes to life or death?"

"I've got news for you, darling," Smith stepped towards the door, "Communism's dead."

Liz remained firmly planted in his path, her arms folded even tighter.

"You've altered my piece so comprehensively, you might at least have thought to remove my name from it."

Smith's eyes lit up. "Ahh! So it's not the content you're worried about, it's being associated with it. Your reputation!"

"My reputation? Stop twisting this."

"And don't forget the recognition you're getting. Every journalist's dream." Smith reached back over his desk and rotated his computer screen. "Look! You've got the front page again."

"What you've printed is no longer my page. It's the exact opposite of what I'd written," Liz roared. "For fuck's sake Simon, I want a reputation for credibility!" She sighed loudly. *Keep calm...keep calm*. She lowered her voice. "Listen. I've spoken to several sources. All credible. And all point to a definite plan here of selective immunisation."

"Do you have absolute, iron-clad, infallible proof of this?" said Smith earnestly. Liz faltered. "Well, not proof proof. Not court of law proof. But there's definitely a plan or plot here. I'm getting there. I've a follow-up with Hendry this afternoon at the W.H.O.'s London office. Says he's got proof of a cover-up. And geo-statistical evidence of—"

"Liz, come on! Statistics? Really?" Smith grinned at her. "Statistics are the best way to hide lies. Researchers locked in labs with no daylight, no fresh air. Rots their brains. And forget journalists, researchers are desperate for recognition. Peer recognition. They crave it. 'Look at me, my numbers are bigger than your numbers.' Anyway," Smith cleared his throat, "I understand Hendry disappeared last night. News desk are reporting his wife's got the police looking for him."

"What! I only arranged the appointment yesterday. Are you sure? His secretary hasn't phoned me."

Smith put his hand on Liz's shoulder, "I must go."

"Fucking hell! The way things are going, I wouldn't be surprised if his body's found naked and zipped inside a holdall."

Smith pursed his lips and slowly shook his head, "I remember you once swore that conspiracists were only a notch away from psychos."

Liz didn't hear a word. "The bloody Roxburgh Institute avoided interview as well! Refused point blank! I noticed you'd edited that out too." Liz saw Smith's face visibly redden.

"Because the Roxburghs don't figure anywhere in this. Don't even go there. That's one lawsuit we'd never win," said Smith.

"So the Roxburgh Institute is not the World Health Organisation's biggest donor?"

"The W.H.O.'s funding is cross-Governmental and wholly transparent," said Smith defiantly. Liz felt his hand slide down her back and a gentle pressure prizing her away from the door.

"Wholly opaque I think you'll find," said Liz. "I've dug so deep… you know me well enough Simon… the Roxburghs *are* the W.H.O.'s biggest sponsors. They even donate the use of their medical research facility in the US."

Face reddening further, Smith forced his hand onto the door knob and began opening the door. "I really have to go. Promise me you won't dig any deeper." And as he headed down the corridor towards an open elevator, Smith called back. "We don't want you falling in, darling."

*

Alone on the balcony of the fifth floor conference room, Smith pressed his phone to his ear. He was looking down at the vast fan of railway lines converging as they ran northwards out of Kings Cross Station.

"Simon." The voice sounded hollow.

"Yes?"

"Thank you for the re-write."

Smith's voice cracked as he spoke. "I'm not comfortable with it."

There was a pause on the line before the reply came.

"You're not comfortable? Want us to fluff your

pillows?" Another pause, "Or are those rent boys still doing it for you?"

Smith bit his lip. *Leave me alone!* He gripped the balcony rail and watched a train five storeys below start its journey north. He imagined himself on it, clutching a one-way ticket.

"And Simon…"

Again Smith held his tongue.

"…about your favourite journalist."

"What about her?"

"We're still watching her. We've warned you twice now. Remember…" The voice suddenly became harsh. "…three strikes and she's out."

Chapter Two

Sitting bolt upright at the front of a café, a hunter scanned the throngs of shoppers. *Bloody sheep. Why do people in crowds always look so dumb?* He watched them milling along the fast-drying pavement, their wet brollies folded. It was the last Saturday before Christmas. This gave stamina to the crawling crowd. And it was becoming increasingly engorged, growing from centipede to monstrous millipede, as the rain-shy added themselves to its stupid bulk. He rechecked the time on his phone. It was precisely 9:33 when he spotted his victim approaching the café door.

"James!" Dangerfield stood to greet him, smiling warmly, his eyes alight. "Hope you didn't get caught in that. Tweed hates rain."

"Shit. I can't believe you've actually turned up," said James.

"Don't look so shocked. I replied to your email, didn't I?"

"This time, yes." James rolled his eyes. "What about all the texts and phone calls. Over what is it... eight years?"

"Can't be!" Dangerfield mocked surprise.

"My sister still refers to you as Mr No Show."

Dangerfield nodded, "How is Liz?"

"A lot better since you disappeared."

"Good to hear. Look, let's find a better table. It's deserted at the back."

The two men chose different routes across the densely tabled café, Dangerfield lying loudly, "You look well."

Frowning, James glanced across at him.

"Although I'm not sure about this!" Dangerfield rubbed his own chin. "James, you're twenty nine for God's sake. That pointy beard makes you look like a professor," Dangerfield nodded. "Oh yeah… I forgot, how is academia treating you?"

As they reached the back of the café, Dangerfield ushered James to the nearest seat and slid himself into the corner with its wide-angled view. He spotted the waitress squeezing her way towards them, cheap pink uniform bulging in all the right places.

"What can I get you?"

"Triple shot espresso for me and…" Dangerfield looked at James. "…James? Wakey, wakey. You still a tea boy?"

"Sorry, miles away. Yeah, sure, tea's good."

"Anything else?"

"Two huge buns!" Dangerfield exclaimed, grinning at her.

She returned the smile, stifling a giggle, and turning, set sail in the direction from which she'd come.

"Fuck's sake, Charlie, I'd forgotten how much of an arse you are!"

"Have some fun, mate. Trust me, life's short." Dangerfield glanced around the café. And waited.

After a shuffling of feet and folding of arms, James spoke.

"That's the thing. You use the words 'Trust me' but where the hell have you been for the last eight years? Were

Liz and I too boring for you?"

Dangerfield remained silent.

"You just vanished off the face of the earth. No response to emails, no phone calls. You didn't even turn up for graduation for Christ's sake! I presume you know you got a First?"

A bunless tray slid onto the table, and with a wink accompanying her smile, the waitress retreated. Dangerfield noticed James's hand shaking as he reached for his teacup. It failed to reach his lips. The cup was lowered, heavily, and with spillage, clattering against its cheap saucer.

"You pissed Liz off! You pissed me off! You just pissed off, full bloody stop!" James shoved his cup and saucer across the table, the saucer teetering on the edge, the cup crashing to the floor. For a second, silence hit the café, heads jerking in Dangerfield's direction, as James reached under the table for the fragments.

"Leave it for the waitress, mate. Quite like to see her bending over."

"You haven't changed a bit, have you?" said James.

Dangerfield was poised for any opportunity. "You're right. I haven't changed." He closed in for the kill. "I'm still your friend." It's so easy, thought Dangerfield, when you know exactly what people want to hear.

James leant forward, elbows on the table, face in hands. "Bollocks to this!" He sat back suddenly in his chair, "I'm gonna explode if I don't talk to someone."

"Hey." Dangerfield reached forward and clamped his hand on James's wrist, "Talk to me." He stared into James' eyes. At the back of the café, further from daylight, the bags under them looked even darker, heavier.

James let out a loud sigh, pulling his arm from Dangerfield's grip. "So what happened to you?" He jabbed at the table. "Eight years. Eight bloody years! I thought Liz and I were your best friends." He shook his head. "Not even a goodbye."

Dangerfield took a gulp from his fast-cooling coffee.

"And when you do eventually reply to an email, it comes from dangerfield@genesis-engineering." James swallowed hard. "Explain that!"

"What's to explain?" Dangerfield quizzed.

"Well, I was with Sir Peter Brown at the Defence Procurement Conference yesterday… I presume you've heard of Brown?"

"Of course. He's my bitch at Genesis." Dangerfield leaned back in his chair.

"He's the fucking CEO Charles," James's voice started to rise, "and when I asked him about you, he told me that he didn't remember you. In fact, he'd never even heard of you."

Dangerfield tried to interject but the man was in full flow.

"And we both know what that means, don't we? If someone doesn't remember *you* Charles, it means that they cannot possibly have met you!"

If silence can be golden, then at this precise moment, at the back of this cheap café, it was shit-coloured.

Chapter Three

Dangerfield kept direct eye contact with James, gauging his expression. He saw a small boy whose favourite toy had just fallen down the stairs and lay smashed in the hallway below.

How much could he tell him? Lying wasn't going to cut it. His GCHQ colleagues were sitting comfortably, sifting through all the garbage humans waste their breath on - the tapped phones and emails, laptop cameras accessed, search histories analysed. Their computer algorithms, feasting 24/7 on billions of spurious connections, had choked on and vomited up irregular, out of context meetings between two scientists in the Defence Industry. And Dangerfield knew both of these scientists. One sat facing him now. Fuck, he shouldn't be on this job. He knew the people involved for Christ's sake. But old Bulstrode, chief honcho at MI6, had insisted that he was the man for the job. Insisted.

Against protocol? Obviously.

Gut feeling? He could do with a shit.

"James. I need you to focus." Dangerfield noticed the frown reappear, the eyes questioning. "I know you're cutting edge in optical physics. Missile guidance right?" James's frown deepened, his eyes narrowed further. Dangerfield continued, "So you must have signed the Official Secrets Act."

James hesitated before answering, "For someone who

hasn't kept in touch, you seem to know a lot."

"So what are you? Level 4?" Dangerfield asked, waiting to be corrected.

James rolled his eyes, "Too high to be sitting here discussing it with you."

"I'm Level 7," said Dangerfield firmly.

James went to speak but then stood up, shaking his head. "You really need to grow up."

"Sit down, James. We need to talk."

"You're unbelievable," said James. He started walking in the direction of the café's door. "There *are* no levels, you dick."

Dangerfield sighed. *Fuck it. No pain, no gain*. He called after him, "Tell me about O'Brien," and watched his old friend come to an abrupt, juddering halt, impressed by the ongoing quiver.

Casting his eyes over the café, Dangerfield noted that, other than the living statue clutching the next table, the place had emptied. Having stuffed their faces, the last dregs of the clientele had been drawn back into the High Street to feed a different addiction. He clocked the waitress, moored at the far side of the café, busy yapping about nothing to nobodies on the other side of the kitchen hatch. *Perfect*. The grubby café had become a clean, clinical space to operate in. He stood to help his frozen patient rejoin him for treatment.

"We've been tracking O'Brien since he left Cambridge."

Not a flicker. "We know he approached you four weeks ago."

Trance-like, James returned to his chair and sat in silence.

"Talk to me, James. We can help you."

"Who's we?"

"Who'd you think?"

"Come on then. I'm curious. Tell me. How did that happen?" said James, sitting back in his chair, folding his arms. "And oh, please don't tell me you'll have to shoot me afterwards."

Dangerfield, noting the aggression, the zero humour, again scanned the café. *OK. Let's do this*. "Remember in our second year at Cambridge, a new Chancellor was appointed?"

"Higson. Didn't he die last year?" James asked.

"Yeah, he did. Well, turned out he was on MI6's recruitment team."

"He told you that?"

"He told me that sacrifices were necessary. Couldn't have spelt it out more clearly. Friends and family." For the first time, Dangerfield glanced down. "You know I don't have any family," and looking directly at James, "so you should understand just how important you and Liz were to me."

Dangerfield saw the man's arms unfold, his hands now resting on the table, his frown receding, shoulders relaxing slightly. *So far, so good.*

"These sacrifices… were they worth it?" James looked straight at him.

Dangerfield held his gaze, batting the loaded question with ease. He had him. "The Greater Good's a fickle concept, mate. By definition it cannot give you *everything* you want."

James remained silent for a minute, nodding gently, his focus over Dangerfield's shoulder.

That's relaxed him, thought Dangerfield. *Just give 'em what they want.*

"Alright. So you probably know I bumped into O'Brien last month at the Paris Defence Conference," said James

"Well, technically he bumped into you," said Dangerfield, "or rather, orchestrated it."

"I know that now. He insisted we went for a beer, which I thought slightly odd as he was completely teetotal at college."

"I remember."

"I tried to get out of it, but he seemed almost desperate. Felt quite sorry for him to be honest." James shook his head, "Crazy huh, now that—"

"What did you talk about?"

"Almost the second we sat down, he was demanding to know if I'd like to be rich. In fact, super-rich was the term he used. Twat. Said I could upgrade from my flat in Sparrow Lane to a mansion if I helped him on a project."

"What did you tell him?" Dangerfield asked.

"Not interested. Happy where I am."

"Did you ask about the project?"

"Nope. All I could think about was how the hell did he know where I lived!"

"Well, O'Brien needs you because he's failing to deliver to his clients."

James hesitated before speaking. "You seem to know a

lot. I presume you know then that five days ago I got a letter from O'Brien?"

"Actually, no." *Interesting.* "What did it say?"

"And later the same day, the shit phoned me."

Bollocks. GCHQ didn't pick that one up! "And?"

James eyes narrowed. "You know what? I think it's your turn to do a little talking. I've recently learnt that trust's a very delicate commodity."

"Isn't it," said Dangerfield, pushing the empathy. "So hit me."

"If you are with MI6, what's your role at Genesis? How the hell is it that Brown's never heard of you?"

"Simple, mate. Industrial espionage. World's rife with it. And so my work takes place under the radar, including Brown's radar."

Dangerfield spotted the waitress drifting towards them and immediately threw her a big smile, giving her the thumbs up, "We're good. Thanks." And as she turned, locked eyes with James again. "You know the stats. Defence is one of the biggest markets on the planet. Trillions of dollars, not billions. And to think, little old Blighty's one of the big boys."

"So—"

Dangerfield interrupted. "Money." He thumped the table. "It's the money. It needs protection. And so my department organises what information Genesis's research team can release to its CEO. The MOD hardly wants Brown nosing around the finer details of what *really* goes on at Genesis. Even though the MOD are the primary shareholder, Genesis has public shareholders too. That's just a sign of the times. And the public demands a public voice. So that's why Brown's so perfect for the job. It *is* all about him. The man's such a puffed up peacock, desperate to show off his plumage. Come on, James, you must have noticed?"

What Dangerfield noticed, was that James looked down for a split second. *Getting there.*

"Brown's so full of himself that there's no room left to take on board the really crucial things that are going on around him." *Was that the beginnings of a smirk? Definitely. Keep pushing.* "He's so over-stuffed with his own opinions that he can't absorb anything else… technical advances, research breakthroughs." Yes, definitely a smirk, noted Dangerfield. *Time to hit him with the punch-line.* "To put it in a nutshell, the prick's the most arrogant man I've ever met!"

Dangerfield saw a smile appear on James's face. *Got him.* "What?"

James's smile grew broader by the second.

"Fuck off!" exclaimed Dangerfield. "Are you calling me arrogant?"

"Well… only completely!" James laughed.

Dangerfield's face also cracked and he gestured a punch. "You fucking fucker!"

Dangerfield knew, that even in man's darkest hour, irony is one of the few tools available with the power to shed light. He also knew he'd managed to re-establish their old bond. A second later, his phone started bleating.

"Probably Q," said James.

"Ha ha, funny. Trust me, the films are nothing like real

life… another tea? I need you to tell me everything."

Retrieving his phone from his jacket pocket, he started walking towards the counter, behind which the waitress sat pretty in pink, filing her nails. Irony, thought Dangerfield. *Love it.*

He took the call.

"Sir?"

"Get him on board."

"Yes, sir."

"Now, Charles. Now."

As Dangerfield returned to his seat, James passed him a small white envelope. Dangerfield opened it and retrieved half a dozen photographs. The first showed a tall woman in her late twenties, sitting in a restaurant, seemingly unaware of the camera. Still attractive, he thought. He flicked to the second. A woman leaving a building. The logo on the wall beside her was that of the Guardian Newspaper Group. Coat collar up, snood hiding her chin, face partially hidden by long, blonde hair, but clearly the same woman.

Dangerfield looked at them one by one and noted that the final photograph was of her sitting on a sofa in front of a roaring fire, next to another woman with long, auburn plaits. They had been shot from the side, but what caught his attention was that the image was framed by brickwork. Photographer must have been in the garden, thought Dangerfield.

"I see Liz has an admirer," he said. "Seems pretty keen."

"These photos were pushed through my letterbox five days ago with a note that said, 'One week to go'," said James.

"Who's the brunette?" asked Dangerfield, unable to help himself.

"It's Amy, Liz's neighbour. I can't believe the slimeball's even been to her cottage, for God's sake!"

"O'Brien wouldn't have taken these photos. What did he say when he phoned you?" asked Dangerfield.

"Told me that if I don't join his project, Liz's life would be in danger. And if I go to the police, the consequences would be even more dire." James eyes flicked around the cafe for a second. "What the hell could be more dire?"

"How did you reply?" asked Dangerfield calmly.

"I told him he was out of his mind." James gathered the photos and stared at his sister's image.

"James, there's something you need to consider."

"What's that?"

"O'Brien *is* out of his mind."

"If that bastard touches a hair on her head—"

"O'Brien's not the driving force here. It's a simple case of blackmail."

"Simple?" exclaimed James.

"Sorry, James, but the choices are straightforward here. Some people choose to go to the police, but more often than not it goes tits-up. And not in a good way."

"What do you mean?" asked James.

"Wake up. The people behind O'Brien are ruthless and have an agenda to fulfil. And at any cost." Dangerfield waited for eye contact. "*Any* cost."

"So what the hell do you suggest?"

"Have you considered paying the ransom?" said Dangerfield.

"What on earth are you talking about? They haven't asked for one."

"I mean join their project…" *Jesus! And this man's a professor?*

"What? You cannot be serious?" cried James.

"Do I look like a line judge? Of course I'm serious. Think about Liz."

"If Tim O'Brien thinks I can be bought, then the man must be out of his tiny little mind."

"Actually, not so little, James. In the Department we call O'Brien, Tri-polar Tim."

"What?"

"Look. We can brief you up in 48 hours. What you need to focus on is Liz's safety."

"Hang on, hang on. What the hell is tri-polar?" demanded James.

"The man's emotions aren't purely up or down, they're all over the shop. He's completely unstable. But there are ways of dealing with him… of managing him. For example, never say no to him directly."

"But that's exactly what I want to say to the skinny little shit. And anyway, I couldn't join his project even if I wanted to. My work's graded Top Secret."

"Of course. But not a problem. I can sort that." Dangerfield reached for James's wrist again and slowed his words. "Just focus on your sister. You know your life wouldn't be worth tuppence if it all went hideously wrong. Everyday you'll be haunted by your wrong decision."

"You disappear for eight years, and now you just turn up and start telling me what to do!" said James.

"I've explained the reasons. Now maybe it's your turn to disappear."

"You know what? It sounds like you've got it all planned out."

"James, it's entirely *your* choice. But MI6 will be behind you." Dangerfield nodded reassuringly. "And eternally grateful."

James put his head in his hands and let out a deep sigh.

"Listen, James, O'Brien flies back to his project next Friday. You should go with him."

"And you know that for a fact, do you?" said James.

"Of course. No one with his background can book a flight without GCHQ in the know. Plus we've tapped the phone at his apartment in Oslo. It's so funny. Each time it sounds like a different person's answering his phone."

"Who the hell would want to live with that creep?" asked James.

"Oh no. The guy lives alone."

Chapter Four

Robert Roxburgh and Karl Lynx made themselves comfortable in a pair of Chesterfield armchairs. The chairs were angled towards each other, separated by a two-tier whatnot in burr walnut. This rare and valuable example of Gillow's work supported two glasses of a blood-coloured, high-protein liquid. Whereas an Adams fireplace and oak panelled walls might normally complement such an opulent vignette, the incongruity of an industrial-sized pump and entirely transparent walls accompanied them. The scene fell way short of a grand drawing room. It was more like a snapshot from a theatrical production of Jeeves and Wooster. The two men, recumbent in their huge leather seats were enclosed, centre stage, in a forty foot transparent shipping container. This perspex oxygen chamber had countless tubes entering and leaving it, and instead of some bow-tie tinkling the ivories, lounge music was provided by the electrical pump gently thrumming in the background.

"I thought you looked different in the elevator. Assumed it was the light." Karl Lynx leaned towards Robert Roxburgh, and squinted. "Have you been in a fight?"

"Karl, if you ever have liver irrigation, your skin will look just like mine. And to be honest, the T-cell injections didn't do much for my complexion either." Roxburgh smiled. "But on the bright side though, Zimmerman says, my ETA's up to 102."

"Why do you always refer to it as ETA? It's not *Arrival*. It's Expected Time of Death. Not going all religious on me, are you? It really doesn't suit."

"Ok, so what's the latest on your expected time of death?" replied Roxburgh, putting excessive emphasis on the word 'death'.

"Well, currently 96, but you've probably heard, I'm in line for new lungs in about six weeks. According to Zimmerman, that should lift it to 103."

"103? You bastard!" Roxburgh laughed. "No, seriously, that's great news."

Roxburgh reached for the glass beside him and sipped his protein drink, his face creasing as he swallowed. "Karl, when Singh gets here, don't let me forget to rib him about the real reason behind his Space Program."

Lynx looked puzzled. "Real reason?"

"I'm sure I mentioned it to you last week."

Lynx shook his head. "Doesn't ring a bell."

"He's not satisfied at the speed of his trans-humanist program. The man has over 20 micro-chips embedded in various parts of his body and yet he's still convinced that meeting aliens, more evolved than we mere humans, is his best shot at conquering death."

Lynx started chuckling. "Actually, yes, I remember now. That's my theory too."

"Oh, definitely. If he had it entirely his way, he'd channel the whole of Earth's remaining resources into exploring space."

A loud beep sounded and Roxburgh called out, "Yes,

Sergeant?"

"Sir, all members of the team are now present on Level One."

"Thank you, Sergeant. Send the gentlemen up and seal the entrance. I want the whole of Level Four switched to 'Lead Box'. No signals whatsoever, in or out. And Sergeant…"

"Yes, sir?"

"That includes all *my* devices."

"Yours too, sir?"

"Blanket close-down. Actually, get Doctor Zimmerman and his med-team out of Level Three and put that on 'Lead Box' as well. Just to be on the safe side." Roxburgh reached for his glass and swigged the last of the crimson liquid. "Look, Karl, a quick word in private before the team arrives for the main discussion."

Lynx also returned his empty glass to the whatnot. "Fire away."

"Couple of things actually. Firstly I'm insisting Mohammed doesn't do any more interviews."

"What? But he ran rings round old Icke and his conspiracy theories on CNN last month."

"Well, yes, all credit to him. In fact I got a real kick out of seeing Icke squirm. But to be honest, Mohammed's becoming more of a liability. The results from his dementia treatment are too sporadic. I'm going to have to bend Zimmerman's ear after the meeting."

"A liability?" Lynx looked perplexed. "But Mo's been a stalwart for years. He crushed that whistle-blower on Fox News last year. What was his name? Middley? Middery?"

Roxburgh nodded. "Well, of course he did. But don't forget, Middleton was *our* whistle-blower, and we chose when he blew."

Silence reigned for a moment.

"Look, I don't mean to take anything away from the man. He's been magnificent in the past, but—"

"A liability?" Lynx repeated. "What's happened?"

Roxburgh's reply was calm. "He nearly blew the lid during last night's live NBC interview."

"You're joking! Live?" Lynx's eyebrows furrowed.

"When I say 'live', obviously we still have the seven second transmission delay. We had to scramble the old boy's last few words."

"What the hell did he say?"

"When he was pressed about the global recovery from the Coronavirus, instead of referring to Covid-19 as a *tragedy*, he actually used the term *trial*."

For a few seconds Lynx sat shaking his head, muttering and cursing repeatedly. Eventually he spoke. "You mentioned there were a couple of things." He raised himself slightly in his armchair. "I know your serious face too well, old friend. What's the second thing?"

It was Roxburgh's turn to pause before speaking. "I want to thank you for your support during all these years we've worked together. And…" He let out a deep sigh, "…in particular for the last few months when fate, opportunity, serendipity, call it what you will, has projected us to the very cusp of the darkest days the human race will ever have to endure."

Lynx bit his lip, nodding in empathy.

"My heart feels so heavy…I can't begin to tell you," said Roxburgh, staring directly into Lynx's eyes. Lynx opened his mouth to speak but Roxburgh held his hand up, stopping him in his tracks. "Our Covid-19 project was a complete success. It gave humanity a peep into the dark abyss into which it could fall. Our Media onslaught spread the fear of God across the whole World. The fear we instilled has ensured our follow-up vaccination distribution was a complete success. Hardly any resistance from anyone," Roxburgh paused for breath, "and furthermore, the team reached agreement on the regional allocation of survivors, you know, those that received the real, genuine vaccine. That, is one massive box ticked. But—" Again Roxburgh sighed deeply, " I want to thank you for promoting the concept of fake news and the development of Deep Fake technology. That, together with years of fostering conspiracy theories, hoaxes, spoof media sites, the whole caboodle, has provided us with the smoke and mirrors behind which we can now distribute our new virus, and provide euthanasia for the human race."

Chapter Five

As Chapel Road evolved into Berry Street, the houses became more imposing and less friendly. Dangerfield threw a left and pulling up in front of the MOD campus, stared into a small screen beside his car until a light flicked to green. He watched as a huge steel barrier, the width of the road, slowly juddered its way level with the tarmac. Parked behind Block 14 and walking towards the main entrance, Dangerfield turned to click the key fob at his black Mini Cooper. Beyond the row of parked cars the long silhouette of the Malvern Hills filled the horizon. Coated in trees, the vast palette of green appeared both languorous and beckoning. He stared for a moment, remembering when he and James were teenagers and their arguments over which paths they might have missed in their bid to mountain bike every inch of them.

Inside the building and several doors later, Dangerfield clocked three people clustered around a computer screen.

“Hey, James!” Dangerfield beamed. “Stanley and Soo-Byn looking after you?”

“Definitely. Stan’s the man.”

A short plump man looked earnestly at James. “Well, I do hope things are beginning to fall into place. Normally I’m given a little more time to do briefings and it’s…” The man paused, scratching the back of his head, a nest of frizzy grey hair surrounding its prize-winner of an egg. He glanced at Dangerfield, "…well, it's not very often we send civilians straight to the coal-face."

"James will be fine," said Dangerfield emphatically. "Any delays, and the Koreans will suspect their latest recruit's been bleating. Anyway, Stan, I'm sure you've noticed how quickly Professor Green here picks things up."

Dangerfield's eyes switched to the slim woman with a jet black pony-tail, her cream dress more like a miniature lab coat. "Our old headmaster wouldn't stop banging on about him!" Dangerfield put his hands behind his back and thrust his chest out, "The boy's bwilliant! Absolutely bwilliant!"

James shook his head. "He only said it the once. You're the one that used to repeat it."

"Jealousy…" Dangerfield looked at Soo-Byn again. "…eats you up and then spits you out."

"Ahem!" interrupted Stanley. "Would you mind if I continued?"

"Fire away, Stan." said Dangerfield, pulling up a chair.

"Now, where was I?"

"You were showing me the network of cameras they've installed around Liz's cottage," said James.

"Oh yes! PASS! Perimeter Alert Security System." Stanley's eyes were shining. "As I was saying, we've given your sister a PASS 5 grading. That's quite rare for an ordinary..." The man paused. "Well, you know, normal person."

"Grade five?" quizzed James.

"PASS 5. That means no person or vehicle can pass within five kilometres of her house without being picked up on camera and vetted. Anyone with a driving licence, passport, UK entry visa, pretty much everyone really, well, we've got 'em!" The man was beaming. "The system scrutinises every face the cameras pick up. Any match with our database of undesirables and it's game over. Hoodies, attempts at disguise, the slightest blip and interception takes place in a matter of minutes. It's standard protocol for royalty, visiting bigwigs—"

James interrupted, "And it's foolproof?"

"It's proved completely failsafe to date." Stanley suddenly held his fist out in front of him, stamping one of his feet down hard. "You shall not pass!" He glanced around expectantly at his tiny audience, his sole takings two polite smiles and a quizzical expression from Soo-Byn. The smile on his own face suggested it was more of a response than his impressions usually received.

"I can't believe there are so many CCTV cameras in the UK," said James, looking at Soo-Byn. "It seems kind of...undemocratic."

"I'm shocked too." She shrugged. "Even more than North Korea. I thought *we* were heavily monitored with a hundred thousand of them. "

Stanley couldn't hold back his enthusiasm. "As I mentioned before Charles arrived, currently six million! And that's only the official ones!"

"So James, you can relax," said Dangerfield. "We've got the facial images of ninety-six percent of everyone in the UK on our database. If Lord Lucan ever tries to return to this country, he's fucked."

"Ninety-six percent? What about the other four

percent?" asked James, his eyes on Stanley. "That's still two and a half million people that have avoided camera detection. They can't all be hermits."

"Troglodytes," said Dangerfield.

James ignored him. His focus remained on Stanley.

"The other four percent?" Stanley put his hand on James's arm. "Oh, you shouldn't have to worry about them. They've mostly been in residential care for the past ten years. I can assure you, with our PASS system of protection, your sister has the best security available."

"But Stan." Dangerfield's tone was deadly serious. "What if one of the Four-percenters sneaks out of bed? What if this decrepit camera-dodger creeps on his hands and knees for miles to get to Liz's cottage? He might reach up to her letter box and empty his colostomy bag—"

"Stop!" James jumped in. "OK. Thank you. I've got the message." He shook his head at Soo-Byn and then turned back to his friend. "Dick!"

"You know what James?" said Stanley, glancing at Dangerfield. "Thinking about something you mentioned earlier, if Charles had been…um…my best friend, I might consider myself very lucky indeed if we'd lost touch for eight years." The man's delight at being the cause of laughter shone from his face.

"Good one, Stan. Very good." Dangerfield stood up. "Listen, James, I know this morning's briefings were wall-to-wall technical. Deep fried missiles with a side of computer chips, right?" James nodded, the remnants of a smile still lingering,

"And I hope Stan's reassured you now on the security

front with regards Liz." Another nod. "So what I propose is that Soo-Byn runs through the peculiarities of North Korea with you, how they're likely to 'manage' you in their territory. We're certain you'll be flown in from China as part of an organised tourist group." He looked at Soo-Byn.

"Yes." The woman nodded emphatically. "And I'll explain how they'll conceal your disappearance from the group when you reach Pyongyang."

"Good stuff!" Dangerfield faced James again. "Any questions?"

"Hundreds," said James. "Could you and I have ten minutes in private first, Charles?"

"Umm, sure. Soo-Byn?"

The woman shrugged. "No problem. See you back here?"

"Cool."

"Use my office," said Stanley, pointing at the door behind him.

Opening the door, Dangerfield gestured for James to enter and was about to follow him when Soo-Byn called out, "Hang on, Charles."

What's she frowning about? He winked at James, "With you in one, mate," and closed the door after him.

"So come on… how?" she asked.

"How what?"

"How the hell did you get him to agree to this?" She glanced at Stanley.

"We're just curious Charles," said Stanley. "We've no protocol here."

Soo-Byn folded her arms. "This situation's

unprecedented."

Dangerfield shrugged. "Every project I run is unprecedented. Probably why Bulstrode demanded I run this one."

"But did you explain to James that MI6 has no one on the ground over there?" asked Stanley. He looked at Soo-Byn. "I mean… we've no one."

"Look, Charles, I survived North Korea for thirty-two very long years. Even I don't understand how I managed to wangle my way out. Believe me, no one gets out."

"Soo-Byn's right." Stanley looked distraught. "He seems such a decent chap."

"You've chipped him, right?" said Dangerfield calmly.

"Yes. Injected it this morning. Which means we'll know the precise location of his corpse when the North Koreans find out he's screwed their whole missile system."

Dangerfield walked the three steps separating them and spoke quietly. "Just do your jobs." He looked Soo-Byn directly in the face. "And if, during your briefing, he asks about extraction, make sure you tell him that everything's in hand."

"What?"

"Tell him, and only if he asks, that he'll receive full details as soon as his work over there is complete."

As Dangerfield turned his back on them, and made for Stanley's office, Stanley whispered, "You mean, you haven't told him he's on a one-way ticket.

Chapter Six

The office of Stanley Hammond, Special Projects Director, would be the most spacious on the MOD campus if it weren't for the rows of floor-to-ceiling glass display cabinets filling the majority of the room.

As Dangerfield entered, he saw James had his face pressed up to the nearest cabinet, studying a stuffed owl.

"Ah! Stan's cabinets of curiosities!" exclaimed Dangerfield. "These are legendary in the Service."

"Bit freaky," said James, as he realised the owl's eyes were a pair of camera lenses.

"Freaky? Not at all," said Dangerfield. "Some of these are genuine antiques."

"This one isn't." James was pointing through the glass at a freshly-excreted dog turd.

Dangerfield's concentration was on a Victorian framed painting. Its naked female subject seemed to follow him with her eyes as he moved from side to side.

"Knowing Stan, it'll be some kind of camera system you're looking at."

"Well, I bloody hope it is, or the men in white coats will be here to collect him," said James.

Dangerfield looked across at where James was pointing. "Oh right! No! I've used them! We were trying to close a Bosnian drugs ring about four years ago. They've got a very powerful listening device inside them."

Dangerfield moved next to James. "They even squidge! So if someone decides to bin them, they still won't realise what it really is."

James screwed his face up.

"Probably the most reliable devices I've ever planted. Even in the good bits of Sarajevo, nobody picks their dog's shit up."

The two men turned into the next aisle of cabinets.

James stopped abruptly. "JESUS FUCK! What the hell is that? Tell me that's not a severed head!"

"Oh, my God! I remember that," said Dangerfield excitedly. "That's Bulstrode's head." The head lay on its side, squashed, its eye sockets empty. "That guy controls MI6 with an iron fist."

"How does he do his job from in there?"

Dangerfield ignored the quip. "Must have been Director General for… well… the last twelve years at least. Imagine a sabre-toothed kitten."

"You ever get any trouble from him?"

"No chance. My immediate boss is the biggest swinging dick in the department," said Dangerfield. "She can handle him."

James snorted.

"That head-sheath was Stan's first experiment in mixing advanced prosthetics with 3D printing. Because I was the newbie back then, and my boss thought my head shape was vaguely similar to Bulstrode's—"

"He is pretty ugly."

"Thanks," Dangerfield smiled. "I was the muppet that volunteered to endure two hours in Stan's laboratory.

Bulstrode and I were filmed making different facial expressions and then software merged our idiosyncrasies for a kind of, you know, best-fit scenario. I know Stan made at least three of the Queen. And by the way…" Dangerfield ran a finger across his throat. "…you didn't hear this."

"Of course," James nodded.

"No one realises the woman didn't turn up for half of her public events. An agent from Special Branch, who was exactly her height, had been donning her mask for years. Stan's first attempt though… Christ! What a disaster! It looked like she was sitting on the toilet, trying to push one out!"

"What's it made of?" asked James, smiling.

"Not sure. Probably some kind of graphenic rubberoid."

"Still bullshitting I see."

"OK, Professor," Dangerfield smirked. "Bastard. Anyway, some futuristic shit."

"So, I'm guessing you just pull it over your head like a condom?" said James.

"Same concept, different head." Dangerfield started opening the cabinet door.

"It's alright Charles, I can see how it works."

"Oh no, I'm taking it!" said Dangerfield, reaching inside. "Always like to do something memorable at the office Christmas party. Like scare the shit out of them! Forget the hype, agents are some of the most boring people you can meet."

"Really?" said James earnestly.

"Ha ha ha… fuck off!" Dangerfield grinned. "Well, think about it. They've usually got nothing to talk about, having signed the Official Secrets Act. They're obliged to make up fake jobs that they can't be caught out on when questioned. They can hardly tell a girl 'Oh, I'm in risk assessment' in case the girl also works in insurance. He's fucked if she digs a little deeper."

"Or not fucked," added James.

"Exactly. They have to tell them that they do something really mundane like a school's zebra-crossing man."

"Makes sense. But I'm guessing, telling a woman your job involves hanging around outside schools isn't the best chat-up line either," said James.

Dangerfield laughed and squashed Bulstrode's head into his inside pocket. "So come on, what was it you wanted to talk about? We'd better hurry. Soo-Byn's desperate to have social intercourse with you."

"Well, I wanted to tell you that, now the shock's worn off, I'm definitely up for this assignment. I shouldn't think like this, but these North Koreans fascinate me. I'm dying to see, you know, technically, how far these guys have got."

Dangerfield looked directly into James's eyes and nodded. "I can understand that. This is your life's focus, for Christ's sake."

"My life's focus?" James looked wistful, "Designing killing machines. How sad is that?"

"Could be worse, mate," said Dangerfield. "Actually… I take that back."

"Don't ask me how I fell into missiles, space rockets, you name it," said James.

"Fireworks."

James chuckled. "Yeah… Fireworks."

Dangerfield, leaning against a glass cabinet, folded his arms. "You've loved this shit ever since your dad took us to that MOD Bonfire Night when we were, what, seven?"

"You've got it," said James. "That was one crazy evening. Remember when that rocket misfired and shot into those crates of fireworks and—"

Dangerfield interrupted, "And the whole fucking lot went off!"

James sniggered. "That bank of rockets came hurtling towards the crowd, about two feet off the ground."

"And we all dived for cover," said Dangerfield, laughing. He cleared his throat. "I've got to tell you, James. I have missed you and Liz."

There was no reply.

Dangerfield carried on, "And I think your attitude here is… well, completely understandable. Part of you must be crapping yourself, but I think you get the bigger picture."

James looked pensive.

"Look, Bulstrode sees this as a rare opportunity that we can't afford to miss. 'Imperative' is the word he's been spouting. In fact, I've never seen the man so animated. Sarah, my boss, swears she almost pissed herself in shock when he told her that the resources available were unlimited." Dangerfield then lowered his voice. "And again, this is off record, but the Prime Minister is backing this. He knows about your involvement."

"Is that supposed to impress me?" asked James.

"Hardly. Nothing ever impressed you unless it was radio-controlled. I just want you to be absolutely clear that you agreeing to get on board is nothing less than heroic."

"Heroes never impress me either," said James.

Dangerfield smiled. "The thinking is that although the North Koreans only have missiles with limited range and poor accuracy, the fact is they're learning. And you of all people must know that. If we can put them back five… ten years, then we've bought some valuable time to try and hit them with democracy from the South."

"What, like the Arab Spring, you mean?"

"God, that was bad judgment on an international scale. But these North Koreans are one crushed homogeneous mass. None of your complex loyalties to tribal systems. These poor sods are so ripe for intervention."

James suddenly stepped right up to Dangerfield. "Now listen to me. I do understand your big picture, but I don't share it. Have you got that? The only picture in my head is one where Liz is safe." Continuing to look him straight in the eyes, "She's not to be involved, full stop. I may have an academic interest in these guidance systems, but that's secondary to Liz's welfare. This PASS 5 Status thing Stan's talking about had better be the Berlin bloody Wall. And you…" James prodded Dangerfield in the chest, "must promise you'll keep her completely outside the loop." He started shaking his head. "God knows what she'll do though, when I become one of the disappeared."

"Don't worry, she'll cope. It's not as if you'll be gone forever," said Dangerfield calmly.

James was now staring over Dangerfield's shoulder and into the distance. "Have you ever boarded a train and it's set off before you realise you are on the wrong one?"

"What?"

"Just a feeling. Can't help thinking, why me? One minute my life's sorted. I've gotten over Cathy. I've been leading a ground-breaking project. And I was looking into the future with a big fat smile on my face." James paused and took a deep breath. "And then O'Brien rolls up." He fixed his gaze back on Dangerfield. "So why the hell me?"

"Simple," said Dangerfield putting his hands on James's shoulders. "Your brain was in the wrong place at the wrong time."

Chapter Seven

The heavy snowfall was now struggling to hide the dead, retreating fast as the temperature headed above zero. Liz crossed her legs, the wooden bench hard and unforgiving beneath her. Except for the frigid breeze occasionally pulling at her hair, she sat motionless and despite knowing it by heart, read the inscription on her parents' gravestone.

Ursula and William Green, Aged 39,
Died February 14th 2001
Little Malvern
'I lift up mine eyes unto the hills
from whence cometh my help.'

"Oh Mum. When did I ever get any help?" Liz closed her eyes and pictured her parents' smiling faces, more from the photo on the sideboard in her cottage she suspected, than from any real memory.

Her gaze retraced her lone footprints in the snow that weaved between gravestones, all the way from the church gate. For a moment she imagined they belonged to someone else. The only other footprints, some on the gravestones themselves, were those of a small bird. And then, there he was. He landed on top of her parents' tiny headstone, tilting his head, flashing his red chest and looking at her suspiciously. And asking what she was doing in his territory.

Sunlight began to streak between the sheets of cloud draped across the sky. Liz squinted towards the silhouette of the church and warm memories came flooding in. The Children's Home had little to offer, but the years before the car accident provided rich pickings. Pancake days, baking gingerbread men and Monopoly sessions dominated her thoughts. Liz was reminiscing about her and James' endless hide and seek sessions when the church bell tolled, brutally jolting her back to reality. A second later and her phone beeped.

Amy: Found James yet?

She stood up instinctively. "Where the hell is he?" Her voice seemed to echo through the cold crisp air, ricocheting off trees and gravestones. And the snapping of twigs underfoot said goodbye to the robin. At the church bell's second chime Liz was already striding towards the car park, straight blonde hair flying back from reddened cheeks. "Call yourself an investigative journalist!" By the time she had reached the rusty kissing gate, she had retrieved her car key and pressed *call* on her phone. All of James' friends and colleagues had responded in the negative. Not a sausage. Not an inkling. Nothing. Other than James being abducted by aliens, a single stone remained unturned. There was one man on earth that she never ever wanted to meet again, but even so she should have tried to make contact days ago.

Chapter Eight

Liz opened her emails to a sudden intake of breath. *Shit, he's replied!* And almost panting, speed-read the message. It was headed up tim-o-brien@oslo-dynamics.no

Hey Bizzie,

Mega surprise to get your message. Not heard a dickie bird from you since Cambridge. Can't help though. Last saw James at a conference over a year ago. Let me know if you're ever in Oslo. Second date?

Liz leapt to her feet. "WHAT! There was no *first* date!" She shivered at the memory of herself struggling and shouting, of O'Brien's groping hands. "You twisted piece of SHIT!"

Her yell, at the extinction of her last glimmer of hope, however small, was complemented by the sound of splintering glass, as the keyboard entered her computer screen. Liz began to shudder, her hands shaking wildly as the carpet screamed towards her.

Episodes like this occurred rarely these days. In the Children's Home, the doctor had said Liz's fits were triggered by emotional stress. Her medical report had stated that it was highly unlikely that anyone surviving such a violent car accident could remain unscathed, let alone nine-year-old twins. Even if they'd largely escaped the physical, there would definitely have been psychological trauma.

Despite lying curled up on the floor of her cottage, Liz was still falling. Falling through darkness. And as she plummeted, a thin white mist began to rush past her that rapidly gained in density, becoming thick cloud, which solidified further, lessening her speed of descent until she finally came to rest, crouching in a wet ditch. Breathing hard, Liz crept up the bank and tensed.

Ahead of her lay a patchwork of fields, the poorly-made quilt rising and falling across a dark landscape. Liz's attention was drawn to the horizon. A clump of trees was creeping towards the edge of the fields. They were more gang than clump, shuffling their feet, forming themselves into a black line against a dark blue sky. And from a gap in this tree line, like a missing tooth, came a burst of high-pitched screaming. Ducking into a nook in the thick hedge beside her, she peeped out. A small car was charging along the lane towards her hiding place. The screaming ripped the air, the deafening roar increasing as the car raced towards her. It was not the car engine roaring, but its occupants. All four were trying desperately to squeeze themselves out of the four open windows. Liz thought she could make out her brother's face and wanted to shout out 'James! Jump for it!' but the words refused to come. And now she wasn't sure if it was him after all. Because their faces had become terribly distorted as if they were competing in a gurning competition.

The trapped passengers' hideous screaming got higher and higher as though seeking a crescendo that refused to arrive. Four twisted faces, each straining skyward in the hope that their bodies might follow. Liz crouched lower into the hollow. Headlights blazing, eight arms flailing, the metal box hurtled past her hiding place. Its headlights continued to carve a path through the rapidly descending gloom as the car raced out of sight.

The line of trees with its missing tooth began to close in on Liz as she climbed out of her hiding place in the hedge. And like a flock of malevolent sheep turning the tables on their shepherd, the trees began herding Liz down the lane in the direction the condemned car had taken.

She started to run down the single track road but at every step her legs felt as though they had doubled in weight. Every few seconds a branch would fly out from the pursuing trees and whip against her bare legs. The cajoling wooden mob was gaining on her, as Liz found herself mimicking the movements of a monstrously overweight zombie. Wherever the trees were forcing her, it was somewhere she knew she didn't want to go. Somewhere ominous.

At the first bend she came to, an unnatural gap appeared in the hedge. Something had violently punched through it. As Liz peered between severed branches her breathing became more laboured. She leaned forward into the gaping hole, holding onto a broken branch to steady herself. Across the dark field she could see the outline of a car that had an electricity pylon growing out of it.

The braying trees had gone quiet and obediently lined up behind her on the other side of the lane, as if patiently waiting to cheer the arrival of a cavalcade of visiting dignitaries. With the trees silent, Liz's attention was grabbed by the familiar sound of a siren. She stood at the centre of the opening in the hedge and looked back up the lane. An ambulance was approaching. At speed.

The fat white vehicle careered round the corner, its siren blarting left and right, leaving cacophonous skid marks in the air. Tree branches reached across the lane and gave it celebratory slaps on the back, one even cheekily pinched its square metallic arse as it left the road, hurtling up the short grassy bank towards Liz.

Leaves hanging off broken twigs in the hedge reached out from either side of her and gently caressed her face, imploring her to remain precisely where she was standing.

Rooted to the spot, Liz felt herself immediately sink into the soil up to her knees.

The ambulance hit her smack between its beaming headlights, ripped her out of the ground and threw her through the gap in the hedge and into the field. Next to her parents' car.

Liz, nine years old again, stared through the passenger window. Her trapped mother was barely half the person she used to be, with her legs on the wrong side of the pylon. She watched her mother's face become horribly disfigured, contorted with the efforts her collapsed lungs were having to exert to try to catch her breath. Her final breath.

Through the gloom, Liz saw James on his hands and knees crouching over their father, a few yards from a car she didn't recognise. This hideous wreck, now mangled coffin, must be somebody else's car.

Liz, kneeling at her father's feet, watched a drop of blood the size of a grape fall from her brother's chin and disappear into her dad's torn woollen jumper.

"Get up!" begged the small boy.

Doors slammed and Liz turned towards the short leafy tunnel through which she had been viciously propelled. Two men in blue uniforms had climbed out of the ambulance that poked through the hedge. As Liz started walking towards them, the faceless medics yelled, "Stay on the scene!"

From behind her she heard another pitiful "Get up!"

"Stay on the scene!" the pair of paramedics yelled again, except this time she could swear their words were accompanied by a funky shake of their hips.

The ambulance was clearly taking part in medical trials to see if 500 Watt speakers, at maximum volume, were a more effective resuscitant than boring old defibrillators. Pumping out at full whack, causing the whole field to shake, was James Brown's 'Like a Sex Machine'. The paramedics, dancing towards Liz, started singing along to the music.

"Get up!... Stay on the scene!... Like a sex machine!"

And as the faceless duo advanced on her, their singing became more raucous.

"Get up!... Stay on the scene!... Like a sex machine!"

Liz broke into a run, her legs thrashing against her living room carpet. And as she looked frantically back over her shoulder, the two men chasing her crossed through the twin beams of the ambulance's headlights. Momentarily their blurred faces gained detail. Liz froze, her heart pumping violently. Two Tim O'Brien's were bearing down on her.

Looking ahead, Liz gauged that there was barely enough space for her to dart between the hedge and the ambulance blocking the hole in it. She dived past the side of the vehicle, the sharp stubs of branch scraping at her, pulling at her skirt. The two Tims followed, the narrow channel forcing them to merge into one, his hands grabbing at Liz's ankles as she fought to complete her exit from the field. One final kick caused a shoe to fly off which clattered against the glass door of her wood burner. Liz rolled over on the floor of her cottage, gasping for breath. As her panting subsided, Liz could make out a gentle rustling around her. Shoulder to shoulder, trees lined the walls of her small living room. They began swaying from side to side and then jostling each other aggressively. Their clamouring became frenetic and they started stamping their huge root-like peg legs. The collective stomping continued, the banging getting louder and louder. And then the shouting started.

"Liz…Liz…LIZ!"

As the trees faded away, torchlight beamed onto Liz's face through her letterbox.

"LIZ, OPEN THE DOOR!"

Chapter Nine

"God, I needed that," said Liz, her blue towel wrapped like a turban, stark above the white bath robe.

"Sit and chill, love." The woman patted the sofa cushion beside her, her voice warm and gentle. "Kettle's on."

"Best friend forever," said Liz.

"Want me to pop next door and grab your meds?"

"Thanks, Amy, but they'll be way out of date."

"Not surprised. I can't remember when your last fit was," said Amy. "How did you sleep?"

"Like a log. Could have been a bed of nails."

"You were snoring like a pig. Could hear it through the wall."

"Thanks, best friend forever."

Amy headed to the kitchen at the click of the kettle. Liz pulled the cord of her bath robe tighter and began flicking through her phone.

"Bollocks. Forgot it's the reunion tomorrow."

"You should go." Amy called out. "Give your mind a break."

"Nah. I need to figure out my next move, now I know O'Brien's lying through his teeth."

"Are you sure?"

"Double-checked it just now."

"So how come the police drew a blank on James."

"They're not interested," said Liz. "Plus that new facial

recog software I'm using is probably outside their budget. I reckon any investigative journalist worth their salt could outrun the cops."

"Ooh, get you!" said Amy.

Liz didn't hear the retort. "So why the hell did the slime ball lie? Says he hasn't seen James in over a year… and yet FaceCog just found a photo of the two of them together, obviously in conversation, only a week ago."

"Where were they?" said Amy, carrying two mugs into the room.

"Defence Conference, surprise-surprise."

"Industrial espionage is my guess," said Amy.

"Where did that come from?"

"Just a guess," said Amy, putting the mugs on the low coffee table. "You did say they were both in missile technology. I'm sure loads of countries would kill to get their hands on military secrets. Well, not kill kill. Sorry, I meant—"

"That's my thinking too," said Liz quickly. She looked out of the small window beside the fireplace, remnants of snow still clutching at the bottom of the frame. "I never thought, even in my wildest nightmares, I'd be emailing Tim Weirdo." She reached for the nearest mug and took a gulp. "Of all the men I would never ever want to make contact with again."

"I thought that accolade belonged to one of your other Cambridge colleagues."

Confused for a moment, Liz stared at her friend. "What? Charlie Dangerfield?"

"That was it."

Liz snorted. "Well, to be honest, I did try cyber-stalking him about a year ago."

"Kept that secret," said Amy, smiling. "And?"

Liz shook her head. The blue towel began to unravel. "Nah. Nothing. Off the grid. Even my FaceCog software couldn't find a trace."

"I've a vague memory that the last time his name came up we'd killed two bottles of red."

"Don't remember," said Liz. Another gulp of coffee and she got up from the sofa. "Gonna get dressed. Where's your hairdryer?"

"Usual place. What's the hurry?"

"Got an idea," said Liz, as she began to climb the stairs.

"Tell me."

No reply. Amy raised her voice. "He might be at the reunion."

"Who?"

Amy yelled up the stairwell. "Mr Dangerous." She could just make out Liz's reply above the hum of the hairdryer.

"That'd be a first."

Chapter Ten

Staring deadpan into the security camera, Dangerfield pictured his boss in her usual tight pencil skirt. *What's she called this meeting for? Bending the rules again?*

Eye recognition complete, the thick steel barrier at the entrance to GCHQ slid silently down into the ground. He put his foot to the floor. The 3.5 litre quad-cam engine, hidden inside the black Mini Cooper, shredded the air. It tore up the fifty metres to the car park. Two security checks later and he was inside the Doughnut.

"Morning, Jack! How's the wife?"

"It's Gerald, sir, and I'm—"

The doors slapped shut behind Dangerfield. Having swipe-passed several more security doorways, a final corridor brought him to an office clearly labelled in brass: Senior Commander Sarah Watling, M.B.A., .S.R.O., D.I.R.. He entered a huge windowless room, its two chairs and desk tiny in comparison. The wall behind the desk was covered in computer screens. Partly blocking his view of this was a woman in a grey pencil skirt, with hair to match. She turned towards him.

"Oh sorry, Miss. Should I have knocked?"

"Very funny. Take a seat."

Dangerfield remained standing.

"Charles, I need to talk to you about something that GCHQ's picked up. And if you think I'm having this conversation standing in these heels, you are mistaken." Watling sat down, crossing her legs.

Dangerfield, with deliberate slowness took the other seat. His go-to image, whenever GCHQ was mentioned, flashed across Dangerfield's mind. He pictured electronic tendrils reaching deep inside a human brain. Occasionally it flipped to bindweed choking a lily.

"Now, about GCHQ's findings," said Watling.

Dangerfield clocked the piercing stare, folded arms and frown.

"They highlight how close you used to be to the Green family. And that bothers me." Her eyes never left his face.

"Hang on, Sarah, that connection's one of the central reasons Bulstrode wanted me on this project."

"Well, I need to give you a reminder, Charles, that in this game everything is expendable."

"Very thoughtful of you," said Dangerfield. "And by everything we both know you mean everyone."

"Look, you pulled a rabbit out of a hat with James, but his sister's a different kettle of fish. She's not going to keep out of this, and I'm not convinced you'll be able to remain impartial."

"I knew exactly what I was doing when I signed up," said Dangerfield, meeting her stare. *This woman misses nothing - give her nothing.*

"I've heard you say that a few times," said Watling. "It's just that Langley keeps stressing that the consequences of this project failing could be... well... catastrophic. That's my assessment too."

"The Americans are always stressing." He could smell

her perfume wafting over the desk. *Classic Chanel.* "They need to take a chill pill. At least *these* fuckers really do have Weapons of Mass Destruction."

Dangerfield watched his boss as she stood up and walked the few steps to a stack of printers. *God, she could be frustrating. But her predecessor was an ugly bastard and nowhere near as sharp.*

The printers were confined in a steel cage, heavily bolted to the wall. Watling entered a code and a second later a sheet of A4 shot from the lowest tray. Dangerfield focused as she bent to retrieve it.

"Read that!" Watling almost barked.

It was headed up 'ISP Connections' and beneath that a record of email communications between a Tim O'Brien and a Liz Green. The words 'James' and 'brother' were highlighted. Dangerfield scanned it and tossed the paper onto the desk. His superior took it and slipped it through a slot in the top of a metal cube next to the desk. A tiny puff of dust signalled the document's final gasp of existence.

"We assumed she'd reach out to all her brother's contacts, however unlikely the link," said Watling. "Hopefully O'Brien's reply will have quelled any further attempt at contact." She was staring at him. "But I can't stress this enough." Her eyes were burning holes, "It's absolutely imperative that Green's sister stops digging. We've worked bloody hard to ensure the trail to Green has gone completely cold. I don't want his sister stumbling on anything that might resurrect him. She's a bloody journalist, for Christ's sake." She folded her arms tightly under her breasts. "Do you understand, Charles? James

Green must remain dead."

Chapter Eleven

Dangerfield stepped through the twin doors of the chapel and into the bright, wintery light. Ahead of him lay the smooth lawns of Magdalene College, manicured to within an inch of their life, and spreading down to the edge of the river Cam.

A banner hanging above the chapel doors, flapping in the breeze, caught his attention. He turned and read '8th Reunion' and shrugged. *First and last for me.*

He scanned the gathered crowd and saw a field of cattle, in polished shoes and sparkling jewellery. Four hundred ex-students constrained by convention. Conforming to code. The men were dressed almost identically, dark-suited, and only the occasional scarf breaking the monotony of their appearance. The women were more variegated, colourful, a few dressed inadequately for a winter's day, cleavage and legs overriding frost bite.

Dangerfield checked his watch. He'd timed his arrival perfectly. Ten minutes since kick-off, and the herd had already formed into its natural groupings. He could see inside their minds. For some, the confidence that had brought them here would have already evaporated. They'd be hoping that the glass of Chablis they'd quickly downed on arrival would hurry up and kick in. He clocked the most extreme sociophobes, already back at the drinks tables, empty glass in hand, desperate for the effects of a refill. *Bet they pre-loaded too.*

For others, clearly, shyness wasn't an issue. As he began to skirt the crowds, he passed thirty former members of the Wyvern Gentlemen's Drinking Club, competing to be heard. Women, the stock market, rugby, political intrigue and how their wives spent their money were being discussed loudly. *Idiots.*

Three years as a fellow inmate at Cambridge and Dangerfield had the lie of the land. On average, the artists were louder than the engineers, and both at least ten decibels above the scientists. These shy, pale, laboratory-bound mice shunned light. And human interaction. He passed a small group of them, huddled together for comfort, discussing the weather, the words diffraction and precipitation springing out. Continuing to circle, he passed the desperadoes and validation queens: I'm not a failure, look, Gucci *and* Vuitton. I'm with the in-crowd. I'm above you, better than you. A success. *Fools.*

Familiar faces shone from the crowds but Dangerfield kept his focus: hunting for Liz.

And there she was. Chatting to two other women. At the far side of the crowd. *Shit, where's Moses when you need him?*

It took several minutes to part the excited and curious waters. He had to run the full gauntlet of 'Charlie darling! I've missed you!', 'Thought you must have been in jail, mate.' and 'I've bought an island.'

Several times Dangerfield's eyes met Liz's before they came face to face. At no point did she return his smile. As Dangerfield made his final approach, the other two women seemed to evaporate, slinking off in some unspoken understanding.

Standing in front of her, he looked deeply into Liz's eyes. And smiled.

Liz folded her arms. "What the fuck are *you* doing here?"

Behind them, the former Wyvern Club members were becoming rowdy, squawking loudly and throwing their bow ties at each other. Dangerfield glanced at them. "Fear of missing out, maybe?"

"FOMO? You? Yeah, right!" Liz said above the din. "Very funny. Why *did* you come? I thought us low-life's weren't worth talking to."

Dangerfield shook his head slowly and smiled. "So where's James? Haven't spotted him yet."

He noted the pregnant pause.

"James couldn't make it this year. Deadlines. You know how it is."

"That's a shame. Was hoping to catch up with you both."

"Why? Is it convenient now, after, what is it, seven… eight years?"

Dangerfield ground a lone remnant of snow into the grass with his foot. "So how's the world of news? Spotted your name more than once in the Guardian."

Liz didn't answer. She folded her arms even tighter. "Tell me about you, Charlie. What have you been doing since I last saw you? Haven't seen *your* name anywhere."

For one fleeting moment, Dangerfield imagined that her big hazel eyes could see right through him. He took a deep breath. "I'm in management consultancy."

"I see."

Dangerfield sensed a mocking twinkle in her eye.

"Well there you are..." he smiled, "...and the job really is as vacuous as it sounds."

"Perfect for you then. So why did you choose it?"

The Wyverns had begun raucously chanting a rugby song.

"You know what, Liz..." He glanced at them again, "...sometimes, I wonder myself."

The chapel bell rang once, the sound deep and tremulous through the crisp air. Balancing on a wooden chair, the college chaplain, with his hands to his mouth, bellowed for silence.

Only seconds into his welcome speech, a dyed blonde appeared from nowhere, planting herself between Liz and Dangerfield.

"My god, Charlie!" she shrieked. "So the rumours aren't true! You're not dead after all!" She laughed, alone.

Dangerfield didn't answer.

"Hey, Rosie," said Liz.

"Hey, Liz," the woman threw back at her, her eyes remaining locked on Dangerfield. "What on earth have you been up to?"

"Busy minding my own business," said Dangerfield curtly.

"You've got your own company? Knew it! Could never imagine you having a boss." The woman was permanently animated, her hands grabbing at Dangerfield's arms as she spoke, the volume and excitement in her voice destroying the chaplain's delivery for all those nearby. She leaned into Dangerfield. "Is it true that you saved a man's life?"

Dangerfield grinned at her. "It's true." He beckoned for her to come even closer and then whispered demonically, "I took my foot off the cunt's throat." *Now fuck off. I'm working.*

The woman jerked her head away and stepped back, unsure of how to react. She broke into nervous laughter and then stopped suddenly, the confusion on her face flicking to panic.

As Rosie vanished into the crowd, the chaplain ended his speech, referring to the arrival of a chilling breeze and cheerfully yelled, "Grub up!"

"What the hell did you whisper to her?" Liz asked.

"Nosey Rosie? Told her I was about to propose to you."

"WHAT?"

"Thought that would pull her plug. Can't stand attention seekers."

"Attention seekers?" Liz cracked a smile. "Pot, kettle?"

Dangerfield, returning the smile, coughed sharply. "Proposal retracted," and taking Liz's arm, led her swiftly across the lawn, with zero resistance.

Inside the banqueting hall, the noise was tremendous. Four hundred chairs scraped out and then in. Four hundred voices switched on simultaneously, jabbering the niceties of arrival at an over-cutleried table before the face-stuffing began. The racket reverberated around the hall, echoing horrifically inside the lofty chamber.

Dangerfield glanced at Liz, noting a faraway look in her eyes. "Are you alright? You look a bit…"

“A bit what?”

“Dunno… preoccupied?”

“I’m fine. Really.” Liz gave a weak smile. “Things on my mind.”

“Life of a journalist, huh?”

“Pretty much.” She looked up at the ceiling, and sighed. “I shouldn’t have come.”

“Look, I've got an idea,” said Dangerfield, glancing across the sea of heads, “How hungry are you?”

“I'm absolutely starving. It’s a bloody long drive here.”

“Ok, follow me.” Taking Liz by the hand, Dangerfield strode between the endless refectory tables, each having consumed a whole oak tree in its manufacture.

The two of them slipped through the double doors that led to the kitchens. The stressed staff all had their heads down, frantically plating up. Approaching the man with the tallest hat, Dangerfield announced, “The Chief Provost's been taken ill. We're to take his meal to his room.”

“God, that's the last thing we need right now…”

Dangerfield took the plate that the man had been holding. “Don't worry, I know exactly what he wants.”

“Thank God for that, sir. Appreciate the help.”

Dangerfield grabbed a large silver tray and thrust it under his arm, tossed half a dozen quail breasts onto the plate and as he headed towards an enormous cage of French fries, he shouted across the noisy kitchen, “Miss Green, do you know what the Provost's favourite pudding is?”

“Well, they do say feed a cold... so maybe we could tempt him with the chocolate truffles with crème de marron *and* the Eton Mess. He loves his strawberries and meringue." She grinned, some of the stress already drained from her face.

Back in the weak sunlight, the puddings wobbled insanely as Liz tried to regain her composure.

"It's like we never graduated," she giggled. "You haven't changed at all."

"Come on," said Dangerfield, pointing to the river, "Let's go and sit in one of those rowing boats." He grabbed a nearly full bottle of Chablis from a table as they headed across the lawn.

They had both forgotten cutlery, so while Dangerfield rowed, Liz fed the two of them by hand. The puddings were the trickiest, the strawberries and meringue becoming smeared around Dangerfield's mouth.

"You'd make a good make-up artist," Dangerfield said, wiping his sleeve across his face.

"For the Joker in Batman maybe," Liz said, reaching to wipe a bit he'd missed. "So tell me, how can a management consultant manage to forget napkins as well as spoons?"

"Forget the detail. Life's about focusing on the important things. Look, I didn't forget this!" Dangerfield held up the bottle of Chablis and passed it to Liz. "Sorry, no glasses."

Liz took a swig and passed the bottle back. "Don't you think, Charlie, that the years just seem to slip by?"

Dangerfield nodded and smiled at her, watching her trail her hand briefly in the water as the boat glided along.

"How *do you* spend your spare time?" she asked.

"Well, seeing as you're asking, I'm trying to write a book."

"Oh yeah? Really? Come on then. What's it about?" asked Liz.

Dangerfield continued pulling on the oars, steadily and firmly, as they approached a wide bend in the river.

"Come on, Charlie. Don't keep any more secrets from me. I know you want to tell me. We both know you love the sound of your own voice."

He smiled. *Damn it, she was just as he remembered her.* "Ok, well... it's about a boy who doesn't have any friends."

"Autobiography huh?"

"Funny. And he gets a nocturnal visit from a really odd character, telling him that he's a wizard with magical powers."

A broad smile appeared on Liz's face, "Hate to shoot you down in flames, but I think you'll find it's been done before."

"Yeah, yeah, but wait. The thing is, he doesn't have any magical powers at all! That's the twist. He goes to school and starts trying to cast all these spells, bragging about what he can do. But none of the damn spells work! He's completely humiliated! To make things worse, the poor thing's even skinnier than his useless wand. The school bullies have a field day."

"Sounds more like a treatise on developmental psychology," said Liz.

Dangerfield returned her big smile. *Keep it going*. "I thought the story could follow his progress through life. You know, how at university he's this skinny misfit. And while studying to be a scientist, becomes this emaciated monster, vowing to wreak revenge on humanity."

"Is there going to be a moral undercurrent?" asked Liz, "Or is it a pure horror story? What about a screenplay? I love a good horror movie."

She reached between Dangerfield's legs and grabbed the bottle of Chablis that was lodged there. "So have you got a title for the book yet?"

"Working on it. What about 'Revenge of the Stick Insect'?"

Liz didn't reply, and took a swig from the bottle.

Surely she's made the link to O'Brien by now. "No, you're right, not very punchy, is it?" Dangerfield followed her gaze. She was staring at the riverbank. "Liz? You're miles away."

"Yeah, sorry." She took another swig. "So who's this weirdo scientist based on? Better not be James!'

Dangerfield laughed, "Think James was about the only normal one in our year. And he was never thin." He watched as Liz swirled her hand in the water again, his attention drawn to the goose pimples on her forearm.

"You know, I'm being reminded of someone who used to take some of James' classes."

"Really?"

"Tim O'Brien. Thin guy. Took physics. Weird mannerisms."

"Tim O'Brien? Definitely rings a bell. Tim O'Brien, Tim O' my god yes! Yes, of course, Triple Jump Tim we used to call him. Every third step he took had to be a small jump."

"That's the guy," said Liz quietly.

"You know, the funny thing is, now that you've

reminded me of him, I'm sure I've met his doppelganger," said Dangerfield.

"Believe me, one is too many," said Liz, shuddering.

"You're telling me! This guy was a French version of O'Brien and one violent bastard."

Dangerfield pulled the oars in and slipped off his jacket. "You're shivering. Come on, you've got bare arms." He stood and the boat wobbled as he leaned towards Liz, reaching behind her and slipping his jacket over her shoulders.

"Thanks, Charlie."

Dangerfield began rowing again. "Yeah, my advice to anyone would be to stay well clear of this kind of fruitcake. One bleeding-heart Francophile felt sorry for the loner and tried to befriend the guy. The next friend she made was St. Peter."

Dangerfield looked straight at Liz to gauge her reaction. *That's quite a frown. Let's seal this.*

"Oh God, poor woman. Do you know what provoked him?" asked Liz.

"Well, that's just it. Could've been anything. His emotions were so explosive."

"Explosive?"

"Imagine you're driving a 1956 Maserati 250F down the M5 out of Birmingham. You're in top, and hitting 12,000 revs. Now, you should be touching 200mph."

"Isn't that slightly illegal?"

"Apparently not, if you're leaving Birmingham."

"Ha…ha…ha... don't be a meanie... my favourite Grandpa was a Brummie," said Liz.

"Ah, that's so sweet... but listen, imagine at 200 mph you suddenly jam the gear lever into reverse. Now *that's* what I mean by explosive." *She'd better be getting this.* "You'd be left writhing in agony amongst the wreckage... not unlike the state they found that woman in, when Frenchie exploded." *Fuck!... of all the inappropriate analogies, but hey, this should keep the mission on track. And it could save her life.* Dangerfield paused from rowing for a second and glanced at Liz. *So why the hell is she smiling?* "To be honest, if you were in the kind of pain he'd left her in, you'd be grateful if the cars exhaust pipe wrapped itself round your neck and squeezed your head off."

"Nice..."

"Although obviously in your case it would be more like a cork flying out of a bottle of Richebourg Grand Cru."

"Thanks very much. Put that way it sounds almost pleasurable," said Liz.

"Oh no, trust me, the popping sound is horrific when your head leaves your neck."

Liz suddenly turned and stared at Dangerfield "You're in Security Services, aren't you." She flicked the surface of the water. "I knew you had to be. Explains why you're untraceable." She flicked again. "James thought my idea was mad and that you were just a miserable bastard who didn't keep in touch."

"If I were a real-life spy we'd be having sex by now, not freezing to death in this rowing boat."

"So, you *are* just a miserable bastard?"

"Afraid so."

"You know what Charlie? You remind me of my Grandpa a little bit, now I come to think of it..."

"The Brummie one? That's really... great." Dangerfield grinned.

"Yes. You've got the same wicked smile."

"Thanks." Dangerfield shrugged, smiled again, and started gently tapping his foot against Liz's.

"Wow, long time since we've played footsie."

"Ha! Centuries. You know, now that you've reminded me of O'Brien, I'd say that he and Frenchie must be like two peas in a pod. I'm telling you, if anyone were to knowingly get involved with old Triple Jump they'd have to be bonkers. Luckily, that French guy's permanently strapped down in a prison's psychiatric wing." *Surely that's done the job.* "I wonder what happened to O'Brien?" Dangerfield noticed that the bottle of Chablis was almost empty and that Liz's eyes looked a little glazed. *No wonder the girl isn't petrified, she's been swigging the whole time I've been spouting.*

"I think James keeps in touch with all the Physics nerds. None in prison that I know of. Think O'Brien went to Norway." Liz raised the bottle "Nearly gone. We'd better head back."

"If we must."

Liz grinned. "Guess what Charlie, we've got something in common."

"What's that then?"

"I love the sound of your voice too."

At that, the little boat ran aground opposite Kings College, scraping to a gentle standstill.

"Come and sit next to me. The view from here's lovely," said Liz.

Dangerfield pulled the oars in and joined her on the short wooden bench.

Liz passed her arm through his and huddled closer. "So… why *did* you disappear? We were friends."

"More than friends, surely?"

"So… why?"

"Tell you one day."

"On our death beds?" She nudged him with her elbow.

"Promise."

Liz pulled the jacket collar up. "I've got another question."

"Fire away."

"Why was it that you never ever seemed to get stressed Charlie? In all the years I knew you."

"Probably just hid it well. Plus I always try to focus on the bigger picture."

"And what's in this big picture of yours?" asked Liz.

"Good question. Well, let's think... I'd definitely have Constable's England as a backdrop and then maybe mix it up with a bit of Dali. Always loved his Autumn Cannibalism... you know, where a loving couple are entwined and helping themselves to spoonfuls of each others' body!"

"Maybe best that we forgot the cutlery after all, then."

Dangerfield snorted. "Maybe."

"Bit of a weird combo, Constable and Dali. Hope you've got Elgar's Land of Hope and Glory playing in the background," suggested Liz.

"Of course! No, all I want is a happy kind of capitalism, where everyone gets rich. Everyone, fuck it. We're all equal. Every single Earthling would have an equal share in this rotating ball of a planet we're all shacked up on."

"But what about Aliens?" said Liz, smiling. "Don't leave Aliens out."

"Actually, fuck it, you're right. Let's include them too. In fact, you've got me thinking. I'm going to come out. Yep! Right here. Right now. With you as my witness, Liz. For years I've been living a lie. But, no more!" Dangerfield suddenly stood and the boat wobbled violently, Liz grabbing the edge of the boat with one hand and Dangerfield's calf with the other. Cupping his hands to his mouth, Dangerfield yelled "I… AM… AN… ALIEN!" the sound carrying through the crisp, still air. And as he sat down, "In my world… no, in my universe, everyone's welcome."

Dangerfield reached for the wine bottle but Liz's hand got there first, his fingers brushing the invisible blonde hairs on the back of her hand as she gripped the bottle's neck.

"So that's where you've been for the last eight years. On another planet!"

*

The noisy vibrations increased as the 747 trundled up the 4 kilometres of the Northern Runway at Heathrow Airport. Looking out of the window, Liz watched the huge glass structure of Terminal 5 slipping backwards.

"Scandinavian Airlines welcomes you aboard Flight SK804 to Oslo. We will be arriving at approximately 13:30 hours, and the weather on the ground is currently unpredictable."

Chapter Twelve

The telephone in Dangerfield's office at MI6 was telling lies.

"She's bought a ticket to Oslo?" *What the fuck*! He leapt to his feet. *After all that crap I gave her, to scare her off O'Brien.*

"Okay, I'll pay her another visit. I presume the Department's instructed the Airline to tell her about the double-booking-blip."

An even bigger whopper sprang from the phone. "In the air?" *I can't believe what I'm hearing! I can't fucking believe it!*

If Van Gogh was standing in Dangerfield's shoes, this time he would have done the job properly. Both ears ripped off, thrown out the window, and heading for the River Thames, seven storeys below. Within seconds Dangerfield sprinted the long corridor that led to his boss's office and shoved her door open. If he'd stopped to read the shiny brass plate on *this* door, he would have read Senior Commander Sarah Watling, S.T.U...P.I.D ...B.I.T.C.H.

"Why the hell didn't you pull the flight?"

Watling sat resolute. "The opportunity wasn't available."

"But I'm always having flights stopped," exclaimed Dangerfield. "Bad weather, defective undercarriage. The airlines are good at making it up."

“Have you been doing this without my authorisation?”

No reply. He moved to the window and stared out at Big Ben and Parliament on the other side of the river.

“So what went wrong in Cambridge?” she asked.

Still no reply. Big Ben started chiming. Dangerfield started banging his head against the glass, matching the chimes. Luckily it was only two o' clock.

“You should have stopped that flight... it will be landing in less than two hours.” He began pacing up and down. “We don't even need to give the airlines a reason. We're MI6 for Gods sake!”

“Don't lecture me, Charles. We always need a reason. And a very good one at that.”

“But the airlines get compensated and there are umpteen excuses they can give the passengers!” *Why is she so bloody calm?*

“Oh really. Indulge me...” Her reply seemed almost playful.

“I don't bloody know! Tell them the wings have snapped off... the tail's bent... or announce that some stroppy steward minced into the cock-pit and yanked the captain's fucking joystick off for all I care! For fuck’s sake, what the hell happened to 'absolutely catastrophic'? Wasn't that the joint assessment of this project going tits-up?”

“Interesting... I've never seen you lose it before. The reason the plane wasn't pulled, as I just told you, was because we didn't get the opportunity. She bought a ticket on her phone at the airport and boarded immediately.”

“But—”

“Listen! GCHQ may be effective, but it’s far from

perfect. You might want to control people 24/7, but the Service can't. Especially when they're on random."

"Yeah, but I laid it on so thick about O'Brien. I don't get it!"

"Well you'd better start getting it! I'm seeing Bulstrode in ten minutes! What the hell am I going to tell him?"

Dangerfield made for the door, "She bought it at the airport? Why so impulsive?"

"For God's sake Charles, she's a woman... in case you hadn't noticed. Although I'm beginning to suspect that you have!"

Dangerfield didn't hear Watling's final words. He was already back in the corridor and running for the lift. It took an eternity to get him to the ground floor. As the doors opened he burst into the huge entrance hall, barging between two men playing Candy Crush on their phones. The impact caused one man's device to fly from his grip and crash to the marble floor. Sprinting for the exit Dangerfield trod on its carcass. *Game over, mate.*

"Oi, you! That's Government property!"

Dangerfield turned and growled before slipping through the double front doors, "Aren't we all?"

Chapter Thirteen

"Tolv hundre kroner."

"What?"

The taxi driver held up ten fingers, and then two fingers. "Velkommen til Oslo."

Liz nodded. "Yeah, yeah, I get the message. You can put your fingers away now. Thanks a lot. I mean takk." She waved her card at the device in his hand, and quickly climbed out of the cab.

Speeding off, the taxi rounded the corner and the street fell silent. Liz pulled her jacket collar up. The place looked desolate. No pedestrians, no parked vehicles, and the only litter, a plethora of street signage. The red Norwegian lettering could have been declaring a chemical disaster zone, given the absence of life. *And this is a residential area?*

She'd been dropped outside a modern, five-storey apartment block that looked more IKEA store than accommodation. Stepping up to the glass entrance, Liz's eyes were drawn to its entry-phone system. The egg-yolk sun, just beginning to slip behind the buildings opposite, was giving the shiny metal box a silvery-orange glow.

Bugger!

She pulled her phone from her shoulder bag. Her call to O'Brien's landline went straight to answerphone. *At least he's definitely out. Thank God.*

Liz leaned against the wall beside the entrance, put her phone away and ferreted in her shoulder bag for her paperback book.

Surely, sooner or later, somebody's got to leave the building.

She'd almost completed two chapters and was engrossed in the discovery of a second body when she heard deep voices approaching from the other side of the door. *Shit!* Shoving the book into her bag, blonde hair flying back, she quickly stepped in front of the glass door. As a man's hand closed on the handle inside, Liz pretended to reach for the entry system's keypad, and then stopping short, smiled.

"Ahh, hi!"

"Hei." The two young men replied together and, returning Liz's smile, held the door open for her.

"Takk." Still smiling, she squeezed past them and headed straight for the elevator. Pressing the call button, the door immediately scraped open, and without looking back she stepped inside. Breathing quickly, Liz stood completely still. Three seconds dragged by before she heard the loud click of the front door closing. She took a long deep breath, focusing on the air filling her lungs, and then her steady exhale. Another deep breath, and again she concentrated on the flow of air entering and then leaving her body.

At the third breath, she felt her heart leap. The sound of scraping jolted her, as the elevator door began to close. *Shit! Someone's called it.*

Half throwing, half sliding herself through the narrowing exit, she was back in the hallway. As the elevator rattled upwards, she started to quietly climb the stairs. At the top of the third flight, she heard it pass her on its way back down. A few more tentative steps and Liz was outside apartment 4A. She glanced behind her and saw a mirror image. Except on this door the brass numerals read 4B and sat above a small spy hole. She could hear her heart beating and knew it wasn't the climb.

I'm crazy. I'm actually breaking and entering.

O'Brien's reply to the email she had sent, while boarding at Heathrow, had been clear. She was welcome anytime, but he wanted plenty of notice, and the next few weeks would be a complete no-no as he'd be out of the country. Her instincts, however, were still telling her to knock. *Maybe his schedule's changed. What if someone else is staying here while he's away? Maybe he just lied and he's actually in!*

If there was one person who'd murdered her trust in anything he was ever to do or say, it was Tim O'Brien. In her turmoil, she was reminded of why she was here. An image of James, aged eight, leaning precariously from the wooden bridge in Priory Park flashed across her mind. He was reaching down, straining to grab her up-stretched arms, as she struggled in the waters below.

Grabbing her purse, Liz extracted her library card. She inserted it in the door crack, just above the lock, and slid it downwards. Two attempts later and she could feel the beginnings of panic. *I spent over an hour Googling this!* Raising her knee against the door, she leaned into it as heavily as she could. *Third time lucky, you bastard!* Pulling the card down hard, the door burst open sending her tumbling into a small dark hallway.

"Thank you bloody YouTube."

Flicking the light switch, she started to close the front door, but at the last second decided to leave it slightly ajar.

Four doors led off the tiny entrance area. Dipping her head into each room, she quickly scanned their contents. Kitchen. Lounge. Bedroom. All three rooms were pristine and devoid of warmth. No friendly fridge magnets, no framed photos, and no cosy slippers. As she opened the fourth door, initial darkness was ripped away by a light springing on. Her ears filled with a hellish whirring sound. Slamming the door shut, she could feel herself shaking. It took only a second for realisation to hit her.

"Idiot!"

She reopened the door of the windowless bathroom, logged the showroom-clean porcelain and closed it again. The automatic fan continued to whirr.

Stepping into the kitchen, Liz was struck by the reek of bleach. Its gleaming surfaces were clear of any utensils other than a kettle, toaster and microwave that sat equidistant from each other. The room would win first prize in any OCD competition. Squeaky clean, and everything precisely placed, except for an open cutlery drawer shouting 'Look at me!'

In the bedroom, Liz stared at herself in the mirrored doors of the wall-to-wall closet and sighed. *Right, Miss Bloody Marple. Where to start?*

Walking around the double bed, she slid the left door of the closet open. She was expecting a couple of suits, the odd jumper and a coat or two hanging limply in a largely redundant space. What immediately bulged towards her, as if just released from captivity, was the theatrical wardrobe of a full Christmas pantomime. *Weirdo! Shit, he'd better not walk in on me.*

Velvet, PVC, nylon and rubber costumes fought for Liz's attention in their attempt to climb out of the over-stuffed closet. The winner was a pink tutu. She couldn't take her eyes off it. Something about its condition disturbed her. Prising it from between Spiderman and a clown's frock, she threw it onto the bed. It was ripped as though the wearer had fallen into a shredder.

Pulling the closet's drawers open, she found smaller garments, neatly folded. Rifling through a rainbow of suspenders, panties and tights, she paused at the leopard skin mankini.

Liz felt tense as she made for the lounge. Bookshelves held only technical literature. Thick tomes on guidance systems, machine code and electronic controls were arranged according to book height. In front of the room's only window was a birchwood desk. Whoever sat at it had a commanding view of Strømberg's Terrasse, four storeys below. A large computer screen and keyboard took centre stage. Leaning over the chair, Liz clicked the mouse. Expecting the display to request secure login details, she jumped when the computer screen went straight to an image of O'Brien. She shuddered at the sight of his stick-thin frame, failing badly to fill a Superman outfit. He also wore an unfeasibly wide grin. Heart rate quickening, Liz sat down. *Result! Still logged in. He must have left the apartment in one hell of a hurry.*

Clicking repeatedly on the arrow, image after image of O'Brien filled the screen. His range of costumes seemed endless, the only common theme being the background. All were selfies, and Liz could see they had been taken in his bedroom with him posing in front of the mirrored closet doors. After clicking through twenty odd pictures in as many seconds, Liz noticed make-up appearing on O'Brien's face. A little eye shadow to start, and then rouge. In the photo of him in a gossamer-thin white bodystocking, his eyes had progressed from mascara to huge false eyelashes. When the image of O'Brien in a pink tutu hit the screen, Liz felt a huge sense of foreboding. Here the tutu wasn't ripped, and thin bare legs ended inside a pair of shiny brown brogues. The make-up however, was so over-the-top, so badly and thickly applied, that any self-respecting drag queen would have immediately driven to the cliffs at Beachy Head and floored the accelerator pedal.

Filled with dread, Liz clicked the mouse again. The image that sprang on the screen made her jolt back in the chair, desperate to distance herself from the horrific intensity of what she was looking at.

With open scissors in one fist, fingers wrapped round the blades, and his phone clutched in the other, O'Brien was standing open-mouthed as though screaming. The pink tutu now looked identical to the one she'd just pulled out of the closet. She could only guess that he'd hacked at it with the scissors whilst still wearing it. The blades must have torn right through, as tiny rivulets of blood trickled down each pale leg and disappeared into O'Brien's brogues. The massive overdose of make-up had been crazily smeared over his face. It looked like he had dragged his fingers frantically over his eyes, cheeks and lips as if he had walked into a dangling cobweb. The blusher, spray tan and scarlet lipstick were now swirled together in a tangle of multi-coloured skid marks. In this photo, O'Brien had obviously been sobbing. His panda eyes were streaming, and had washed mascara over the mess of streaks. No amount of concealer could help now.

Liz closed the page and stared at the blank screen. She felt drained. A few seconds passed before she pulled the chair in sharply. "OK… let's do this."

She clicked on the 'History' tab. *This guy definitely lives alone!* O'Brien hadn't deleted the history of websites he'd visited. Some sites were unsuitable viewing for children. Others were unsuitable for every living creature on Planet Earth.

Feeling sick, she clicked on 'Documents' and scanned the list of filenames. The name 'James Green' jumped out at her. Her heart was pounding. Opening the file, Liz thought she must be imagining what she was looking at. The photograph had been taken through French windows. Its two subjects were sitting on a sofa. Their faces could not have been more familiar to her.

Despite all the disturbing images she'd just witnessed, the one in front of her right now shocked and distressed her the most. Why was a recent picture of her and Amy on this freak's computer?

She was given little time to dwell on it. The 'ding' of an elevator burst in her ears. Her whole body jumped. *The bloody door!*

Leaping from the chair, she raced into the tiny hallway. Through the slim crack, she could hear footsteps. Options raged in her head as they approached.

Diving into the bedroom, Liz frantically scrambled underneath the bed, banging her head hard on the frame. The gap was so tight that she had to keep her head turned sideways, her forced view on the world, a very narrow slot towards the doorway.

She heard the quiet click of the front door closing, the pad of steps getting closer. With each breath, her back squashed against the underside of the bed frame. Liz watched helplessly as a pair of shoes filled her field of vision. A pair of highly polished brown brogues.

Chapter Fourteen

"Wrong side of the bed. Didn't I teach you anything?"

The brown shoes looked familiar, but the voice didn't make any sense. Liz stayed frozen under the bed, her back pressing against the hard ribs of its wooden frame. Her view changed to one shoe and one knee. And then a face. The shockwave scrambled every cell in her brain.

"Here. Let me help."

Liz assumed she was in some weird, twisted dream. She sensed the bed lifting off her back. Her mouth opened, but no words even attempted escape. A hand reached out to her and she took it as if she'd been hypnotised. As she began to stand up, the words started forming.

"What the hell? … What the hell? … What the bloody hell?"

"Heard you the first time," replied the face. It was smiling.

The slap could not have been louder, as Liz's open hand slammed against Dangerfield's left cheek.

Her wrists were instantly grabbed and she felt her whole body shaking. No fit, just full-blown rage. A thousand questions, pent-up frustrations and stress exploded.

"What the hell's going on? What are *you* doing here?" She was shrieking.

Dangerfield let go of her wrists. He walked to the end of the bed and stared down at the empty street below.

"Hello? I asked you a question!"

The streetlights had come on, their low energy bulbs glowing weakly.

"Start talking, Charlie, or I swear on my parents' grave I'll push you out of that bloody window!"

Still with his back to her, Dangerfield's reply was calm. "Why did you come here, Liz? I thought I'd warned you off O'Brien."

"What! Why am *I* here? I'm here to find James. Remember him? My twin brother! Your friend! At least he *was* until you fell off the planet."

"I didn't have a choice in that little matter." His reply sounded flat.

"No choice? Your fellow Aliens abduct you, did they?" Liz's voice was on rapid-fire. "Yesterday you could barely remember O'Brien's name and now you've beamed into his apartment like bloody Spock! So, why are you here? Face me, damn it!"

Dangerfield turned and stared directly at her, his lips pursed.

Liz's mouth suddenly fell open. "Hang on! How come you're not surprised to see *me*? How did you know I was coming to Oslo? Oh my God…" Her hands sprang to the sides of her head, "… you're tracking me!"

Exasperation peaking, Liz let out a roaring yell. "You know where my brother is, don't you? Where is he? Tell me where James is!" She took a step towards Dangerfield, and with a mimicking lilt in her voice, "Hi, Liz. So where's James? I was hoping to catch up with you both." She stepped closer. "Management Consultant my arse! Chief

Bullshitter more like!"

The man's eyes were fixed on her like a rabbit's caught in the main beam of the 6.30 Express from Grand Central.

"You'd better start talking Charlie or I'm going straight to the police. I'll bang on the door of Number 10 if I have to."

Dangerfield came to life.

"Cup of tea?"

"What?" Liz exclaimed. "What planet are you from? Do you understand English?"

She stepped up to him and tried shoving him backwards. "Where's James?… Where's James?… Where's James?"

Dangerfield caught her wrists again.

"Listen. He's overseas. On a project."

For a moment, Liz couldn't speak. Then, "You're lying! If it was that simple, he would have told me."

"There, you've got it in one. It's not that simple." He released her hands. "Now, tell me Liz, why couldn't you just accept the 'missing person' line?"

The look Liz threw at him questioned the man's sanity.

"Okay, okay. I'm forgetting you two were virtually conjoined. Look, let's move to the lounge and I'll tell you what I can."

"Oh, don't worry, you're going to tell me everything! And *then* I'm going to the Police." As Liz left the bedroom, she heard, "Did *you* trash this pink tutu?" But her thoughts were elsewhere. *He's alive!*

Liz sat on the edge of the cream sofa, her arms crossed tightly, and watched Dangerfield as he followed her into the lounge and then headed for the kitchen.

"Sod the tea! Talk!"

Turning to face her, he was confronted with a steely look of expectancy.

As Liz listened to Dangerfield explaining about the photo of her and Amy that still filled O'Brien's computer screen, she could swear someone had turned the apartment's heating system to max.

"Are you getting this, Liz? If you tell anyone about James's recruitment by Intelligence, you'll put his life at risk. Just as yours would have been if James hadn't gone along with O'Brien's demands."

"He did this for me?"

"Yes."

"And he's in danger?"

"Not if everything goes to plan."

"And if it doesn't?"

Dangerfield shrugged.

The room was bursting with silence as Liz paced back and forth. Eventually she spoke, her voice more controlled.

"Do you have any friends, Charles?"

"You're joking right? MI6 doesn't even allow you to take prisoners."

"I thought as much. Everyone's expendable as far as you're concerned, aren't they."

"Someone's got to do this job."

"Yeah. Sure." Liz nodded. "Yesterday on the river, you talked about your ideal world. Well, what's the point of your Land of Hope and Glory if you've no friends to enjoy it with?"

This time, Dangerfield's mouth stayed shut.

"It's basic!" Liz exclaimed, "You protect your friends and family above everything." Liz tried reading his facial expression. "What happens if you ever fall, Charlie? Who's going to catch you?"

Suddenly the room seemed eerily quiet to Liz. The man she had thought she knew had turned his back on her again and was staring out of the window at the full moon that hung in the darkening sky.

"Look, Liz, I was never going to fritter my life away in the city, gambling with other people's money." He turned to face her. "And thirty years of assessing some fat corporation's account books wouldn't be my idea of fun either."

"So your current job's fun is it?"

He ignored Liz's question. "Joining Intelligence was a difficult choice. I had to make sacrifices."

"So you sacrificed your best friend!" The tempo in Liz's voice suddenly rose. "Why did you let James go? Why not just go after O'Brien? That's the bit I can't get my head round. Doesn't seem that complicated."

"Welcome to the real world."

"Don't patronise me!" Liz thumped the side of the sofa. "After what I've just been through!" She sighed deeply, burying her face in her hands. Seconds later, she looked up, surprised by the sound of chuckling. Dangerfield was standing at the desk, his hand on the computer mouse.

"What's so damned funny?" She noticed he'd clicked through to the selfie of O'Brien in the ripped tutu, crying. Phone held up in one hand, scissors in the other, thick multi-coloured make-up smeared madly all over his face.

"Have you seen this muppet's face?" Still chuckling, Dangerfield threw her a glance. "Jackson Pollock must be in town."

"You think you're so bloody clever, don't you? You haven't a compassionate bone in your body. The man obviously needs psychiatric help with serious identity issues."

"You're right there. He thinks he's a garbage can."

Liz shot up from the sofa. "You're the fucking garbage can! You're full of crap!" She headed for the door. "I must need therapy even more than O'Brien. To think I once thought there might be a chance for us, you arrogant bastard." She turned to leave.

"I'm just doing my job."

Turning back to him, Liz yelled in his face, "Then fucking well do it, and get my brother home!"

"Promise me you'll keep schtum. Trust me Liz, it's 24/7 out there. Evil never sleeps."

As Liz strode out the front door, she called back, "Now you mention it, *you* always had trouble sleeping."

Dangerfield turned and stared out of the window. The orange moon, a perfect circle, hovered in solitude against the night sky. His thoughts focused on the way she had glared at him as she left the apartment. That was the point at which he knew the link between them was severed. He knew soldiers who'd had their legs successfully re-attached. But this was different. This felt permanent.

Then he thought about his dad. '*Remember, son, before a calm sea, angry waves must crash.*' Dangerfield shook his head. *Nah. Too late. This boat has capsized.*

As his mind continued to wander aimlessly over the past, he was drawn repeatedly to the three years that he had shared an apartment with Liz and James. It dawned on him that those Cambridge years had been the only time in his entire life that he hadn't felt lonely.

Opening the lounge window, he gazed into the dark sky. Mid-way up its black canvas, some thief had replaced the beautiful moon with a rotting slice of carrot.

"BOLLOCKS!" Dangerfield's yell disappeared over the rooftops of Oslo and into the night.

Where's Groundhog Day when you fucking need it?

Chapter Fifteen

Thrusting into the sky, it sparkled brighter than a blood diamond. The British architects had named it The Space Tower. Journalists from the China Daily News were calling it The Rocket. But the residents of Shanghai knew exactly what it looked like. This superskyscraper, the latest proclamation of Chinese economic development, screamed 'Up yours!' to the rest of the planet. And scheduled for today, at precisely 11.00am, was its official opening ceremony.

Julie Hong had no say in what she was to wear for this morning's ribbon cutting. After ordering two teenage girls out of his bed, her gargantuan boyfriend, Bong, had waddled into her adjoining room, grunted, and tossed onto her bed a grey trouser suit and a pair of shoes as flat as rice paper. He didn't want her head blocking his view of the British Ambassador's face when she stood between them translating.

Bong Wu's journey to immense wealth had been spectacular. At thirty, he'd accepted a five million dollar unsecured loan from the Nanking branch of China's Construction Bank. By sheer coincidence, the branch director's daughter was simultaneously fast-tracked via the British Embassy in Beijing to St Paul's private school for girls in London. Twelve years, and as many bank directors' children later, the Bong business empire was now financing

China's tallest skyscraper.

The opening ceremony was taking place inside a huge pair of temporary hemispheres, one of which contained a full orchestra. At the cutting edge of plastic engineering, they were designed to keep smog out and protect the gilded guests within. Inflated to bursting point, the two domes nestled against the foot of Bong's monolithic statement like a shaved ball sack. Although at street level, these anti-pollution domes looked more like giant buttocks.

Today had been billed as the year's biggest event in the Shanghai calendar. TV crews, the national papers and the city's mayor had all descended on Shanghai's Pudong district. Even four senior members of the Politburo had been flown in early that morning from Beijing on one of Bong's private jets.

The TV cameras focused most of their efforts on China's top girl band as they trotted neatly up the red carpeted stairs and disappeared into the translucent entrance tunnel. All four teenagers had had their hair dyed grey, the colour of Bong's company logo. Everything had its price. And in Bong's eyes, everyone could be bought. China's favourite TV comedian, its prime TV news presenter and the latest singing sensation from Taiwan, all lined up obediently to be photographed with Bong. Their smiles threatened to split their faces in half.

This event represented the pinnacle of Bong's achievements. Twelve years of promises and lies. His threats of violence. Actual violence. All congealed into this morning's extravaganza. Even he couldn't believe he'd made it here. For God's sake, he was the son of a factory potter from the industrial choke of Shenyang, a city of eight million nobodies. Ten minutes ago he'd shaken hands with a Vice Premier of the State Council. And the British Ambassador to China was due at his event any minute now. He was going to milk these two for sure.

Chapter Sixteen

Peter Clark, Britain's long-standing Ambassador to China had endured his umpteenth flight from Beijing to Shanghai. The landing had been precarious. And now he was being driven recklessly to the 'Grand Opening' of yet another tower block. The staff driver from the Shanghai Consulate had his nose to the grinding traffic and hadn't replied to any of his questions. Even the one he'd asked in Mandarin.

Lesser cars kowtowed to the black Mercedes 600, pulling aside before its flashing headlights. But even so, the traffic was intense. He was late. And the constant sound of car horns had him on edge.

Each time he'd dropped in on his staff at the Embassy's Branch in Shanghai it had involved being introduced to some regional Bigwig. Same old routine. Shake a bunch of hands. Smile a lot. Keep the local Ferrero Rocher down. Reassure categorically that their proposals were under consideration. And state that the British Government welcomed every opportunity to 'bring our two great Nations to a closer understanding'. Blah Blah Bloody Blah.

But today?

Today was different. So different. The Foreign Office had given him a specific mission. A vital message to deliver.

As the car pulled up outside a gigantic pair of pollution domes, he quickly ran through in his head the instructions he'd been given; Speak to Bong. In private. Focus on the Rare Earth Metals he'd been selling to British companies. Make it known that the British government is aware of their source. Geological proof that a significant proportion of his recent shipments of REMs had originated in North Korea. Remind the dodgy bastard of the International Trade Embargo with North Korea. And insist…

The car door was yanked open by Dominic Baker, Clark's Second Secretary. He'd been in the job for two whole weeks.

"Hello, Sir. Just in time!"

"Dominic. How are you?" asked Clark as he climbed deftly out of the Mercedes. "Where's Bong?"

"Good thank—"

"Bong. Where is he?"

"Right… er… follow me."

Clark strapped his smile on as he followed Dominic up the red carpet and into the plastic entrance lobby. Someone shouted, and lines of photographers swivelled on the spot to capture the latest arrivals. Their path became blocked by other guests, and the calls from the photographers increased as word of who Clark was, spread like wildfire.

"Speed it up, Dominic. I need to grab Bong before the programme kicks off."

Pursing his lips, Dominic skirted around a ridiculously blinged couple posing for the cameras. Several photographers side-stepped their colleagues to try to stay level with Clark and Dominic as they leap-frogged other guests.

"I think that's him," said Dominic nodding in the

direction of a cluster of people surrounding a surly looking guy holding court.

"Which one?" asked Clark quickly. "Mr Happy?"

"Yep."

Clark gave a knowing nod to the closest of the guests surrounding Bong, and smiling broadly, forced his way between them with Dominic in his slipstream.

"Hello! Ni hao! Ni hao!"

Bong levered one man aside, faced Clark and spoke quickly to the exquisitely dressed woman standing beside him. Clark was transfixed by the woman's smile. And when she spoke, momentarily forgot why he was here.

"Mr Clark. We are so happy you could make it." She shook Clark's hand and gesturing to the fat man beside her. "This is Mr Bong Wu."

Bong broke into a grin and spoke loudly in Mandarin, addressing all the people around him.

Clark proffered his hand and it hovered for an eternity until another quick exchange between the woman and Bong.

"Congratulations, Mr Bong. Shanghai's tallest building. Excellent!" And still clutching Bong's hand, Clark moved his face closer to the woman's. "Sorry, I didn't catch your name."

"Ah! It's Jia Li. Call me Julie. Much easier!" She hit him with her smile again. "Julie Hong".

"The thing is… Julie. I need a quick word with Mr Bong. In private."

Another exchange in Mandarin.

"Mr Bong says that you are very welcome. He is

looking forward to this evening's even more exclusive party in the Penthouse when you and he can talk at length."

"But—" Clark began.

Loud music filled the air, and the guests within the two pollution domes all turned towards a stage where four girls, moving provocatively, stepped up to four microphones. Clark put his hands to his mouth and half yelled into Julie's ear.

"It's urgent. Mr Bong. Two minutes. In private."

Julie flashed a worried glance at Bong. "Maybe later? After the Opening Ceremony? The ribbon cutting takes place straight after this song." She glanced at Bong again. "These are the X Girls." Julie looked quizzically into Clark's eyes. "China's biggest girl band? Mr Bong paid a lot of money to get them."

Clark had been to enough Grand Openings to know it was now or never. Before Bong consumed alcohol. Before competition for the guy's attention grew exponentially.

Clark held up two fingers. "Two minutes."

The girls began to sing, the guests roaring as they scrabbled to attach their phones to selfie sticks. The pollution domes reverberated with the monstrous increase in decibels.

Again Clark put his hands to his mouth and yelled in Bong's direction.

"RARE… EARTH… METALS!"

These were three English words Bong clearly recognised because Clark saw the man's forehead furrow deeper than the Mariana Trench. And his fists clench.

So Clark hit him first.

"It's about Pyongyang."

Chapter Seventeen

Bong stormed towards the back of the pollution domes, guests scrambling aside.

Money didn't talk here. It screamed.

A middle-aged dribbler, unable to take his eyes off the X Girls, bounced off Bong's tremendous girth, only the density of the crowd keeping him upright.

In Bong's wake, Julie Hong kept pace, glancing back at Clark every few seconds. Clark knew to keep right on her heels. But Dominic, newbie in China, busy throwing apologies left and right, got swallowed by the crowd as its parted waves crashed back together.

Without turning once to see if Clark was following, Bong marched up to a row of girls holding a golden tape across the glass entrance to his two thousand foot dream. Spaced evenly, each girl held the tape up with one hand, a pair of golden scissors the size of garden shears in their other.

As Bong ducked between the central two girls, the tape caught across his forehead. Even above the live music, Clark heard Bong yell, followed by the clattering of garden shears against marble paving slabs.

The X Girls were between verses, and as they danced suggestively, the bass cranked up, thumping madly. Clark could feel the air throb and imagined the giant pollution domes bursting at any second.

In front of him, the androgynous tape holders were no longer expressionless. All looked distraught, the scissorless one in tears, her mascara already on the run.

Behind the tape holders, Julie started remonstrating with Bong, gesturing for him to calm down. Grabbing him by the arm she pulled him towards the huge rotating glass doors to the Space Tower. Clark was right on their tail but stepped into the next glass segment, partly to give Bong and his P.A. a moment of privacy, partly to maintain a detachment to facilitate the completion of his mission. To deliver first hand, and in private, a very simple message.

Clark, gesturing to Julie, tapped his watch. But she was completely absorbed in the squabble with her boss. Now inside the Space Tower itself, away from the crowds, Clark took in his surroundings. He was familiar with the Chinese design theme of 'more is more' but this building's entrance hall took the biscuit. The ceiling, three stories above them, was a trompe l'oeil Sistine Chapel. Except this mural featured an outer circle of peasant rice planters, and as Clark's focus moved to its centre, they became factory workers and then besuited office workers clutching laptops. And at the epicentre, surely that wasn't Bong shaking hands with Mao Zedong, with the two of them sitting on clouds and in the lotus position? It was so crass and so corny that Clark found it amusing. He was repeating Napoleon's words in his head, 'from the sublime to the ridiculous' when he was interrupted.

"Mr Clark, I'm sorry. We must be quick. Mr Bong must get back for the ribbon cutting."

Bong's ruddy and gleaming face was staring at him, the

man's arms folded, prepared for battle.

"Of course." Clark cleared his throat. "So briefly, the Royal Geological Society has confirmed that more than half the Rare Earth Metals that Mr Bong has been selling to British companies, are not originating in China as he claims in every single contract, but are undeniably proven, in fact, to be from North Korea. I am—"

Julie held up her hand.

"One moment, please." As Julie translated into Mandarin, Clark focused on Bong's face. No raised eyebrows. No curled lip. Not a twitch.

Julie gestured with her hand for Clark to continue.

"I am here to inform Mr Bong directly, on behalf of the British Government, that these trades are illegal and must stop forthwith. Mr Bong cannot plead ignorance of the International Trade Embargo on North Korea. If—"

Again, Julie held up her hand, and as Clark watched Bong's facial expression whilst she translated, the man's cheeks became no redder. No increase in sweating. Nothing.

When Julie gestured for him to continue again, Clark decided to wrap things up.

"If it is discovered that even 1% of future REM shipments contain any material of North Korean origin, then we will be forced to go public. And while the British Government may have a little embarrassing egg on its face, you, Mr Bong, will have a tarnished reputation that would remain with you for the rest of your business career."

After translating and listening intently to Bong's reply, Julie looked distinctly uncomfortable.

"Mr Bong says…" she began, but turned back to Bong swiftly, appearing to clarify something. "He says not to worry about embarrassing egg as he can give the British Government a flock of embarrassing chickens."

Clark was unfazed. His negotiating skills had helped put out fires all over the world. Palestine. Sarajevo. Ireland. His reputation had had the Foreign Office pleading with him to continue as Britain's Ambassador to China long after the standard diplomats' innings. The story of him flipping a furious Chinese Colonel from drunken anger to drink spluttering laughter was legendary at Foreign Office dinner parties. In the 1990's, during a highly charged meeting, Clark had promised to have Britain's Governor of Hong Kong, Chris Patten, shot, and to return Hong Kong to Chinese ownership immediately. As shock silenced the room, he'd then yelled the word 'But…' and paused for four long seconds to garner the attention of everyone present, '… only on the condition that China give Britain Taiwan'.

Clark breathed deeply before replying to Bong.

"I'm sorry. I don't think you understand. If Mr Bong fails to desist from mixing REMs from China with REMs sourced in North Korea immediately and forthwith, we will be open and honest with the World Trade Organisation. We will put our hands up and admit that Mr Bong misled British Companies and the British Government." Clark folded his arms. A statement of intent. To punch home his closing gambit. "How do you think your Japanese customers would react? And your American customers? We would be seen as the innocent party in this. Whereas you would most definitely not."

Julie turned to translate. And at the end of it Bong shrugged. His reply was short.

"Mr Clark, Mr Bong says that you are opening Pandora's Box. He asks how would the WTO respond to learning of two British citizens actually working in North Korea?"

Clark took a moment to absorb this before responding to what he considered childish. He'd been here a thousand times before. New kids on the block. Immature diplomats from emerging economies, straw-clutching because they hadn't done their homework. Stroppy negotiation by tantrumatic children caught red-handed.

"Please tell Mr Bong that that is a preposterous suggestion."

Even before Julie had started translating, Bong was talking again.

"Mr Bong asks if you would like… I think you say in English… a little more meat on the bone, yes?"

Clark didn't bother replying. His job as postman was done. He was content to leave the parcel on Bong's doorstep. No signature required.

"Mr Bong says that there are two British scientists assisting North Korea with their Nuclear Missile Programme. He saw them last week. In the city of Kusong. 120 miles west of Pyongyang."

Clark's reputation for thinking on his feet suddenly meant nothing. Bong had ripped the carpet from under them. He looked upwards, desperate for inspiration. His gaze fell on Mao Zedong, sitting cross legged on a cloud.

The guy seemed to be grinning at him. For the first time in his career Clark's mind went blank. He couldn't think of a single clever retort. And even if he could, he wouldn't be able to deliver it. The music had stopped. The crowds were roaring. And Bong had gone.

Chapter Eighteen

The roads through Shanghai's Pudong district were less choked now, but it had begun to drizzle, and denied the Merc any increase in speed.

"Sorry I lost you, sir."

Dominic's sheepish tone barely entered Clark's consciousness.

"You're new. You'll learn," said Clark. *Shut up* was what he meant.

"So how did it go with Mr Bong?"

"Routine." Clark was abrupt for good reason. A million thoughts were colliding in his head. *What the hell just happened?*

"So what was our objective there, sir?" Dominic glanced nervously across at his boss. "I'm keen to learn from an expert."

Clark shook his head, "Today's lesson… expect the unexpected."

Dominic had hoped his open-ended questions would trigger more of a conversation, but Clark's intonation said 'End of'.

The rest of the journey was in silence, Dominic staring out of the window, Clark deep in thought, and the swish of windscreen wipers and the occasional car horn their only accompaniment.

At the British Centre on Garden Square a barrier arm

raised and the diplomatic car pulled up outside the Shanghai Consulate. Dominic jumped out and while struggling to open an umbrella, raced around to Clark's side. But Clark had already mounted the three stone steps and was charging towards the entrance.

Ignoring the guard's salute, Clark slipped through the double doors, only nodding greetings to other Consulate staff as he steamed through the building.

"Hey, Sophie."

"Oh sir… I wasn't expecting… Mr Hughes is out until—"

"Tomorrow. I know." As Clark turned the handle to his First Secretary's office he paused to face her. "Sophie, it's a lock-in. No one's to disturb me. Got it? No one."

"Yes, sir. Of course, sir."

Clark closed the door behind him, stared up at the ceiling and let out a long sigh. "Shit!" Crossing the office, he pulled a mobile phone from inside his jacket and slumped behind a huge desk. A couple of taps on the phone and he was on a deepfake app that MI6 had downloaded for him. He scrolled through a long list of pre-recorded conversations. Not one word was spoken by him, but in every conversation one of the voices sounded identical to his.

Clark picked the receiver up from the office landline and laid it on the desk. Before placing the mobile against it, he clicked on Chinese Currency Fluctuations. As Clark's sound-a-like greeted another robot and began discussing, for the benefit of any phone hackers, the economic impact on British exports to China, he moved to the window and retrieved his personal phone.

He knew exactly who to ring. The Foreign Office could wait.

Clark looked out across a small empty quadrangle. The drizzle seemed to be easing. The window opposite looked like one-way glass, so he slipped behind the long blue curtains before dialling and speaking into his phone.

"Nineteen."

The line seemed to go quiet forever before someone eventually replied.

"Yes."

"Bulstrode? It's Peter Clark."

"Yes."

"Ahh. Look, slight issue."

"Yes."

As Clark quietly detailed the morning's verbal conflagration he was not interrupted once. And when he'd finished, Bulstrode seemed to have only one question.

"Does anyone else know of this? Anyone witness your conversation?"

"But surely the man's talking nonsense."

"Peter. Were there any witnesses?"

"What difference does it make? It can't—"

Bulstrode's volume increased. "Peter! Any witnesses?"

"Well yes. One. His P.A. Julie something… Julie Hong… but—"

"And Bong's inner sanctum?"

"Only us three. I'm guessing I'll meet them at this evening's dinner party. I could—"

"Hang on. Give a me a second."

The line went quiet. Clark stared up at the ceiling again. His breathing was faster. So was his heart rate. And someone must have turned the heating up.

In the background, coming from the mobile he'd placed on the desk behind him, he could hear what sounded like himself droning on about a renewed fortitude with regard to the symbiotic relationship between the U.K. Government's import and export tax policies…

The rattle of the door handle made him jump. He thought he could make out Sophie's and Dominic's voices. And as footsteps led away Bulstrode's voice burst back in his ear.

"You've been taken ill."

"Sorry?"

"You are not to attend tonight's dinner."

"But—"

"The Foreign Office concurs. You will not be attending. It could severely impact ongoing intelligence operations." Bulstrode paused as if waiting for any potential response, but Clark remained silent. Bewildered.

"What you heard this morning has Top Secret classification. Peter, do you understand? It didn't happen. You heard nothing."

Chapter Nineteen

Sweat poured off him, water bottle long empty. Ten miles. Two circuits of Tai Tam Park. And still petrol in the tank.

Dangerfield gazed across Victoria Harbour towards the skyscrapers of Kowloon. Running. Cheapest therapy going. An hour to reflect. An hour to process Liz's finger-pointing.

And her direct hit.

He hooked the heel of his trainer over the handrail at the water's edge and as he stretched his calf muscles, checked the running app on his watch. A personal best. And by some margin. He should piss Liz off more often.

Dangerfield stretched his other leg, then headed off. Uphill. Up or down were the two main options on Hong Kong Island. Up to Bangers & Mash, his go-to café. When in Rome… fuck that.

Towards the end of Perkins Street, three girls, Filipinos, stepped out from a doorway. Blocking him. On purpose. On business.

For fuck's sake. Dangerfield shook his head in despair. It was eleven o'clock in the morning, no sun, cold breeze blowing. And they were in hot pants and crop tops.

Dangerfield saw traffic lights. One wore red, one yellow and one emerald green.

"You three must be freezing." Dangerfield's watch claimed ten degrees but with the biting wind he reckoned four degrees max.

"What about you?" Emerald pointed at Dangerfield's bare legs.

He wiped the sweat from his forehead and dramatically shook his hand twice at the pavement. "What do *you* think?"

"Who you run from?" said Yellow, invading his personal space, her huge brown eyes quizzical, suggestive, rehearsed.

"Myself mainly." Dangerfield made a step towards the kerb. "How old—"

Red and Emerald interrupted together. "Old enough."

Yellow stroked Dangerfield's forearm, "Hey, big boy."

"Boy? I'm nearly old enough to be your father."

Red ran her hand down his other arm, "Come on then, Daddy."

As Red's delicate cold hand reached Dangerfield's watch, she jumped. It had begun to vibrate. Intensely.

Dangerfield saw Bulstrode's code on the screen. He held it to his ear and answered loudly, "Smith, Hong Kong Police."

The girls, looking shocked, retreated immediately.

"GCHQ *said* your phone was on vacation in Hong Kong. Not part-timing for the Chinese, I hope."

"Not a bad idea, sir. But no. Not on vacation either. Time out."

"Well, time's up, I'm afraid."

"New job?"

"Yes and no."

"I don't do cryptic," said Dangerfield. He heard

Bulstrode clear his throat.

"I didn't get a chance to congratulate you about James Green. You ticked all the boxes there. Don't know how you persuaded him. Excellent work. Excellent."

"I sense a 'but'…"

"But there's a fly in the ointment."

Dangerfield glanced at the girls huddled in the doorway. They were in deep conversation. In Filipino. Hushed, but urgent. They looked agitated.

"Does this fly have a name?" Dangerfield asked.

"Your man Bong."

"What? Bong Wu? I've an agent watching him."

"Well, there's been a radical development. Completely unexpected. A link between Bong and James Green."

"How the—"

Bulstrode didn't break his flow. "And our assessment is that if Bong knows about Green, then both Green's survival, and the mission, could be compromised."

Dangerfield could feel his heart rate rising.

"I cannot stress enough how vital, how absolutely imperative it is, that Green completes his task."

Again, Dangerfield tried to speak. Bulstrode ignored him.

"Some good news though."

Dangerfield waited.

"You're being promoted."

"Thank you."

"You're being made British Ambassador to China."

"I see."

"For one evening."

"When precisely?"

"Tonight."

Dangerfield stared at the sky. *How the fucking fuck?* He took a deep breath and looked around. The girls had vanished. He hadn't even noticed them slip away.

"Is this a 'need-to-know', sir?"

"Of course."

"I'll have to contact Sarah though. I'm due on the Cyprus job. She'll have to find a replacement."

"Keep Watling out of this. She's not code-cleared. Don't worry, I'll talk to her." Bulstrode paused. "Listen. This operation is Top Priority *and* Time Critical."

Dangerfield checked his watch screen. Call ended. A second later it buzzed again. He read the encrypted message. Instructions. More detailed than usual. Shanghai. He checked the time. Nine hour window. Five to get there. Two to prep. Fuck it, Bangers & Mash it is.

He turned the corner. The girls were standing beside a parked car, the driver yelling at them in broken English, clearly angry at the girls' failure to earn. Fear was written across their faces. Red suddenly recoiled from a punch to her stomach.

Dangerfield checked the street. There could have been tumbleweed.

No traffic. No pedestrians. No witnesses.

No excuse.

Sprinting the ten yards, Dangerfield snapped the pimp's prodding finger backwards. Before the yell began, he grabbed the man's wrist with both hands and yanked so hard there were five witnesses to the click of dislocation, the pimp's head clubbing the top of the car's window frame. With one foot on the car door, Dangerfield used his body weight to wrench even harder. The man's head flipped out of the window, a right fist to the temple silencing him.

Dangerfield could feel the anger surging, filling his head, his muscles firing up as he ripped the man's body through the open window. It flapped onto the pavement. Lifeless, but breathing.

He turned to the girls.

"Waitress. Study. Anything. But for fuck's sake, not this!"

Dangerfield opened the driver's door, threw the meat back inside and with his foot, shoved it onto the passenger seat.

"I'll take him to hospital." As Dangerfield climbed into the driver's seat, he picked up a stray brick lying in the gutter and tossed it onto the pimp.

"And don't worry, you won't see this shit again." Dangerfield smiled at them. "Unless he gets good with a wheelchair."

Accelerating away, Dangerfield threw a left and then a right onto Henderson Road. Eighty metres ahead lay a ninety degree turn. And a brick wall.

He slowed the car to ten and opened the door.

Edging himself off the driver's seat, he dragged the deadweight with him, leaving it slumped across both seats. The instant the brick touched the accelerator, Dangerfield felt the car surge and the door try to close. He pushed against it with his left hand, and gripping the steering wheel with his right, planted both feet firmly on the door sill. And jumped.

He hit the ground running.

As the car continued to accelerate and break away from him, Dangerfield gauged that its impact speed with the wall would be thirty-five. Maybe forty.

He slowed to a halt and took a last glance before sprinting back the way he had driven. *Run Forrest, run*. He reckoned six seconds and counted down as he anticipated the wonderful sounds of impact. The twist of metal, the shatter of glass and the crack of airbags.

Six seconds exactly.

"Fucking user," Dangerfield growled, against the sound of jammed car horn. He turned left onto Black's Road. Glass fronted offices, closed for the weekend. His head flicked right. Someone was staring at him. Another runner. Same shorts and top. Staring hard. Accusingly.

Dangerfield looked his reflection in the eye.

"You can fuck off as well."

Chapter Twenty

All day, Bong Wu had been on fire. He could do anything he wanted. This morning, at the Grand Opening of his Space Tower, he'd grabbed the British Ambassador by the short and curlies. And this evening he was going to yank them hard. The whole world was bowing before him. 'It's my world, my planet', he'd murmured under his breath that morning, as the umpteenth dignitary had proffered their hand.

Compared to the extravagant opening ceremony, this evening's dinner in the penthouse was designed to be a far more intimate event. Everything had been going exactly to plan. Until fifteen minutes ago. The Ambassador hadn't looked well on arrival, and immediately after the meet and greet, disappeared into the bathroom to be heard retching loudly. Bong was furious to see his window of opportunity close as Clark made his excuses and left. And it didn't help that only Clark's Second Secretary remained. How dare he not bring his First Secretary. The insult was eating at him.

The Foreign Office had sent Dominic Baker to China two weeks earlier and he was out of his depth. Three years in Nairobi as Communications Officer was proving to be of little use now that he'd been promoted to Second Secretary on a completely different planet. The stats didn't add up for him either. He may have achieved a First in Classics but out of 1.4 billion Chinese people, the sum total of those who knew any Latin or Ancient Greek was zero.

When he left Oxford at twenty one, he'd never done a day's work in his life, and yet curiously his CV had been bulging. Dominic's father had handed it in personally at Whitehall. Viscount Baker and the Foreign Secretary, in matching ties, had shaken hands more elaborately than a couple of rap stars.

Dominic could hardly have refused the transfer to China. His father had been insistent. So here he sat, one cold January evening, two thousand feet above street level, at a huge dining table that seated twenty people, none of whom were talking to him.

Sitting on either side of Dominic were two of Shanghai's countless billionaires. Neither spoke a word of English. It wouldn't have mattered if they did. Both had their backs to the junior diplomat, talking to their other neighbours. Why the hell hadn't he taken his boss's advice and left with him? His dad would have been proud of him, though, for insisting on staying. He could guess his thoughts on the matter, 'Get your feet under the table son. Clark's retirement's well overdue.'

Always keen to outdo the Japanese, the Chinese host had gone one step beyond sushi. The food on the plates wasn't merely raw, it was still alive. Spread evenly along the length of the immense dining table were five 'Lazy Susans', each covered in bowls of various sizes. Some containers were filled with innocent-looking leaf dishes. Others played more of a restraining role. A fish, staked to a wooden platter in front of him, kept slapping its tail. He could swear it winked at him. Tonight was his introduction to rice wine, and if any of the guests had even bothered to look in Dominic's direction, they would have guessed. Every minute or so, a prawn would leap from a large central bowl. One landed on his empty plate. He swigged from his tiny glass again. He'd already had so much that he no longer noticed it being topped up by silent, over-attentive staff. He told himself he was suffering this for Britain. If only his taste buds weren't so fucking patriotic. He tried to ignore the large lobster whose flesh had been scooped out and then returned to its own back on a thin bed of ice. It flexed its huge claw every few seconds. When the clawed leg suddenly flicked out and knocked his champagne glass over, he leapt from his chair.

"Right! That's enough!"

The talkers around him didn't miss a beat. If anything, their volume seemed to increase. He glanced at his fellow diners. All were engrossed in loud conversations. Sitting back down, he felt lonely and exposed. Although totally ignored, he assumed that everyone there must have acknowledged his embarrassing predicament.

Dominic's attention was suddenly grabbed by the attractive girl in the figure-hugging purple dress, whom he'd noticed his boss trying to talk to earlier. She got up from the far end of the table, pulled a phone from her purse, and headed for the balcony. He watched her intoxicating progress, hoping at least to catch her eye. But it was as if he wasn't there. He was feeling too awkward, too out of place to have the confidence to talk to her. *What was the point? No one here spoke English anyway.*

He picked up his chopsticks and tried to fish a peanut

from a small bowl on the far side of the table. Five pick-up attempts later and he just wanted the world to swallow him up. He felt so isolated in this noisy room. *Fucking chopsticks*. A little voice in his head started toying with him, urging him to stick them in his own eyes. It wouldn't have mattered if he did. In less than two minutes, blindness would be the least of his worries.

Bong looked across at Julie, leaning against the balcony, her purple dress billowing ever so slightly, her silhouette surreal against the dark sky. The full moon seemed to hover just above her head. From where he sat he could see no skyline, only sky. Shanghai had a multitude of tower blocks and yet none as tall as his. He was top dog. *This is my city now and you're all gonna have to look up to me whether you like it or not.* It was the year of the snake. His year. No wonder he felt lucky. In less than one minute his luck would run out.

Julie's phone began vibrating. Even Dominic could hear the loud 'Big Ben' ring tone.

"Charlie? Give me some good news," she said.

Dominic couldn't believe his ears. That was definitely English. *At last... someone to talk to.* He got up, clumsily, rice wine pumping through his veins.

"What do you mean, leave now?"

Dominic stumbled towards her, intending to hover nearby until her phone call had ended. It seemed rude but for Christ's sake, he'd just found an escape route from this hell.

"Stop shouting, Charlie. I can't leave now. Listen, I've learnt there's two British scientists in North Kor—"

*

It could have been Fireworks Night the way burning bodies spewed out of the top of the two thousand foot Roman Candle. They soared into the night like a flock of scared crows before falling back to earth, violently slapping pavements, roads and the roof of one overstuffed minibus.

Dominic, legless for the second time that evening, cleared the balcony, bits of champagne flute randomly embedded in his face. His pulped corpse flew northwards before hurtling down into the welcoming arms of the building's wall-mounted wind turbine. The horizontally rotating blades made a terrible job of dicing him. His father would be distraught. He hated chop suey.

Julie's tiny frame, pressed up against the balcony when the bomb exploded, was squeezed out between the metal rails like sausage meat from a mincer. Her mashed body hung from her left arm that still gripped the top rail with its three remaining fingers. The one with the Cartier eternity ring on, a present from Bong, had been the first to go.

Of the twenty-four victims, Bong had by far the greatest mass, so gravity pulled on him the hardest. As he fell, it held him close to the building, accelerating him directly towards the midpoint of the two plastic domes below. Despite owning twenty-six gym complexes, this was the first time his body had ever been ripped. Metres of intestine, unravelling from his gaping belly, wrapped themselves around his neck, as if trying to strangle the man who had cruelly overworked them for so many years. On impact, his huge body burst, leaving a sticky wet mess wedged between the cheeks of the twin pollution domes. A shit gone wrong.

Chapter Twenty One

As Dangerfield watched the bodies flying into the night sky, he knew one of them was Julie's. He just knew.

He'd recruited her. Played her. And lost her.

Leaning hard against the balcony rail of the Century Hotel, Dangerfield looked across the river at the billowing smoke. He'd turned The Space Tower into a giant lit cigar.

At job completion Dangerfield rarely looked back. Hell knows why he'd booked into the Century. Maybe it was to maximise signal strength in his desperate attempts to call her. Maybe in the hope of witnessing the failure of the incendiary device he had planted. That was bollocks. He knew it wouldn't fail.

He rubbed the back of his head. Clark's mask had been tight. The sense of compression lingered, and more than once on his way to the Century Hotel, he'd touched his face to confirm he was no longer wearing it.

He kept picturing Julie's face. It wouldn't go away.

"Fuck!" He starting talking to himself, "My hints were so obvious!" He kicked the balcony. "And why did she take so long to answer her fucking phone?"

Bulstrode's orders couldn't have been clearer. *Close Bong down now. Make a mess. Leave confusion.* More time and he could have organised a simple poisoning. *Immediately,* Bulstrode had insisted.

He hated scum like Bong with a vengeance. Illegal

trading was one thing. Only money. There were international trade groups, laws and diplomats to pursue that kind of crime. But this fat bastard had shat on several corporations, leaving his arse-prints at the crime scenes. They took all the risks financing digital research and cutting-edge technologies, and this low-life would trot up and steal the fucking lot. Bong had funded industrial espionage. And in MI6's books, high-tech secrets were sacrosanct.

"Yeah. This fucker was responsible for Julie's death." At least I've removed Bong Wu from the planet, the fly from the ointment, a potential spotlight on James.

It was quiet, the roar of the explosion having dissipated. Dangerfield knew the sirens from the Shanghai police, ambulances and fire crews were only minutes away. And in those minutes, a single thought filled his head. *What's the point of your greater good, your beautiful world, Charlie... if you've no friends to share it with?*

"Bollocks."

Confidence was King. Even a micron short of arrogance. It had always worked for him. Big time. His whole life he'd felt in control. Invincible.

Now he'd discovered a chink in his armour.

And that chink was Liz-shaped.

Chapter Twenty Two

"Ching Dao Supermarket." The voice was high, the three words staggered.

"Finkel." Dangerfield poured his coffee, his phone pressed to his ear.

"Hoo yoo? Wah yoo wan?"

"Finkel." Closing his eyes he breathed in deeply, the coffee vapour flooding his nostrils. "Your accent's shit."

"How yoo git numba?"

"It's complex. I pressed 'Finkel' in my contact list."

"Damm yoo!"

Dangerfield swapped the stained aluminium coffee pot for a milk carton.

"Listen." White swirled in the black. "I'm calling in that favour you owe me."

"Typical!" The voice was deeper now, and distinctly East Side New York. "Someone saves your life and two seconds later they're crawling back with their hand out."

"Yada, yada. Actually it's two years, but hey." As Dangerfield took his first gulp of coffee, his gaze fell on the small photo of his father, Blu-Tacked to his kitchen wall. He turned to the window and looked down on the warehouse roofs below. "I need help getting in somewhere."

"Which club is it this time? The Groucho?"

"Funny." He watched a tiny fork-lift truck, eight storeys

down, jerking its way between a pile of toy-sized pallets and a miniature yellow lorry. For a second, he pictured his dad and himself playing Lego. "I heard you screwed up in Pakistan, so Langley hung you out to dry in North China." Dangerfield took another gulp of coffee.

There was a pause on the line. And then chuckling.

"Ah, I get it. You're jealous of my promotion."

"Not in the slightest, mate. Mazel tov and all that crap. I've got to cross the Chinese border, and you can help."

"Beijing off the British Airways schedule? Try Delta. Their stewardesses! Hubba hubba or what? When they bend over to reach the window seats... Wowzers! Those round tushes in those tight uniforms—"

"Ok, Finkel, calm down. Make sure those images stay in your wank-bank. How *is* Anna by the way?"

Finkel started chuckling again.

Dangerfield swapped the phone to his other ear. "Listen, screw up there mate and a legion of men would dive into your shoes. And trust me, if we weren't mates…"

More chuckling. "She has a nickname for you."

"Really?"

"Yes. It's Charlie Chutzpah."

"Sweet."

"Believe me, it's no compliment. And you know what's ironic?" Finkel didn't wait for an answer. "You, preaching about fidelity, when even your initials are seedy."

"Actually, you're wrong. They're C.A.D."

Finked laughed again. "I rest my case."

"Well, get off mine, and tell me the best way to cross into—"

“Hang on! Hang on! So what does the A stand for? Actually, don’t tell me. I can guess.”

“Ha, bloody ha. Now listen. I need to cross the Chinese border, just North of Dandong.”

The phone went silent. Dangerfield found himself looking at the small photo of his father again. After a couple of seconds, he heard a deep sigh at the other end of the phone. Playtime was over.

“That’s the border with North Korea.”

“No way! Really?” Dangerfield couldn’t help himself.

“What the hell are MI6 up to?” Finkel was almost shouting.

“It’s an extraction…” Dangerfield’s voice trailed off. “And, erm, it’s sub-covert.”

“Sorry. Didn’t quite catch that. Did you say ‘sub-covert’? I do apologise, I’ve only been with the CIA for twelve years. I haven’t come across that term before.”

“MI6 will be outside the loop on this one.”

“Oh, right. ‘Sub-covert’ huh? Got it. For a moment it sounded more like Dangerfield-speak for I’M A FUCKING LUNATIC!”

Dangerfield pulled the phone away from his ear. He started to pace around the small kitchen. *Ok, let’s get this over with.* With the phone to his ear again, “Listen, David. I fucked up. And now I need your help. It’s as simple as that.”

“What? But… you don’t do cock-ups. At Langley we call you Mr. Meticulous. Christ’s sake, Charles, it was only your obsessive attention to detail that saved my bacon in Syria.”

"So, what's the payload of a military drone?"

"Sorry?" The man sounded as if he'd been addressed in gobbledegook.

"You heard me. I'm 180 pounds."

"Is that sterling or your weight?" Exasperation in the man's voice was clear. "Ok, Charles. Here it is. Firstly, the whole point of a drone is that it's unmanned. U… A… V. Get it? Unmanned Aerial Vehicle. And secondly, what crazy-shit drugs have you taken?"

Chapter Twenty Three

The door to the True Love Club was shaking in its frame. As Dangerfield approached he could feel the vibrations of its pumping sound system through his shoes. *Nice choice, Finkel.* It was eight o'clock in the morning. The two minute walk here from Dandong railway station had been relatively tranquil, despite the rush hour pecking order being in full swing. The occasional car overtook the few mopeds that weaved in and out of the many cyclists.

The Club stood on the Chinese side of the Yalu River, above the grey waters that form a territorial border. On the other side of the river lay North Korea. The milk-yellow sun hung low and heavy in its skies as if reluctant to rise. Above the Club's pulsing door, neon lctters spelt the words 'True' and 'Love' in both English and Mandarin, separated by a large red plastic heart, a light within it randomly flickering on and off. *Someone needs a doctor.*

Pushing the door, Dangerfield stepped inside. The club-by-night, café-by-day concept wasn't working. The place was deserted. Stackable plastic chairs were badly arranged around matching white tables. On a low stage designed for two pole dancers, more plastic furniture had been thrown up against the steel poles. Spotting the sound system at the side of the stage, Dangerfield made for it, yanking the plug from the wall, the sudden silence ringing in his ears. Walking to the nearest window he pulled its long blinds open, and was about to sit at the adjacent table, when a man ran in through double swing doors behind the stage. His outburst in Mandarin ground to a halt, as he took in Dangerfield's face. The man remained silent, looking confused as Dangerfield sat down and returned the stare. After a few seconds the man spoke, his English economic.

"No foreigner come here!"

Dangerfield made a point of scanning the room, taking in the cheap furniture and a badly framed print of Mao Ze Dong, hanging cock-eyed above a serving hatch.

"You're joking! I'll spread the word."

Folding his arms, the man's eyes burnt into Dangerfield's.

"What you want?"

Dangerfield leant back in his chair and ran his fingers through his hair.

"Oh, I don't know. How about a cup of tea and… do you do toast? Ding sha lo?"

The man screwed his face up, and without answering, marched behind the stage and yelled through the serving hatch, before disappearing back through the double doors.

Through the window Dangerfield watched the expressionless faces of cyclists gliding by.

"Come on, Finkel."

Moments later the double doors swung open again and a girl in a pink and white striped blouse, with a matching short skirt, started re-positioning the white plastic tables, tucking the chairs underneath. She kept glancing at Dangerfield as she stacked two tables and four chairs and carried them out of the club. Dangerfield watched her progress as she then moved around the club, distributing menus.

A couple in their twenties, deep in conversation, entered and sat next to the other window. Having greeted them, the waitress hurried to raise the blinds. As she hovered to take their order, Dangerfield's focus switched to a taxi pulling up outside. A tall thin man, in a dark suit got out and headed for the club, his shock of ginger hair making him stand out from other pedestrians. He peered around the club door.

"Busier than I remember."

"Finkel." Dangerfield stood, extending his hand.

The man shook it weakly. "So. You made it." His tone reeked of disappointment.

"Sha Bi," said Dangerfield.

Eyebrows raised, Finkel gestured outside. "Let's get some peace and quiet." He waved at the waitress, spoke to her in Mandarin, and then turned back to Dangerfield. "You ordered anything?"

"Not sure." said Dangerfield. "My Mandarin's a bit basic."

"You're telling me. Do you realize what you just called me?"

"What? Sha Bi?" Dangerfield grinned. "No idea."

Finkel responded with a grimace.

Outside the sun was still weak and low. The two foreigners attracted passing curiosity from the stream of locals making their way to work. More customers arrived, and the café started to fill. The waitress brought them two cups of tea, and as the café door closed behind her, Finkel cleared his throat.

"How did you get here?

"Flew to Shenyang, then bullet-trained it.

"Train?"

"I think better on trains."

Finkel remained silent and sipped from his tea, only speaking after he'd returned the empty cup to the table. "Anyway. It's done."

Dangerfield nodded. "Thank you."

"I'm not wasting another breath telling you what a fucking idiot you are."

"OK," said Dangerfield.

"The drone's from a joint US-Chinese company, basically a knock-off of the Northrop Hawk. As you requested, the Ground Control Station will drop you in woods, a half kilometre from The Pyongyang Missile Research Centre in Kusong."

Dangerfield sipped his tea.

"So… in a few minutes you'll leave here and head to the Golden Shopping Plaza on Dong Hao Street. Level two. The booth selling the worst fake phone covers you can imagine. Ren Jin will leave her colleagues in charge."

Dangerfield began to speak.

"Shut up and listen, Charles. I've told her to expect a tall English guy in about half an hour. She will drive you to a UAV test facility just south of Dandong. There'll be no practice take-offs or landings. You'll be straight in the air and flying for around forty minutes." Finkel stared hard into Dangerfield's eyes and shook his head. "You're a fucking idiot."

Dangerfield sighed deeply.

"I'll be honest with you, Charles. I never expect to see your face again."

"OK, David. Like you say, it's done. Just give me a minute, yeah? Which way's the john?"

Finkel snorted. "Don't worry, if I were in your shoes, I'd be shitting myself too. Probably a triple-flusher." He shook his head. "Past the stage… double doors… on your left."

Alone, Finkel scanned the street, fidgeting nervously with his phone. Several customers passed him as they entered the café, each transfixed by his ginger hair. Eventually he pressed the call button.

"Xorba."

He shoved the phone back in his pocket, and slammed his fist on the plastic table.

"Fuck!"

The Club door opened once more, and a tall Oriental man in military uniform stepped out and sat down opposite Finkel, staring directly at him.

"It's taken. Sorry. Jingba."

The man stayed sitting, silent, and staring.

"Dui bu qi. Sorry. Jingba," repeated Finkel.

From the man's Oriental mouth came perfect English.

"You said you didn't expect to see my face again."

Chapter Twenty Four

Slipping through the crowded shopping mall, Dangerfield searched for a stairwell. The four-storey complex was a maze of narrow aisles bordered by small booths, crammed with identical offerings of fake Louis Vuitton or the latest Nike knock-offs. The air was ringing with frantic negotiations. As Dangerfield squeezed his way through the crowds, sellers sprang forward with instant smiles that faded just as quickly when they registered his military uniform. Stepping back they reluctantly nodded at him. Approaching the back of the mall, Dangerfield spotted concrete stairs leading upwards. Before he'd made even the first step, his path was blocked by a woman in black leggings and a bright yellow top, with Daffy Duck sequined across its front. A small red and black handbag, in the shape of Mickey Mouse's head, hung from her right shoulder.

"Mr Charles?"

Dangerfield resisted replying.

"I'm Ren Jin," the woman extended her hand. "My American friend tell me you have change of nationality."

Dangerfield remained expressionless, whereas her face suddenly lit up.

"Ah, meiyou! Sorry, I mean… I think word is… race?"

Dangerfield shook her hand but stayed silent. The woman began staring at him, spellbound, her gaze analysing every detail of his face.

"I can't believe it," she spoke slowly. "You look like one of us."

Dangerfield smiled politely, gesturing in the direction from which he'd just come.

"Shall we go?"

"OK." Ren Jin nodded and led the way back through the mall and out onto the street, the whole time her eyes flicking back and forth to Dangerfield's face. Guiding Dangerfield around the building and to a small parking lot behind, she pointed at a blue Hyundai. As they approached the small car she turned to him and smiled, "I think you are crazy-man."

"What do you mean?" asked Dangerfield.

"My friend tell me you are Daredevil charity worker."

"Ah!" Dangerfield exclaimed loudly. *Fucking hell, Finkel. Clever boy!*

"Yes, that's me! Totally crazy!" Dangerfield winked at Ren Jin feeling the slight friction of rubberoid against the skin around his eye.

He watched as she unzipped one of Mickey Mouse's ears, pulled a key fob from it and clicked it at the car.

"Cute handbag."

"Thank you," she replied and, looking up into Dangerfield's face, "I still not believe you real Englishman."

Dangerfield shrugged. "All part of the stunt. YouTube's so competitive now. You've really got to push the boat out if you want the 'views'."

"YouTube." Ren Jin nodded. "Not popular here. Access difficult. Government controls media."

Dangerfield grinned at her. "Surely Gangnam Style got past the Great Firewall of China?" He started to do the moves.

"Of course." The woman's smile was becoming a permanent fixture. "Please…" She opened the rear passenger door.

Dangerfield shook his head. "I prefer the front."

As he was driven out of Dandong, Dangerfield realised that for once he felt nothing when the traffic lights appeared to be against him. No frustration. No irritation. Only acceptance. Instead of being an adrenaline-charged challenge that he would normally run full pelt at, the task ahead seemed more like a dark cloud to be avoided. As he gazed at the stationary traffic on the other side of the junction, he was startled to realise that Ren Jin had been staring at him. He smiled at her as the lights went green, and a couple of seconds passed before a huge open-backed lorry behind them blew its air horn.

"Aah!" Ren Jin jumped in her seat. "Xorba!" Flustered, she pulled away quickly, the car's small engine racing loudly. "Sorry."

Dangerfield could see her cheeks reddening.

"No worries," said Dangerfield calmly. "Do you play GTA?"

Ren Jin flashed her eyes at him, obviously keen to maintain her focus on the road, on the job she'd been given.

"Sorry?"

"Grand Theft Auto?"

She shook her head, her cheeks still flushed.

Dangerfield signalled straight ahead with his hand.

"Better let you concentrate."

Silence continued until Dandong lay behind them and the road had deteriorated significantly with pot-holes everywhere. Ren Jin worked hard to avoid them, the little car veering right and left, but in places they were too numerous to miss and the two occupants jostled together as the car shook. After hitting a particularly deep pot-hole, Ren Jin was lifted clear off her seat as the car bounced, with Dangerfield's head hitting the cloth lining of the roof.

"Sorry!" cried Ren Jin, grinning nervously.

"Don't be." Dangerfield grinned back. "It's like a theme park ride."

Another mile or so of being jostled and the road suddenly became wider, smoother, with a solid white line down the centre. Their route had been devoid of buildings for some time, just open road surrounded by immense fields laid out with long lines of crops disappearing into the distance. Looming up, Dangerfield spotted the first man-made structure he'd seen for a while, a huge billboard in the shape of an arrow. As they drew closer, the words SINOFLEX AERO came into focus.

"We arrive now," said Ren Jin, slowing the car and indicating right.

Having made the turn, she looked across at Dangerfield.

"So what Charity you raise money for?"

"Ahh!" Dangerfield struggled to think. He felt tense. Apprehensive. "It's… truly… tragic." He shook his head. "It's… er… for children with hearing difficulties."

Ren Jin looked across again. Dangerfield could see confusion on her face. He gestured a short person with his hand, then did a Prince Charles impersonation before whipping his hands away from the sides of his head.

"You mean deaf children?"

"Pardon?" Even before the word had left his mouth, Dangerfield cringed at his own reply. *Fuck!* He blamed the dark cloud that was drawing closer.

Ren Jin looked stony-faced. "My daughter is deaf."

Chapter Twenty Five

Three metre security fencing bordered both sides of the road. As the small blue Hyundai approached the expanse of aircraft hangers that made up Sinoflex Aero, Dangerfield could see that two entry guards had almost completed the opening of the security gates.

"Lucky timing," said Ren Jin. It was the first time she had spoken for several minutes.

"Not luck," said Dangerfield, as the guards waved them through. "There were cameras at least a mile back."

"Ahh." The reply was half grunt, the ready smile dead and buried.

Having parked at the end of a short row of cars, Ren Jin pulled her phone out of Mickey's mouth and made a call. The short conversation was in Mandarin but Dangerfield could tell she was upset. She offered Dangerfield her phone. Even as he took it she avoided eye contact. He quickly got out of the car and shut the door.

"Finkel?"

"Your contact at Sinoflex is Mr Wei." The voice was instant and matter of fact. "The man spent three years in Tel Aviv on an Israeli drone project."

"So?" Dangerfield couldn't help himself. *What the fuck's eating me?*

"So? What do you mean, so? And so, therefore, he speaks decent English. What's wrong with you, Charles?

I'm telling you, if I didn't owe you, I'd put the kibosh on this dumb ass idea of yours in a nanosecond!"

"Yada yada. Hurry up, I've got a plane to catch."

There was silence for a couple of seconds before Finkel spoke again.

"Wei is the only one who knows your destination. The rest of the ground crew think it's some hair-brain charity stunt, so I suggest you run with that."

"Yep!"

The clouds circling in Dangerfield's head were getting darker, ominous and buffeting.

"If anyone can help you pull this off, it's Wei. And listen… don't piss this one off. Sounds like you've already cost me a bundle for the latest hearing aid tech."

"Oh fuck. Yeah. Get her the best. I'll pay." Dangerfield looked across to Ren Jin. She had remained in the car, sitting with her head down, arms crossed.

"Don't worry, I'll sort it. She's sweet. You, my stupid friend though, need to focus. This drone was a surveillance prototype. Never carried weapons, only lightweight cameras so I hope you've been on a diet."

"Calling me fat?"

Finkel ignored him. "Only got it because it's due for decommissioning. Wei also said something about an invisibility cloak."

"Thinks he's Harry Potter, does he?"

Again Finkel carried on. "A lot of it went over my head. Got some high-tech Teflon coating that lends itself to… anyway, talk to the man yourself. He's a bit of a genius."

Dangerfield growled, "Which bit?" then snatched the

phone away from his ear. *Why am I so fucking angry? Calm the fuck down.*

"What the hell's bugging you? I'm pulling in serious favours here," said Finkel. "If this little charade doesn't stay under the radar—"

A sudden loud rumbling behind Dangerfield made him turn quickly. The nearest hanger doors were opening. He watched as the two massive silver metal sheets separated, revealing a dark vacuous space. At its centre stood a huge winged insect.

Dangerfield could still hear Finkel's voice dragging on.

"Drone, drone. Spit it out, Finkel," he jested, trying to lighten his own mood.

Dangerfield spotted what had to be Wei and two boiler suits walking towards him. The man in the suit and tie was not smiling. No one was smiling. Snapping the phone off, Dangerfield walked round the car, tapped on the driver's window and waited as Ren Jin wound it down.

"Thank you," he said quietly.

As Ren Jin took the phone from him, she kept her gaze forward, her head remaining down. Dangerfield could feel the breeze strengthening. A waft through the open window caught Ren Jin's long black hair, revealing her face. Dangerfield was rooted to the spot. Tears were running down her cheeks. Suddenly he understood why he felt anger growing inside him. He was about to hand control over his life to the complete strangers walking towards him, and the tension was ripping at his insides. His father's voice rang in his head. *Shit happens. Deal with it.* He knew Ren Jin was crying for her daughter and he saw in her tears her love and determination. Reaching in through the open window, he put his hand on her shoulder.

"You," he swallowed hard, "are an amazing mother."

Whereas I... am a twat. Not waiting for any response, he immediately strode towards the three men, smiling broadly. *Let's get this show on the road!*

"Mr Wei, I presume." Dangerfield held his hand out to the man in the suit and tie as he drew close.

"Ni hao," said Wei, his face expressionless as he shook Dangerfield's hand. He motioned to the two tall thin men paused behind him. "Mr Shao and Mr Liu are my ground staff and will assist you today."

"Then I, and the deaf children of the world, salute you." said Dangerfield, nodding. "Will you not be involved yourself, Mr Wei?"

Wei paused before replying, as if weighing up what he had been asked.

"I am your pilot."

"Of course!" *Of.... bloody... course!*

" Would you like to see ground station?" asked Wei.

" No need. Like a flight simulator right? Live camera feed. Commands via satellite link." Grinning, Dangerfield rubbed his palms together. "Show me the beast!"

Wei pointed towards the silver drone. "Xorba!" The two lank, angular, virtually identical boiler suits walked briskly towards it, deftly manoeuvring their way around and beneath the aircraft. As they untied cord stays and loosened a short tarpaulin harness from its belly, Dangerfield saw worker insects preparing their queen.

Wei reached up to the harness. "You lie here," then

pointing towards the drone's tail, "your feet go in that cloth loop we have specially made."

"Ok." Dangerfield nodded, "And my arms?"

"You will need them free to undo harness on landing. So, if you reach out to brackets under each wing where surveillance cameras are fixed…"

Dangerfield stooped under the harness, and stretching an arm out beneath each wing, was just able to close his fingers around the two metal fixtures.

"Has anyone tested this?"

Wei's face broke into a smile, "Mr Finkel said you were joker."

An intense rattling made Dangerfield turn suddenly. Shao or Liu was clattering a height adjustable hospital trolley towards them.

"Optimistic, aren't we," said Dangerfield.

Wei ignored him. " This to help you slide in harness."

Three minutes later, Dangerfield was suspended horizontally beneath the drone, legs together, arms outstretched.

"Finkel mentioned an invisibility cloak?"

"Ah, yes. This aircraft has ceramic and Teflon sheeting. But, very old technology now. More than 2 years old."

"Ancient. So people on the ground can't see me?"

"Oh, they can see you. It is aircraft that will be difficult to see." Wei paused and then held his arm straight up above his head. "They will see Superman!"

Dangerfield smiled. "Thank you. But I don't think Superman had a ten foot jet pack strapped to his back." He took a deep breath. *I look more like Christ the Redeemer overlooking Rio!*

"So," Wei's voice intensified. "I will keep you low altitude, low speed, less than one hundred knots, so breathing no problem."

"Sounds good."

"Flight should be simple…" said Wei, as he backed away from the craft, maintaining eye contact with Dangerfield, "...unless we lose satellite link."

The two ground crew started pushing the drone out onto the short runway. Out of the corner of his eye Dangerfield spotted Ren Jin running towards him. The two men waved her away but she ignored them. As she approached him, he noticed her smile had returned.

"Good luck!" She then held her phone to Dangerfield's ear. He heard a familiar voice. "I was thinking—"

"You again?" Dangerfield winked at Ren Jin and mouthed silently to her, *thank you.*

"I was thinking, that this has to be as ironic as life can get."

"How so?"

"That I'm helping the man that saved mine… to lose his."

Dangerfield snorted. "Not going to cry, are you Finkel?"

"I want you to know that it's not too late."

"What?"

"It's not too late to change your mind," Finkel insisted. "We can ground zero this whole thing."

"As my dad used to say, it's always too fucking late."

"So that's where you learned to swear."

"It's about the only thing the bastard did teach me."

"Listen, Charles, you do realise that if the North Koreans catch you, you'll be used for propaganda. They'll absolutely crucify you."

"Look Finks, enjoyed chatting and all that, but, I'm gonna have to take off. You know how it is, things to do, people to see." Dangerfield nodded to Ren Jin and she pulled the phone away from his ear.

"Ren Jin. Thank you. I'd wave, but…" He raised his eyebrows at her.

She started walking backwards, waving as she did. After a few metres she turned and jogged towards her car.

Dangerfield's body suddenly jolted as the drone's tiny turboprop engine fired into action, the aircraft jerking into motion. Controlling his breathing, keeping it deep and slow, he recalled his boyhood trips with James, gliding at Pershore airfield. He remembered the intense jolt, and explosive bang of dissipating tension, the moment he'd pulled the release trigger for the metal winch rope connecting them to the old Land Rover that had towed them high into the sky. His life had been entirely in the hands of the unknown pilot sitting immediately in front of him. And he remembered the flood of excitement that overrode all fear, as they glided silently in the sky, between heaven and earth, the odd buffet of wind, the occasional bird flapping across their path. It had been both exhilarating and peaceful at the same time.

As the drone taxied down the runway, picking up speed, Dangerfield recalled Finkel's final words. *If they catch you, they'll crucify you!* He glanced at his arms outstretched under the wings and smiled to himself.

"THEY'RE TOO FUCKING LATE!"

Chapter Twenty Six

Suspended face down, five feet off the ground, Dangerfield's body shuddered in the harness, the concrete blurred beneath him. Suddenly the front end of the drone lifted into the sky, his vista expanding dramatically. Pale yellow fields stretched before him, leading to a dense carpet of dark green forest. The blue Simpsonian sky, that accompanied his and Ren Jin's drive out to the research aerodrome, was now clogged with swollen cumulus clouds. As he felt the adrenaline surge, he fought to keep his breathing under control.

Levelling off at thirty metres, Dangerfield's window on the world had shrunk to a sixty-metre circle directly below him. A small concrete bunker zipped beneath, followed by the airfield's perimeter fencing, its razor wire winking at him. He knew his rubberoid mask was cutting-edge, but sweat was sweat. *Thank fuck it's freezing up here.*

For the next ten minutes Dangerfield acclimatised to the rapid airflow across his body, his focus on maintaining a steady breathing pattern. The view beneath him was so repetitive it had become hypnotic, the drone now skimming above an endless ocean of fir trees. Only the sudden appearance of the Yalu river broke their spell. Tensing, Dangerfield scanned the waters below. The river appeared still, its surface opaque as if beginning to freeze. He could see why Wei had chosen this point for the river crossing. It was at an extremely wide section on a slow bend. Who would attempt escape from North Korea by swimming the river at its widest point? As the drone crossed the far riverbank and entered North Korean airspace Dangerfield saw no signs of border guards, watchtowers or other military installations. His only threat seemed to be Wei's piloting skills.

The east side of the river had no visible bank, just an immediate return to the thick carpet of firs that inclined steeply upwards. As the drone's engine growled louder, its nose jerking skywards, Dangerfield's body slid back in the harness. He gripped the camera brackets more tightly and forced his head back against the drone's metallic belly, straining to look ahead. Nothing. Nothing but an endless ocean of trees that coated the landscape. The fronds at the tip of one freakishly tall fir slapped his arm. Instinctively Dangerfield looked across at both guidance cameras. *Thanks, Wei!* Trying to gauge his speed, he recalled a drive in a 6.6 litre Maserati with the hood down. Just like today, he'd had passenger status only. No input. No control. At least he knew and trusted that driver. This Wei guy owed him nothing. And as if thought alone had summoned the drone's remote pilot, Wei's broken English suddenly bleated in his ear. *What the fuck*? It took him a second to remember the radio link.

"Mr Charles. We have problem."

"Excellent!" Dangerfield flicked his head from side to side trying to locate the microphone. "Can you hear me?"

Wei continued, "My staff make mistake on fuel. I give mileage to destination. He multiply by exactly two. No more than that. So, must be direct flight. No detour. Fuel for there and back only."

A loud crackle, together with the whistling of air passing Dangerfield's ears, made Wei's next sentence indecipherable.

"Hello?" Dangerfield was almost yelling. "Where's the problem?"

"I study route from coordinates Mr Finkel gave me."

"Ok?" *Get to the fucking point*!

"You go to Kusong."

"Mr Wei! If you can hear me… I know! I gave Mr Finkel those coordinates." *Fuck's sake*! Dangerfield fought to suppress his frustration. "So… Mr Wei, what's the problem?"

Wei didn't break from his monologue. "Kusong area difficult terrain. Many mountains."

"It's also seventy percent forest, so track just above the tree-line. Yes?" *Fuck, is this radio link only one-way?* "You've live camera feed, haven't you?"

There was a pause before Wei spoke again. "Most of time."

"Ahh! You *can* hear me!"

"The problem, Mr Charles..." Another pause. "… is that airport lies between you and destination."

"Yes, Taechon Airport. Just skirt it." Dangerfield shouted, "Go round it. You told me the drone was invisible to radar detection. Keep me low and I'll be under the radar too." More crackling. "Just don't lose the satellite link!"

"I'll do my best. Mr Finkel say he get my son into Harvard. He also say I not have to scrap this old UAV myself... that you probably do job for me."

"Mr Wei. Trust me. This drone *will* be returning to you… in just a few hours."

There was a pause before Wei spoke again.

"As long as satellite link not break."

Cheer up for fuck's sake. "Just trace the tree-line to precisely the coordinates that I… that Mr Finkel gave you."

No response.

"Hello?"

Silence.

Pessimists! Who needs 'em? The fronds at the tip of another fir tree suddenly slapped his arm and Dangerfield smiled to himself. *Oh yeah... Me*!

Pushing his head back against the cold fuselage, Dangerfield could see the forest he had been skimming, rising up ahead. For the first time, turbulence caused his body to shudder. His hands were freezing so to compensate he repeatedly squeezed the camera brackets to increase circulation. The rapid airflow was also beginning to make his eyes water and so after blinking hard he dropped his head and allowed the dark green blur of forestry below to fill his field of vision.

What felt like another ten minutes passed. Dangerfield spent the time practising a handful of short Korean commands, yelling them into the wind. He couldn't help grinning, every time he repeated 'Dak-Cho Byung-Shin!'

More turbulence and Dangerfield glanced across for the umpteenth time at both eight-foot wings, clocking the fuel pods at their mid-points, each with a camera installed directly in front. He knew he'd been gaining height for some time and strained to look at the view that Wei should be sharing with him from the live camera feed. He was tucked in just below a long mountain ridge and gauged he was into the final stage of his flight before Wei would bring him down into the huge valley that housed the two hundred thousand inhabitants of Kusong City. A large proportion of these people laboured within North Korea's secret military establishment. Dangerfield knew the establishment's name. It *was* Kusong City.

The airflow pulling at his military uniform began to lessen, the green forest sliding more slowly beneath him. Looking ahead, Dangerfield spotted a track that traversed down the mountain, cutting a rare path through its canopy of fir trees. Something was moving. As the drone got closer, he made out a small cluster of goats together with their herdsman. The invisibility cloak might be keeping the drone beyond the hungry gaze of any radar systems, but the noise of its engine, only thirty metres above the ground, caught the man's attention. He was staring up at the drone, shielding his eyes with one hand. Dangerfield couldn't miss this chance to test his raw Korean. As he passed overhead, he yelled, "Shi-bal-non!"

He hoped the man would shake his fist at him, proving he'd got the pronunciation right, but instead, he fell to his knees, bowing instantly.

Bollocks! Must think I'm his supreme fucking leader!

As the prostrate herdsman slipped out of view, Dangerfield felt the drone turn and begin to descend. Wei seemed determined to trim the forest, as proud treetops frequently clipped the aircraft's wings or Dangerfield's body. Instead of taking the most direct route to the valley's basin, the pilot chose a more gradual approach, flying the drone diagonally across the mountainside, the hum of its engine becoming softer. Dropping lower into the valley, Dangerfield kept his focus to the left and recognised, at the head of the basin, Taechon Airport.

God bless Google Earth.

The single runway meant limited passenger traffic, but as Dangerfield's gaze followed its huge length he could see it had the capacity to receive some of the largest cargo planes on Earth. Blinking to clear his watering eyes he also made out the demarcations for a single helicopter landing pad. Except there were three helicopters perched there, like mosquitoes drawing blood.

Someone's in town.

Ahead, Dangerfield could see the forest's edge disappearing into the distance. It formed a natural border to Kusong City, that sprawled across the valley, a Legoland in monochrome. There were few buildings over two storeys high, with crude cubism the dominant style. Closing in on the outskirts of Kusong, the drone continued to slow up, its engine note lowering considerably. Fifty metres from the forest's edge, Dangerfield recognised the narrow keyhole-shaped clearing amongst the trees that he'd identified using satellite cameras back in London. He'd thought it the most secluded place to land; over a twenty-four hour period, zero human activity had been recorded there.

"Descending. Prepare to land." Wei's voice sprang from nowhere. Dangerfield struggled to hear, the man's voice competing with a sudden increase in background noise.

"Great job, Wei!" As Dangerfield yelled, the drone shifted violently, its right wing thrashing through tree tops.

What the fuck!

From the corner of his eye he saw one of the guidance cameras suddenly flick upwards.

"Riiii!" Wei's high pitched screech fought against a massive mechanical roar as Dangerfield felt the drone lurch downwards, branches striking at his chest through the canvas harness. Twisting his head in every direction he struggled to catch a glimpse of the source of the sound.

Wei yelled again, "Zhi Sheng!"

Dangerfield didn't need a translation. The ugly whirring sound ripping the air, and vibrating in every cell of his body, could only be one thing.

The powerful downdraft from the helicopter's rotating blades continued to force the drone into the dense forest canopy. Branches bending wildly, the drone's engine screamed as it thrashed its way towards the clearing.

And as quickly as it had begun, the cacophonic invasion was over, the pervasive sound of beaten air dissipating as the helicopter continued towards the airfield. The drone made a final upward surge before dropping rapidly towards the flat grassy hollow carved out of the thick forest. The impact was relatively smooth, the drone bouncing only twice on its three wheels as it ran to a halt, half way up the clearing.

"FUCK… THAT!"

Dangerfield could feel his heart thumping. Unclipping the harness's tension hooks with frozen hands, he half-fell, half-lowered himself to the ground. He touched his face, checking his disguise. His uniform had also survived, the canvas harness having acted as front line defence. Breathing deeply, he quickly scanned the immediate area.

Wei's voice was hesitant, almost apologetic. "Sound crazy… but… maybe… helicopter not see us?"

"I'm all for workplace equality, but a blind pilot? Really?"

"I not see them."

Dangerfield punched the fuselage. "That's *my* theory screwed."

Dangerfield looked in the direction of Kusong. He thought he could make out the beginnings of a path.

"Listen, Wei, what length of run-up do you need for take off?"

"Thirty metres. Trees very high."

Dangerfield grabbed a camera bracket with one hand and a harness hook in the other and started pushing the drone through the ankle length grass.

"Mr Charles. Any damage?"

"I'll survive."

"Sorry. I mean UAV."

"Yeah, yeah," Dangerfield glanced at the underside of the drone. "Dents and scratches." He looked back down the three parallel lines of squashed grass. *That'll do.*

Ducking beneath a fuel pod he started to rotate the vehicle, leaning his full bodyweight against its fuselage. As he heaved its bulk around he felt something drip onto the back of his neck. Followed by another drip. And another. His brain froze.

Shit. That's not rain.

Chapter Twenty Seven

Heading for the narrow pathway that led from the clearing, Dangerfield stopped in his tracks and stared back at the drone. He focused on the front corner of the left fuel pod until another drop fell. Wei's words clawed at him. 'There and back only. No spare fuel.'

"Bollocks!"

Breaking into a run, he headed for the gap in the trees. The undergrowth had been cleared, but overhanging and intertwining branches put most of the path in shadow.

The drone was parked at least half a kilometre from the edge of Kusong and its missile control centre but that was definitely the sound of someone yelling, the voice rasping through the thin crisp air. Following the rough track to the edge of the forest he breathed deeply, the scent from the pines soporific, easing the pain in his battered chest. The yelling continued. Short and sporadic. And familiar. It reminded him of his probationary days at MI6, the obligatory Royal Parade jobs in London, hanging with bored plain-clothes from Scotland Yard. It didn't matter what language the shouting was in. These were orders. Military orders.

Hidden behind the thickest tree trunk, Dangerfield watched as four hundred North Korean soldiers, grouped in a perfect rectangle, slapped the ground with their cheap military boots. *Shit! Must be a missile testing day.*

He pulled his jacket tightly over his shoulders and spotting a crease in his khaki trousers, brushed it out vigorously. Scanning the tight formation of soldiers standing aggressively to attention, he grabbed the military cap from his inside pocket and pulled it into shape. He brushed his sleeve over the peak's shiny crest and whipped it onto his masked head. Another deep breath, and stepping out from behind the tree, Dangerfield made straight for yelling man.

"Major Tom to Ground Control.... Coming to getcha!"

Chapter Twenty Eight

Dangerfield headed crow-flies towards the military flash-mob. As the circus of four hundred soldiers performed final rehearsals before Kim Jong's arrival, he thought about his dad. About Liz. About any freaking thing that would grab his mind and completely fill it. He didn't want to think about the ramifications of this stunt going wrong. It couldn't go wrong. He'd studied Lebov's method of childbirth as an undergrad. Maximum sensory overload for maximum distraction. For women; from pain. For him, right now, right here; from having any kind of a wobble. He had to be utterly convincing in the role. This was opening night at the Royal Opera House. Ridiculous costume? Check. Audience? Check. Rehearsals? Fuck!

Dangerfield's mind raced, flipping all over the place. *I'm about to play a Major in the North Korean fucking Army! Yeah right! Who's landed in a Tardis and just appeared from nowhere*. He glanced down at himself. *At least I look the part. If an obese Italian can play the love interest in Verdi's operas... Come on!*

A hundred metres to go. The main man was still yelling instructions. The guy had them goose-stepping on the spot, all looking left, in the opposite direction to Dangerfield. His thoughts leapt back to his first year at Uni and the one term he'd tried role-playing with the Cambridge Footlights. One term too many. He pictured Schofield and Fotheringay arguing over whether Strasberg's Method Acting or Stanislavski's 'system' was the superior doctrine, and with such indignant voracity that he'd assumed it was all an act. When he'd realised the pretentious gits were playing themselves, two egotistical peacocks strutting about on stage as if their lives depended on it, he'd wanted to bang their heads together. They were in their final year. In more ways than one, if Dangerfield hadn't controlled himself. Career in acting? Exit stage left.

Fifty metres away. *No one's even looking!* Dangerfield tried to imagine the mindset of a North Korean Major, cognitive cogs whirring in his brain. Surely his role would be the transference of fear? The fear he would hold towards his superior, he would dish out to those below. Pass the Parcel. Simple. Just don't let the music stop.

Thirty metres. Dangerfield started marching. *Fuck... fuck... fuck... step... step... step... Building's... concrete... Single... storey... Sky... is... blue... Clouds... are... white... I... could... die... James... could... die... O'Brien... will... die... I've... got... a... mask... on... Nobody's... looking.*

Another short sharp yell tore the air and four hundred heads simultaneously flipped to the right.

Dangerfield smiled to himself as he returned the stare from eight hundred dark eyes. He took a quick deep breath and then half-snarled, half-barked a vaguely Korean sounding word. Expert linguistic analysis was unnecessary. In that split second these four hundred men understood it perfectly.

The tone of Dangerfield's growl and the braiding on his uniform said only one thing.

Eat my shit, bitches!

Chapter Twenty Nine

Four hundred arms flew up as four hundred left boots slammed against concrete. Dangerfield didn't break a step as he nodded at the solitary man standing nearest to him. Heading directly for the building he gestured to the man to continue. *I could get used to this.*

Dangerfield could swear the two soldiers guarding the entrance had been trained in door opening. The grey steel doors were yanked open simultaneously and so precisely that he found it comical. As he passed between them, he glanced at their faces. But he knew this close-up test of his mask carried little weight. These two were blinded by fear. Fear of provoking a reaction. Any reaction. Dangerfield could read their minds. *We don't exist. Please don't acknowledge us.*

As the doors closed neatly behind him he found himself in a bland vestibule. Facing him hung a large framed photograph of a grinning Kim Jong offering a bunch of delicate white lilies to a group of undernourished children.

Another pair of grey doors, wooden this time, and at each side a steel framed stool, its yellow drop-in cushion embroidered with the Supreme Leader's face. *Kimbo would love these.*

A sudden pit in his stomach caused him to freeze on the spot. Beyond the doors Dangerfield could hear someone talking. He felt his mask contort against his skin as he squinted violently, preparing his ‘fuck you’ face. *Hang on… hang on… that’s English!* Dangerfield sat on one of Kim Jong’s jaundiced faces and leaned in towards the doors. *Bingo! That’s Tim O’Brien alright.* He’d listened-in to enough of the man’s phone calls recently to recognise it instantly.

“Still can’t believe that Chinese programmer screwed the North Koreans over, with his parasitic generic algorithms,” said O’Brien in his distinctive tone. “Sabotage or what? If it wasn’t for that selfish idiot I’d have sorted this weeks ago! *And* I wouldn’t have needed your help.”

Dangerfield tensed as he heard footsteps approaching, relaxing slightly as they faded again.

“At least he got what he deserved. So happy they let me attend. This Chong chap! He’s brilliant! A bazooka… a bloody bazooka! At twenty feet! You should have seen the Chinese guys head explode. It was...” O’Brien snorted, “…spectacular!”

Craning even closer to the doors, Dangerfield heard the same footsteps repeatedly approach him and then fade. *Someone’s nervous.*

The monologue went on for so long that Dangerfield wondered whether O’Brien was actually alone. He peered through the tiny gap between the doors. Despite the familiarity of the face, seeing it in 3D again, for the first time in years, jolted him. A decade earlier at Cambridge, in all MI6 images taken since, and here today, O’Brien’s face looked innocent. Almost pretty. His head was small with delicate features. Except for the eyes. They were large like an inquisitive rabbit’s. Dangerfield struggled to match what he was looking at, to the image he and Liz had seen in Oslo with its gallon of smeared make-up.

A chair scraped the floor loudly.

"Chinese bastard! Who programs in basic Fortran these days? Fortran Seventy Seven fine! I would have coped. But Fortran Four!" O'Brien's voice continued to whine but Dangerfield could swear the guttural cough he heard came from a different source.

"You know what, we've so much in common. Cambridge, both programmers, this project I brought you in on. I tell you, when this is all over I think we'll be good friends."

"Talking to yourself again, O'Brien?"

Dangerfield's heart almost missed a beat at the sound of James' voice. His instinct was to burst into the room, but a nagging doubt as to whether the two men were alone held him back. He pressed his ear to the crack between the doors. That was definitely keyboard clatter he could hear.

"Um, yes. I mean n…no" The man started stammering. "Well, y…yes. I…I…"

"Okay. New chip's bedding in. Should be ready to roll in five," said James.

"G…g…great. But w…why the hell didn't I think generic algorithms? It was so humiliating! I'm Lead Programmer at Norse Defence… the very reason the Koreans head-hunted me, and I had to go c…c…cap in hand and tell them I needed help! That Chinese traitor! China and North Korea are supposed to be on the same team. That bloody traitor!"

"Give it a rest, O'Brien. Maybe the Chinese are the good

guys."

"Wh…what?"

"No-one chooses to live next door to 'the neighbour-from-hell'. I almost feel sorry for China. Imagine having to deal with an aggressive nutter sitting on your doorstep 24/7."

"What do you mean?" O'Brien's voice was almost childlike.

"Why would the Chinese help Kim Jong tuck a nuclear weapon down his pants, when he's been threatening to fuck everyone in reach? I can't believe these guys were so dumb as to execute the Chinese programmer."

"He was a traitor," said O'Brien defiantly.

"*He* was a traitor? You don't get it do you?"

"Get what?"

"North Korea relies on China because they've no one else. On the international stage, their Leader's known as 'Kim Jongy no-mates'. Hey! Maybe you two could be friends?"

"Sh…sh…shut up." O'Brien sounded like he was about to start sobbing. "But they're on the same team! China trades with the North Koreans!"

Behind the two men's voices, Dangerfield could hear the regular tapping of fingers on keyboard. *Surely they're alone?*

"Who gives a shit. Let's finish the job and get out of here," said James. "Look, maybe for the Chinese it's an act of Charity. I don't see any other countries queuing up to help North Korea's starving millions."

"B…but—" O'Brien started.

"But… the North Koreans *need* China just to stay alive. End of. It was plain dumb of them to bite the only hand that feeds them."

"That programmer didn't feed them. He poisoned them."

"Think you'll find his sewing bad seeds in their guidance software is what's kept North Korea safe. Any successful missile launch from them would effectively be shooting themselves in the foot. The international military backlash would wipe them off the face of the planet. *You've* harmed the North Koreans more by uncovering what he did," said James.

"Technically, you discovered it. And now you've solved it. And I tell you, Ch…China and K…K…Korea *are* team mates."

"You really think China's that stupid? More like a case of keeping your friends close and your enemies closer. Now, come here and give me a hug."

"Wh…what?"

Dangerfield smiled to himself and stood up. The two men *had* to be alone.

"Now, a little bit of merge and purge and… we… are… outta here!" said James. "Elvis is leaving the—"

Charles Addison Dangerfield, temporary Major in the Korean People's Army, stepped into the room.

"Oh! Hello?" James looked up at Dangerfield. O'Brien swivelled on the spot.

"Ahh... you're not General Chong." O'Brien sounded like a disappointed child. "Is he here yet? I've good news."

Dangerfield scanned the room. Two doors, one window.

He then stared at James who was sitting in front of a screen rammed with code. Dangerfield's smile pulled at his mask.

"Hello?" O'Brien was hopping from foot to foot. "Do… you… speak… En…ga…lish?"

Dangerfield looked straight at O'Brien. "Shut up and sit down!"

Mouth agape, O'Brien fell into the nearest chair. Dangerfield saw James' expression also change. His eyes repeatedly flashed from Dangerfield to his computer screen and back again.

"Time to go." Dangerfield crossed to the window and gauged the most hidden route back to the forest's edge. The keyboard rattle behind him was getting faster. And O'Brien was stuttering again.

"We've s…s…solved the guidance software problems on the M…M…Multiple Launch System. Where's General Ch…Chong?"

Ignoring him, Dangerfield crossed to James' desk. His friend seemed to be playing Flight of the Bumblebee on the computer's keyboard, his fingers madly flapping across the keys.

"James?"

No impact. The man's frown was deepening, his concentration solely on the computer screen. He was repeatedly stabbing the return key.

"What's up?" said Dangerfield.

O'Brien was back on his feet.

James eyes were glued to the screen. "Fucking Hell!"

"Hello, James? It's me, Charlie. It's a mask" Dangerfield could see beads of sweat forming on the man's forehead. "What's wrong?"

"FUCKING HELL!" James leapt to his feet, still jabbing at the keyboard.

Chapter Thirty

Dangerfield flew backwards as James launched at him, pushing him against the wall.

"I'll tell you what's wrong!"

Dangerfield tried to speak but the man was on fire.

"You talked me into this! Save your sister! Save the planet! Instead, I've as good as triggered World War Fucking Three!"

Allowing himself to remain pinned to the wall, over James' shoulder Dangerfield noticed O'Brien shaking. "What the hell are you talking about?"

"This isn't *my* programme! Your lovely Professor Shitface at the MOD must have switched the computer chip! Thanks to me the North Koreans now have a missile guidance capability on a par with America!"

James gripped Dangerfield's uniform, pulled and then slammed him back against the lab wall. "AND WHAT THE FUCK IS *THIS*?"

Ignoring the spittle, Dangerfield felt two hands scrabbling at his mask. He tried to grab James's wrists. "Don't touch the—"

It felt as if both of his cheeks had been torn off as the mask was ripped from his head. The blood rush was intense, anger beginning to erupt. Behind James, Dangerfield could see O'Brien had stopped shaking, his shocked expression replaced with a grin.

Taking a deep breath, Dangerfield held James wrists tightly. "I haven't got a Scooby what's going on mate but I'm getting you out of here. Now!"

A shrieking noise stole their attention. O'Brien was fist-pumping the air.

"Pay Day! Pay Day! Pay Day!" Yanking the door open O'Brien leapt into the corridor. Dangerfield shoved James aside and lunged headlong at the man, his fist breaking O'Brien's nose.

"Try May Day!"

Bouncing off the corridor wall, clutching his bleeding face, O'Brien hurtled towards the entrance lobby. Dangerfield, scrabbling up, yelled at James. O'Brien began shouting for help, a new nasal tone to his voice. Dangerfield's rugby tackle was messy. He caught only one of O'Brien's ankles, the guy slumping against the entrance door and kicking back, striking Dangerfield's forehead. As James appeared in the lobby, O'Brien pulled the entrance door open and, screaming wildly, threw himself out. Diving after him, Dangerfield grabbed O'Brien's legs and started dragging him back into the building. James reached to help but something momentarily fazed him. The two guards outside had their backs to the entrance. They were frozen in mid-salute, legs bolted together, attention locked on a large central figure amongst a group of uniformed men walking towards them. Reluctantly their heads flipped back to the sounds of three foreigners grappling on the floor behind them. Their mouths fell open, the turmoil and confusion of what to do clear in their eyes. With O'Brien back in the lobby, James quickly pulled the door shut,

Dangerfield silencing O'Brien with a skull-slam to the concrete floor.

"Back to the lab!" said Dangerfield, slamming the massive bolts on the door.

"Hang on… was that...?" said James, shaking his head in disbelief.

"No." Dangerfield swivelled O'Brien on the spot and started pulling him by an arm. "Help me drag this piece of shit. I've an idea."

"So that wasn't Kim Jong himself and his fucking army staring at us?"

"No. Shut up and help."

Both men hauled the dead-weight down the corridor and back into the lab. Dangerfield kicked the door shut as James started shoving the computer desk towards it.

"Leave it. Or they'll know we came in here."

Whilst dragging O'Brien towards a bank of steel drawers, Dangerfield pulled a small gutting knife from his pocket and gestured towards James.

"Give me your arm."

"What?" James was staring at the glinting blade.

"Your location chip. Give me your arm."

James screwed his face up.

"Look, the world's just flipped and you're chief witness. My instincts want you off grid… now!"

Looking nervous, James stepped forward.

"Relax. I had the same until 24 hours ago. Soo-Byn embedded it under your right arm, yes? It's digital. Relies on body heat for energy. Come on!" Dangerfield didn't wait. He grabbed James's arm, ripped his shirt sleeve open, and with his knife, deftly nicked the skin covering a miniscule lump. Instantly he squeezed out a locator chip the size of a rice grain and jumped back to where O'Brien lay. Slapping O'Brien's face hard, Dangerfield held the chip to the man's mouth. "Luckily it's not choosy whose body heat it powers off."

James was frowning.

"It was only a nick for fuck-sake! Open that window."

James didn't move. He was staring at O'Brien face. "O'Brien's not going to be opening his mouth any time soon." James's voice wavered. "I think he's dead."

"Dead?" Dangerfield slapped him even harder, O'Brien's head flopping violently. "Selfish bastard!" Dangerfield dropped the locator chip into one of O'Brien's bloodied nostrils, closed his mouth over the man's nose and blew hard. "At least it'll work until he's stone cold. Anyone interested in your whereabouts will assume you're still here for a few more hours. Let's move!"

"To where exactly?" James looked exasperated. "And why?"

"Because you're as good as dead now you're surplus to requirements."

"Whose requirements? The North Koreans' or MI6's?"

Dangerfield stopped dead in his tracks, his eyes boring into James's "We've no time for this. Let's just say, I got you into this, and now I'm getting you out." Dangerfield forced himself to stay calm, "Window?"

As James turned to open the small window behind him, Dangerfield yanked the large bottom drawer out from the metal chest next to him and half lifted, half threw O'Brien's torso into it. His legs remained folded over the drawer front. James looked back from the window.

"What the hell are you doing?"

Dangerfield didn't respond. He was holding O'Brien legs vertically above the man's body with one arm, his other slashing his knife across the back of the man's thighs. With blood streaming into the drawer, the scalpel-sharp blade sliced through cloth and flesh in one fell swoop, detaching all tendons and muscles in its path.

"Jesus Christ, Charles!" James looked like he was about to retch.

Again, Dangerfield didn't reply. He flapped the man's legs over, until his feet sat at either side of his head. Jumping up, he then flamboyantly kicked the drawer shut.

"There! Didn't spill a drop."

"Why?" demanded James, as he climbed out of the window, "Just why?"

"Out of sight, out of mind… I'm OCD… how long have you got?"

The answer came instantly. Shouting began echoing down the corridor.

Dangerfield followed James out of the window, closing it quickly behind him.

"Come on!" Dangerfield darted across the quadrangle at the rear of the building. At its far side, a low wall beckoned and the two of them slumped into it, crouching low.

"Where the hell are we going?" James' eyes flashed between Dangerfield and the window they'd raced from. "The airport's the other way."

"We need to reach that forest." Dangerfield pointed

across the two hundred metres of grass. “That way.” He gestured with a nod of his head. “That route avoids the eye-line of the army at the front.”

“What’s the plan?” said James. “Are we jogging back to London?”

Dangerfield ignored him, his focus on a soldier who’d rounded a corner.

“You do have a plan, don’t you?”

Dangerfield shook his head. “Ye of little faith. Of course I have a plan.” *At least I did until you ripped my fucking mask off!*

“So that’s a no then.” James’s head dropped and staring at the ground, sighed deeply. “Hang on. How the hell did you get here?”

“Aircraft,” Dangerfield replied quickly, “It’s in a clearing in those trees.”

Looking up, James suddenly put his hand on Dangerfield’s shoulder, “Uh-oh! Look!”

“Well spotted.” Dangerfield tried to hide his sarcasm. He sensed the lone soldier he’d been watching was nervous, his step tentative, as he continued to circle the rear of the building.

“We could outrun him easily!” said James, twitching, desperate to move.

“And his bullets?” Dangerfield placed a hand on James’ shoulder, pushing him back down behind the wall.

“Oh yeah! Twat!”

“Just wait. They’ll be busy in the building. Hopefully confused. Keep your eye on the window. We’ve got to time this right. As soon as scaredy pants is out of sight.”

"But I saw hundreds of soldiers just now," said James, panic entering his voice.

"Parade soldiers," Dangerfield said calmly.

"Explain?"

"Synchronised dance troupe. Purely to entertain Kimbo."

"I knew it was him! Shit!"

"Don't worry. One gunshot and they'll do synchronised pant-kakking"

"I might join them," said James quietly.

Dangerfield's tone hardened, "So what the fuck happened back there? Wrong chip? Old Prof Hammond never makes mistakes."

"You know O'Brien was promised a million to sort their guidance system out, but failed," said James, talking quickly.

"Failed? How? Thought he was Chief Geek?"

"I discovered a Chinese programmer had hidden algorithms in the North Korean's existing software. A kind of malware that gobbled up the chip O'Brien tried to install."

"I know you're Super Geek, but why couldn't O'Brien sort it?" said Dangerfield.

"The programming was written in Fortran Four, not Fortran Ninety," said James.

"In English?" said Dangerfield abruptly, his focus fixed on the soldier.

"He couldn't communicate with the existing programs because they were written in an extinct language."

Dangerfield glanced back at James, "Extinct? We're

talking computers, right?"

James shrugged. "Programming languages evolve constantly. Be like Liz trying to edit an article written in Sanskrit."

"So you speak this ancient computer dialect right?" Dangerfield snorted, "Forgot you majored in Geek History." Dangerfield tensed. "OK, he's disappearing behind the other complex. Give him another few seconds."

James started talking more rapidly. "So I designed some sneaky little algorithms myself and hid them in the replacement microchip your professor gave me. To the North Koreans it would appear as though they'd got a fully functional multiple launch system. They'd never find my insidious little demons. I doubt any programmer could have."

Without turning round, Dangerfield grunted. "Don't bang your head on that cloud."

James talked over him, excitement growing in his voice, "Unless of course Kim Jong ever has the balls to actually press the red button. Then, BOOM! Their whole system would be taken to Ground Zero."

"But that's how I understood the Grand Plan," said Dangerfield, gesturing for James to speed up. He put his hands on the low wall. "Ready?"

As James shuffled next to him, Dangerfield looked him straight in the eyes. "So what the hell's gone wrong?"

"Having synced the new microchip with their old software, I've just confirmed that my buried algorithms will never, ever be found."

"Well, that's exactly what you wanted wasn't it?" said

Dangerfield.

James's volume increased. "They'll never be found because they're not bloody there!"

Dangerfield stared at James, "What? Are you sure?"

"Hang on, I'll just go back and check… Of course I'm fucking sure!"

"I don't get it. Did someone wipe the chip?"

"Swapped! Only explanation." James' breathing was getting faster. "And when I tried to abort the bloody thing, it slammed the door in my face, locked me out and threw away the key." James shook his head. "Do you realise what I've done? I've just activated North Korea's membership of the Nuclear Club."

"Who? Why? How? I don't get it." Dangerfield's brain was filling up.

"Only one option," said James.

"Yes?" Dangerfield's attention was solely on James, his back now to the open space between them and the forest.

"The only time the chip wasn't with me, was when Professor Hammond said his boss had sanctioned a final seal of approval from some guy from the U.S. Defense Department."

"His boss? At the MOD?" Dangerfield's mind was racing.

"Not the MOD. He said the sanction came from MI6."

"WHAT!" Dangerfield's jaw dropped. "Name?"

James shook his head. "Shit… can't remember."

"Guy from US Defense… Name?"

"Again… sorry. All I know is he came by helicopter, landed next to Block 14, and breezed through security.

Took me twenty minutes and I'm English!" said James.

"And you reckon he switched the microchip?"

"It's the only answer. He had it five minutes. Hardly time to log in, let alone review any of my coding. Seal of approval, my arse."

Neither of them had noticed that the soldier had retraced his steps and that another soldier had joined him.

"This MI6 guy," Dangerfield urged, his attention completely on James, "try harder."

"Hammond only used a surname. Could have been a woman."

"This is fucking nonsense! Why would MI6 and US Defense actually hand North Korea nuclear missile capability? The exact opposite of what we've been striving for."

Before James could reply, both men were jolted by the sound of the lab window slam open behind them, shouts bursting from it.

"Bollocks." Dangerfield turned and leapt the low wall to be confronted by two soldiers, both pointing rifles at him. As James landed next to him, Dangerfield could hear his Dad's voice echoing inside his head, *DIS... COM... FUCKING... BOB... ULATE!*

Dangerfield began waving at them, a huge smile on his face.

"Hello! Anyoung!"

He growled at James from the corner of his mouth. "Follow my lead."

"I can't speak Korean!"

"Neither can I. Smile and wave, mate. Smile and wave."

Even at twenty yards Dangerfield could tell the two soldiers were uncertain what to do. He bowed deeply to them and slowly raised his arms above his head and pirouetted.

"What the hell are you doing? said James under his breath.

"Dance or die." Dangerfield began an impression of Krishna, bending his knees outwards, his hands clasped in prayer to his chest. "Do it!"

As James attempted the Sugar Plum Fairy, one arm stretched ahead of him, Dangerfield began twirling repeatedly, his arms outstretched in a sweeping gesture of love and affection. Each twirl brought him a yard closer to his confused prey, his ear-to-ear grin camouflaging his attack. On one soldier's face Dangerfield noticed a reluctant smile hovering, on the other, pure distress.

"Pimp it up," said Dangerfield.

"How exactly?" James started performing a terrible Hakka, his tongue flashing in and out.

"Ok, Funk it up." Dangerfield began singing 'The hills are alive with the sound of music' and prancing from side to side. Lost in the madness, James began gyrating suggestively, switching to a Cuban mambo with an exaggerated thrusting of his hips, each short leap bringing him closer to the soldiers. Inside his head Dangerfield conjured the Rolling Stones playing 'Paint it Black' and started to sing, "I look inside myself and see my heart is black…" His gaze never leaving the soldiers, he could see that one now wore a definite smile, the other on the verge of meltdown. As Dangerfield's memory failed him, James took over, his appalling Elvis appealing to Smiler.

"Hey, Homeboy! You still Beatbox?" said Dangerfield as he moonwalked around James, the two of them closing in on the soldiers. At five yards, Dangerfield was grinning inanely, his arms outstretched towards them as if addicted to love, Robert Palmer ringing in his ears. Smiler began laughing, overcome with placebic joy. The other soldier, overdosed on confusion, fell to his knees.

"Time for Sophie Ellis-Bextor," said Dangerfield, turning his back on the nearest soldier. James nodded his understanding.

The bicycle kick had been Dangerfield's legendary move on the school football pitch. Today it was clumsy, but he still yelled 'Goal!' as his boot kicked Smiler in the head. Crouching over him, as he passed into unconsciousness, Dangerfield saw James snatch at the other soldier's rifle. Refusing to let go and yelling in Korean, the soldier pulled James off his feet, the two struggling violently on the ground. As the soldier rolled over, still screaming for attention, he attempted to get up, until Dangerfield silenced him, by stamping on the back of his head, and grinding his face into the grass.

Shit!" James pulled at Dangerfield's arm. From the far corner of the complex a swarm of soldiers were surging towards them. "Please don't start dancing."

Sprinting, the two men headed up the grassy bank. "Some dance-off!" yelled James. "Reckon I nailed it with my mambo."

"Bullshit! I owned you with that moonwalk." As Dangerfield edged ahead and made for the clearing he noted that no weapons were firing. *'Capture alive', I'm guessing.* Entering the forest, Dangerfield yelled, "Don't look back," and whipped along the overgrown path. Within seconds he was in the clearing and jamming his hand on the drone's start button. "Wei!"

No answer.

"Wei! Wake up!"

The reply was calm. Familiar.

"Satellite link very poor."

"Wei, take off in twenty seconds."

James came crashing towards him.

"What the…"

Dangerfield put his face right in James's, and yelled, "Don't ask!... You're outta here… Controller's called Wei… There's the microphone… Get in this harness."

"But…"

"It's a fucking drone. Lie back and enjoy the ride. You're in business class. Three hundred and sixty degree views. No screaming kids. Well, maybe one. FUCKING DO IT!"

The engine noise grew as Dangerfield attached the last harness hook. His friend looked like he was going into shock. Shouts could be heard filtering between the trees.

"Listen, you can trust Wei. He's piloting you. He'll put you in touch with my mate Finkel."

"What about you?" shouted James above the noise of the engine.

"Forget me. Listen. Nobody's expecting you, so back in London, ask for my boss Sarah. Sarah Watling. Or Bulstrode. He's head of MI6. Explain what's happened."

Dangerfield saw James eyes light up.

"Bulstrode? That was it! That was the name of the guy that sanctioned the swapping of the chip."

"WHAT?" Dangerfield had to yell over the engine noise. "But he's been head of MI6 for years! Why would… FOR FUCK'S SAKE!"

Dangerfield had to leap sideways as with a jolt the drone jerked forward and started to run through the clearing. As the drone lifted over the trees, it slipped beyond the ridge and dropped out of sight into the adjacent valley, the sound of its small engine drifting out of earshot. And Dangerfield stood there. Transfixed. He continued gazing into the blue sky at the point at which James had disappeared from view. Silence enveloped him, wrapping him in swaddling clothes. Soldiers surrounded him, confused over what to do. But Dangerfield was in another time and place. He pictured Liz's face and tears began to form. Everything was out of his hands now. Nothing more he could do. More soldiers joined the fray, taking turns to shove him with their rifle butts. A smile crept onto his face. His friend was on his way home. Time to let go. Let fate do its eternal job. The rifle butt to his head initiated concussion. For a single second the impact brought him back to reality, his senses flaring momentarily, before the lights went out. And in that second, he heard the desperate yelling of soldiers, saw their frozen breaths and nervous expressions. He caught the taste of his own blood tinged with the smell of engine oil. And as he fell, he felt the splash of liquid up his thighs as his knees slumped into a deep puddle of drone fuel. *There and back only… there and back only.*

Chapter Thirty One

The Roxburgh Institute of Life Sciences was at the forefront of medical experimentation. Billy, the monkey with two brains, had been created here. As had the Vascular Department's albino cat, Milky. The lovable moggy had two hearts. If she survived the programme of T-Cell injections, her nine lives might start to become an actual possibility.

Although the literature stated that the Institute was attached to Harvard University, a modern Berlin Wall separated it from the rest of the campus. Harvard's undergrad architects described the wall as art deco, whereas the college's artists, in rare moments of sobriety, saw only Le Corbusier's stark cubism. Everyone agreed though, that the two-metre thick white blockwork, that surrounded the Roxburgh freak show, definitely made a statement. It said, 'KEEP OUT!'

The huge complex of buildings that made up the Institute, and the cutting edge medical research that took place within its white walls, was entirely funded by private enterprise. So private that even its Financial Director didn't know where the money came from. All she knew was that, however big the bills were that landed on her desk, the money to pay them was always there.

Security at the Roxburgh Institute was absolute. Access to certain parts of the site required iris, fingerprint and DNA identity checks. It would be easier to break into Fort Knox. At the centre of the sprawling medical complex stood a four storey windowless cube. Only ten people on the planet had Triple-A passes for this building. And none of them were doctors.

Anyone waiting while their ID was checked, at the only entry point in the perimeter wall, might imagine that their skiing holiday had just begun. The sky was azure blue, whereas the lower half of this world was entirely white. Every building, every walkway, and everybody in sight, all wore the same colour. Snow blindness was a possibility. This morning it was the British Prime Minister's turn to wish he'd packed his sunglasses.

Chapter Thirty Two

Standing in John Blake's way was a mirrored door, military thick. He'd been told to wait there until it opened. *Great! From Prime Minister to schoolboy in under a minute.* Glancing over his shoulder, he quickly scanned the empty quadrangle behind him. *At least no one can see me.*

Four storeys above Blake, last minute discussions were taking place. Ten men were finalising the best way to break the catastrophic news to their visitor.

Shifting his weight, Blake leaned towards the reflective door and stared at himself.

He shook his head. He looked exactly as he felt. Exhausted. Leaning even closer to his reflection, he lingered on the finer details of his face. His mouse-brown hair was exactly in place. But the grey at his temples was definitely spreading. A bunch of blackheads drew his face right up to the glass.

Blake was oblivious of the man in military uniform standing not twelve inches from him, scrutinising his every twitch. On the other side of the mirrored door, looking out through its one-way security glass, the guard stared dutifully into Blake's eyes. Remove the door, and anyone would think the two were about to kiss.

Blake hated being so obsessed with his appearance. Press photographs were the worst. He would always glance briefly at other people in group shots, whether they were flood victims or his fellow world leaders. But his focus would always quickly return to his own image. Were his eyebrows getting bushy? Did his smile look sincere enough?

Fighting to disguise a yawn, Blake twisted on the spot, and checked his profile. He patted his stomach. At least Sandra had been right about this suit.

Why the hell are they keeping me waiting? Scanning the Institute's other buildings, he imagined he was caught in a blizzard. His surroundings were entirely white. And he could swear everything was beginning to swirl.

The flight from London had been terrible. He hadn't managed a single minute of sleep. The turbulence had been constant, and had come entirely from inside his head. He seemed to be stuck in repeat mode, the same thoughts running over and over in his mind. Maybe it was a symptom of shock? He couldn't stop thinking about everything that had happened in the two weeks since, miraculously, the electorate had returned him as their Prime Minister. But shit, his second bite of the cherry was already turning sour. Surely, after the Covid pandemic, the world deserved a rest, a holiday, some normality? Apparently not. Everything was going wrong at the same time. Afghanistan had imploded. Taiwan was shitting bricks. NATO was falling apart. Crisis after bloody crisis. North Africa, West Africa. Just when he'd thought agreements had been brokered, they were suddenly broken. Peace didn't stand a chance.

He couldn't help but smile though, when he recalled how his new Foreign Secretary had made him promise that if the next two weeks were anything like the previous two, then he was to shoot her in the head.

And back in Blighty, the disparate unions were attempting to shout from the same hymn sheet, against all the cuts he'd been pushing through to help pay for the billions borrowed during Covid. But hey, at least on this front, time was on his side. He knew he had until Hell froze over, before they'd get *their* collective act together.

The most shocking event though, that had dominated his thoughts over the last two weeks, and the one that he was still pinching himself about now while standing outside The Roxburgh Institute, was his re-election a fortnight earlier. How? Just how? The election had exploded in controversy. The Opposition were still reeling from the shock result. The favourite had fallen at the last fence and in spectacular style. Four days before the vote, the Opposition Leader, Geoffrey Moore, had been exposed. Pollsters had put him miles ahead. That was before photographs emerged of him giving head. Both Moore and the Bishop denied it violently, claiming they'd been photoshopped. The Shadow Cabinet was immediately up in arms, accusing the Press of being a bunch of Bishop-bashers. Moore found himself on a very sticky wicket because the journalists' unnamed sources had all corroborated. By Election Day, the damage was done. As Black Rod ceremonially banged on the House of Commons door, the newspapers' coverage immediately switched to the turmoil unfolding around the world.

Blake started fantasizing that he'd brought Black Rod with him today. With no bell to ring or handle to rattle, he imagined the man in full regalia smashing his Mace down hard on the mirrored door.

Through the door's one-way glass, the guard could see the frustration growing on the visitor's face.

Blake's visit to the Roxburgh Institute had been fraught from the moment he'd arrived. At 2.45pm, Blake had been forced to inform his personal secretary, back in Whitehall, that his phone would be switched off for one hour. He'd failed to mention that Roxburgh's Security Department were about to confiscate it. His arguments about diplomatic rights had fallen on deaf ears. Edward Bulstrode, Director General of MI6, who'd alerted him of this virtual summons to the U.S. in the first place, had stepped in to mediate. Over a secure phone from London, Bulstrode had reassured Blake that this meeting was likely to be important enough to over-ride any and every possible phone call that he might receive.

They might agree on the status of the meeting, Blake thought, but Bulstrode was wrong about the importance of every incoming call. There was one person on the planet, one very small person, for whom he had an open-all-hours policy. Here in Boston, under a broad blue sky, it had just gone 3.00pm. Luckily, going by the clocks in London, Emily should be fast asleep by now.

Blake checked his new watch, a Rolex 800. Gold hands peeped from behind a huge central diamond. *Fifteen bloody minutes. I perform an electoral miracle and they treat me like this? Jesus!*

His thoughts wandered to the evening when he'd received the exorbitant gift, now strapped to his wrist. The whole Cabinet had been presented with the same watch at the surprise post-Election party. Staff had scrambled to pull the event together. No provision had been made for a celebration because, until four days earlier, the whole country had expected them to lose. Speeches had been rapidly re-written, champagne rushed in by the crate, and a mass of bunting and banners bought in. When it came to the unexpected watch presentation, the Ministers had all protested. They claimed that after four years of peddling austerity, accepting such ostentatious gifts would be obscene. At an emergency Cabinet meeting the following evening, the first five minutes was spent flashing them at each other. After one eagle-eye had spotted that the central diamond on Blake's Rolex 800 was considerably larger than everyone else's, the second five minutes of the emergency meeting saw the male members of the Cabinet in regression.

"John's Crown Jewel is the biggest!" "Apparently not as big as the Bishop's!" "But he's got more than Moore!"

As endless versions of the same puerile joke exasperated the female Ministers, news broke that the North Koreans were carrying out more long-range missile launch tests.

"Use your magic wand on them, John!" quipped the Home Secretary. "If you can bring the party back from the dead, surely—" The woman's words suddenly stopped mid-sentence as she recognised her horrendous faux pas.

The Education Minister started chanting, "Phoenix!… Phoenix!... Phoenix!" As he continued chanting and punching the air, he watched the look of horror spread across his colleagues' faces. The confusion growing on his own face immediately gave way to a silent gaping mouth, as he too made the unfortunate connection between his one-man-chant and the tragedy unfolding in the Prime Minister's private life.

In limbo, standing outside the door to the very heart of the Roxburgh Institute, Blake's thoughts jumped from that awkward Cabinet meeting to Emily. He'd partly excused his performance in his previous term as PM on all the time he'd spent at St Bart's Cancer Centre. Six years of treatment. Six years of hopes, raised and dashed. His brave, beautiful Emily. Six years old. The hospital had sent her home because she was sinking so fast. Even the lifeboat was taking on water; her doctors had started using the T word.

Eleven years of marriage and yet he hadn't gained the slightest inkling that Sandra was capable of such intense anger. Firstly with God, and then with the doctors. This morning in Downing Street it had been his turn to feel her fury.

"How can you even *think* of leaving the country? *She* needs you NOW! WE need you now."

Only when Special Protection Officers pulled up outside Number 10 did she stop being angry. She went berserk. The oil painting of Winston Churchill now lay smashed on the hall floor. He'd stupidly tried to explain.

"John! You are one man! Can't the sodding world wait just once?"

As the armoured Jaguar Sentinel set off for City Airport, Blake felt that on this occasion, waving seemed inappropriate. The look Sandra gave him, as he was whisked away, made him shudder inside. In all his years of visiting disaster sites, attending funerals of terrorists' victims and witnessing the horrific consequences of military interventions, this look was something completely new to him. He thought he'd seen every expression a human face could reveal; love, anger, happiness, anguish, betrayal. So this was what abandonment looked like.

Looking up, Blake scanned the four storeys that reached skyward immediately in front of him. A grey cloud was peeking over the edge of the building's skyline and beginning to contaminate the bright blue expanse. A final check of his Rolex 800. It was almost ten hours ago to the minute since he had been sitting on his daughter's bed, with his arm around her.

Emily's arm had been wrapped around her favourite teddy. The number of soft toys she'd received from well-wishers over the years was into three figures. Yet, despite her bear having lost an eye, and having only one leg, this was the one she loved. It had always been there for her, day and night. A faithful friend.

"Why are you crying, Daddy? I'm not crying." She'd thrust the bear in his face. "Look! Teddy's not crying."

Blake watched his reflection shake its head. *You idiot! What the hell are you doing here?* He raised his fist to bang on the glass door. But at that instant the huge mirror swung quickly inwards. A clack of boot heels and a sharp salute greeted him.

"Welcome, Sir!"

He stepped inside.

"This had better be good news."

Chapter Thirty Three

As the elevator door closed behind him, Blake felt something he'd never experienced before. Official duties had obliged him to enter a multitude of secure locations, from high security asylums across Britain to military correction facilities within a grenade's throw of Baghdad. But right now, here in the hub of the Roxburgh Institute, he felt more prisoner than visitor. Sealed in and quietly gaining height he found himself compelled to stare up at the square-lensed security camera trained on his face. An inexplicable sense of guilt washed over him. Suddenly he was on his way to the school principal's office again, reddening cheeks undermining his innocence. For God's sake, all the boys had parped Bagshaw's new bicycle horn. It wasn't his fault it had chosen to take its final breath at his turn. Five minutes in the school-head's office and he'd received two more red cheeks.

The elevator clicked to a halt on Level Four and Blake's mind jolted back into gear. Stepping into a long, white, doorless corridor, he found himself reaching to tighten his tie. The walls were lined with pressed orchids, each in a shallow white box-frame. Delicate and dead, they were spaced a couple of metres apart, each with its Latin name stamped into its surrounding mount. *What's with the obsession with orchids?* Their presence triggered Blake's memory of seeing similar box-framed plants six months earlier when he'd last met Roxburgh's inner circle.

But that had been an entirely different venue. The wall behind the reception desk at the private Mann Hotel in Monaco had been plastered with the square-framed beauties. He remembered having just completed check-in there when the U.S. President Paul Keats had walked through the entrance door, shadowed front and back by security operatives. Before they had even exchanged greetings, Tomasz Mann or 'Media Mann' as bloggers had christened him, stepped out from nowhere, eyes permanently in stare mode and with a huge mad smile strapped to his face.

"Hey, Paul, John, good to see you together!" Mann had made an exaggerated gesture of looking over their shoulders, "So where's Ringo?"

Their weak smiles had matched their handshakes.

"Sorry about that. Couldn't resist it," Mann had started rubbing his hands together like an obese kid who had just inherited a chocolate factory. "So, Paul, I've put you in the Paradise Suite again, and John, I've told them to put you in Heaven." He'd taken them each by the elbow and had guided them towards the elevator. Keats had made to speak but Mann had cut straight across him.

"Now, look boys, we've got a lot to get through, so if you want to freshen up, we'll fetch you in fifteen. Ok?"

Blake had understood the tone in Mann's voice. In no way had he invited reply.

Blake smiled briefly to himself as he remembered the joke he'd shared with the President those six long months ago in Monaco. In the elevator on their way to Paradise and

Heaven, he'd told Keats that if Mann were ever to make it to the real thing, he'd probably tell God to 'shut up and listen'.

Today, at the heart of the Roxburgh Institute in Boston, the absence of doors strengthened Blake's sense of imprisonment. But after taking a ninety degree turn in the corridor, he immediately felt less isolated. At first glance the man walking towards him looked familiar. It took a whole second to dawn on him who it was. They shared the same tailor. And barber. And wife.

"What the..." *Again?* Fixed above *this* mirrored door was a security camera identical to the one in the lift, except for a flashing red light mounted below it. When red flicked to green, Blake felt his temperature suddenly rise.

Chapter Thirty Four

Ten pairs of eyes were boring holes in him. Blake barely took in the stark room with the simplest of Scandinavian tables at its centre. Instead, his eyes flicked from face to face as the door closed behind him.

"John, welcome!" said Robert Roxburgh, his greeting warm and upbeat. "Do join us." Roxburgh gestured to the only unoccupied chair at the end of the table nearest to Blake. Half of the faces were immediately familiar to Blake and after a second or two a couple more clicked. But three were completely unknown to him.

"So, the Inner Sanctum. To what do I owe this great honour?" Blake asked, as he sat and pulled his chair in.

"Your election. That was some win," said Karl Lynx, "A huge majority. Huge! And from nowhere. You are seriously empowered now."

"Thank you," said Blake tentatively. He nodded at the other men around the table, naming only the ones he'd actually met before. "Thomasz. Mohammed."

Four men lined each side of the long table. And at the far end sat Roxburgh and a sharp-suited Chinese man.

"I think you'll know most of the faces here, but I don't think you'll recognise George Ascot and Ashram Singh." Roxburgh gestured towards the pair, but made no attempt to introduce his over-tailored neighbour. Nodding at the two men, Blake noticed there were no papers on the table in front of anyone. No laptops or phones. Nothing that would suggest a typical meeting. There were only two items on the table. Newbie face, George Ascot, whom Blake assumed was a centenarian, had a glass of water and a foil of tablets laid out in front of him. The man was staring at Blake so intensely and with his mouth agape, that Blake assumed he was either trying to read his mind, or had, at that very second, died of horror.

"Now John, firstly, can I on behalf of everyone present, extend our sincerest best wishes towards your daughter," said Roxburgh. All but the dead man nodded in agreement, "Obviously, you must be devastated by the news."

Blake felt his heart sink. The mention of his daughter brought back an instant wave of guilt. Thirty minutes at the Institute and he still had no idea why he'd been summoned here. What were Bulstrode's words? It had to be immense.

Blake folded his arms, irritation niggling at him.

"Thank you, gentlemen. And on that very note, I hope you appreciate the sacrifice I've made in coming here today. And so I would equally appreciate it if you would kindly elucidate. Naturally I would like to be getting back to Emily as soon as possible." Blake couldn't hold back a deep sigh. "Time is more precious to me now than it could ever be."

Roxburgh didn't answer and seemed content to extend the silence as he appeared to gather his thoughts.

Looking around, Blake's gaze met only staring eyes.

"Gentlemen, you have me at a disadvantage. You haven't given me the slightest clue as to why you've asked me here, and so, let's just say, my breath is bated." Blake hoped they'd pick up on his impatience this time.

Robert Roxburgh cleared his throat.

"Well, John, you've just referred to time, and how precious it is." Roxburgh's eyes flicked around his audience. "Time indeed." The man's eyes were now locked on Blake's. "Time is running out. Not merely for your daughter, but also for the whole of humanity."

Blake frowned. *Stop mentioning my bloody daughter!*

"In fact, time *has* run out." It was Roxburgh's turn to sigh, "Sea levels and global temperatures continue to rise. Our rivers are polluted with chemicals, and our atmosphere with methane, as a result of the mass-farming practices required to feed our ever-expanding population." After a deep breath, Roxburgh shook his head, "John, the stars could not be any more mis-aligned—"

"The ultimate shit-storm!" threw in Mann, "And we humans only have ourselves to blame! We needed Greta Thunberg thirty years ago!"

"Thomasz, please…" Roxburgh's voice intensified. "The Code Red warning for humanity has just been upgraded. A decision has been made and seconded by everyone seated at this table. A decision that will benefit the progress of humanity."

"I'm all for progress," said Blake quickly.

Roxburgh held his hand up. "Please allow me to finish."

Blake opened his mouth to reply but held his tongue.

"The scale of this decision is unparalleled in magnitude throughout the entire history of mankind. And we know…" Roxburgh paused momentarily, "that your initial reaction will be one of disbelief. But…" Roxburgh shifted in his chair, "this decision is the result of every single other possibility having been utterly exhausted."

Blake glanced around the room as he listened. Every pair of eyes seemed to be trained on him. The format was similar to his weekly Cabinet meetings, but the sheer weight of attention focused on him was far more intense than his Cabinet ever gave him.

Dead Man began struggling to get to his feet, his chair scraping loudly. But as his body started to shake, he gave up, slumping back down and blurted out loudly, "There are too many of us!"

Thomasz Mann put his arm on the man's shoulder, "Thank you, George. Succinct as ever."

Roxburgh nodded. "George has said what many have said over the past few decades. It is the ultimate unspoken truth. There *are* too many of us."

Blake took a deep breath. *Where the hell is he going with this?*

"We are beyond 'peak oil' and 'peak gas', and why? Because we've reached peak population. In fact our population peaked many years ago." Roxburgh frowned. "John, you must understand this? Your very own David Attenborough said as much."

Blake nodded in agreement. "Of course. Definitely. We need to address this urgently. I believe part of the UK's Committee on Climate Change has an ongoing discussion with the W.H.O. and as part of its directive we—"

"John. It's too late for discussions. Fifty years too late." Roxburgh, again, glanced around the table. "Nothing is up for discussion any longer. This is why you are here today."

Roxburgh leaned forward in his chair. “We want you to be in charge of COBRA’s Disaster Management for Northern Europe. We want the UK to be a detached force and manage the aftermath across that whole region of the planet. That’s why we gave you BREXIT.”

“*Gave* us BREXIT?” Blake fought to remain sitting. “And what disaster? It sounds like you’re planning one?” Blake shook his head. “Nice try but you’re a bit early for April the First!”

Roxburgh sighed loudly. “It’s ok, John. Listen. Hear me out.” Again Roxburgh shifted in his chair, “Our work here at the Roxburgh Institute is not merely focused on medical research and life extension,” Roxburgh nodded in Dead Man’s direction, “but for over forty years we’ve intensely monitored the earth’s resources. The resources that not only enable our continuing survival but, more than tread water, allow us to *progress* in terms of communicating with the rest of the Universe.” Roxburgh looked around the table, a few of the men catching his eye. “But the fact is, we’re not even treading water. We are drowning. As a species we are going backwards. And that is irreversible unless we act now.”

Blake couldn’t stay silent any longer.

“Act now? Are you proposing to bump a few of us off? Really?”

“Preparations have been going on for nearly two years. And you, John, have been selected as a key player in the management process.” Roxburgh was nodding as he spoke. “Our population is about to come down by eighty percent.”

Blake jumped to his feet. “Eighty percent! That’s

around six billion people!"

"Ok, listen." Roxburgh remained sitting, his voice staying calm, "I did say that your first reaction would be disbelief, but we have exhausted every humane approach." Roxburgh started counting off his fingers. "First, China's one child policy." Roxburgh glanced at the man with no name, sitting beside him, whose expression had remained stoic until now. Blake noticed a weak grin begin playing across his face.

"That alone has cost us trillions of dollars over the last forty years. And now, despite all our attempts at negotiation, the Chinese refuse to maintain that policy. Stating internal reasons, they recently terminated it. Full-stop." Roxburgh then nodded in Thomasz Mann's direction. "Secondly, we've been promoting same sex marriage through every media channel possible. God, John, the list is endless. GM food distribution to take the edge off passion. Free condom distribution across the whole of Africa. Provoking the Arab Spring. Libya. Syria."

Blake couldn't believe what he was hearing. "You provoked the Arab Spring?"

Roxburgh put his hands up. "John, we've tried everything to try to curtail our population growth. SARS, Ebola, Chinese Bird Flu. You have no idea how hard we've worked to steer a path ahead for our species."

Throwing his arms in the air, Blake turned towards the door and then turned straight back.

"You're planning to murder six billion people? WHAT!"

Thomasz Mann chirped up again, "Otherwise we're

irreversibly destined to be living back in caves sooner than you can say, 'G'day, Monkey'. And the short journey there will involve wars, starvation and prolonged suffering for virtually everybody as resources dry up." Mann proffered his arms. "Hey… John… it's a cull. A human cull. Not badgers. Not Koalas, but a different species' turn. Our turn. The latest virus we've developed will spread instantaneously, suffering limited to forty-eight hours and with minimal pain. The North Koreans will take the blame and hats off to you, sir…"

"Me? What the hell have I done?" Blake could feel a wave of heat surging through his body.

"Your sterling work implementing our immunisation programme across the UK for a start."

"But wasn't that the W.H.O.'s recommended programme?" Blake stared at each man in turn. Nothing. "OK! STOP! I'm going now. And when I wake up, this will all have been just a fucking nightmare." He felt as though he could explode at any second. "I WILL NOT BE PARTY TO YOUR GENOCIDE!"

Robert Roxburgh stood up for the first time, his tone suddenly harsh.

"We own the banks. We own the media. And Blake, therefore… as you well know, we own you."

Blake turned and made for the door. Exasperation? Desperation? Resignation? He had no idea what he felt. But as he left the room and closed the door behind him he knew one thing. He was closing it permanently on madness, insanity and lunacy all rolled into one fucked-up ball.

As the door was about to click shut, Blake heard six

simple words. Six words that blew the door off its hinges.

"We can save your daughter's life."

Chapter Thirty Five

Blake was sitting in the back of one of the Roxburgh Institute's private cabs, and being returned at speed to the airport. He was trying to block from his mind the previous hour of his life by focusing on crucial phone calls. He'd updated his private secretary on his flight details and ETA, and ticked off two of the most urgent messages that bellowed at him for replies. But, however hard he tried to concentrate, Robert Roxburgh's final six words kept punching a hole in his focus.

"Can we go any faster?" Blake asked loudly, addressing both men sitting in the front of the huge, black Lincoln Navigator.

"Maybe a touch, sir," the driver threw back, "but the speed limit is fifty."

His colleague glanced at Blake. "We're in good time, sir. Your flight for London doesn't leave for another hour."

"Right. OK. Thank you," said Blake, trying to conceal the frustration in his voice. He stared out of the tinted side window. But couldn't see anything. Not even the blur of buildings as the Limo sailed past them. All he could see was Emily's face.

He closed his eyes.

And she was still there. Smiling at him.

And clutching her lifelong friend, Teddy.

When the Lincoln drew up at the airport, he even forgot to thank the driver as he climbed out.

His thoughts were gnawing at him. Consuming him.

As Blake was escorted through the airport to one of its private suites, he walked in silence, offering no pleasantries, lost in his own head.

He waved-away three different waiters before they accepted the message and left him alone in the corner seat, furthest from the caviar bar.

He retrieved his phone and stared at his screensaver. Emily.

He hit FaceTime and waited an eternity until Sandra answered.

"Hi. You done over there now?"

"I love you," Blake's voice waivered.

There was a pause before he heard, "Are you ok?"

"Just wanted to get that out the way. Look..." Blake glanced over at the bar, "… how's Emily?"

"She's fine at the moment."

"Good, good, good… that's good." Exhaustion washed over him and he sighed deeply.

"You look shattered."

"Yeah, well…" another deep sigh "… long day. Can I speak to her?"

"I put her to bed over an hour ago. You're at the airport, right?"

"Yeah, yeah. Can you wake her?"

"No… not really. What time do you fly in?"

As Blake answered, Sandra's face suddenly turned away from the screen.

"Hey sweetie… hang on, John… you OK, darling?" Sandra pressed the rotate button on her screen and Blake could see Emily slowly making her way down the stairs, one hand reaching up to the banister, the other dragging Teddy beside her, by his one and only leg.

Welling up instantly, Blake called out, "Emmy! Hi, sweetheart." He quickly wiped a tear before it ran, and glanced over at the bar again.

"Slowly, darling… slowly. Look who it is. Come and say hello to Daddy."

Another tear welled but Blake let it run, focusing on his phone screen. "Hey, sweetheart. I've missed you."

The camera rotated again and Blake watched his daughter scramble onto her mother's lap, with Teddy sitting on hers. Sandra stroked Emily's thinning hair, pulling it away from her face. "Couldn't you sleep, darling?"

"Teddy woke me up."

Blake laughed. "Really? Naughty Teddy."

"Naughty Daddy."

"Aah… OK."

Emily raised her teddy bear and bounced him up and down on her knee, on his single leg. "Look. He's hopping mad with you."

Blake laughed again. "Well, tell Teddy, I'm bringing him a present back from America."

Emily hugged her bear tightly. "Teddy says, what is it?"

"Tell Teddy it's a surprise."

Blake watched his daughter whisper in her bear's ear.

"I miss you, Daddy."

From the corner of his eye, Blake caught a steward heading his way. “I miss you too, sweetheart.”

“Your flight’s ready sir. Priority boarding is now.”

“Thank you,” Blake replied without looking at the guy.

“Safe journey, John.” Sandra blew a single kiss. “Ok darling, say ‘night, night’ to Daddy. He’ll be here to have breakfast with us when you wake up in the morning.”

“Night, night, Daddy.”

“Night, night, sweetheart.” Blake could feel himself welling up again. “Night, night, Teddy.”

Emily made her bear wave. And then she was gone, the screen blank.

Chapter Thirty Six

The concrete floor on which Dangerfield had been dumped was freezing. In the darkness, he rolled onto his hands and knees, the rough surface tearing at his skin.

Why the hell was he naked? Remaining crouched and breathing deeply, his senses began to return. What seemed total blackout became fractured by a thin crack of light peeping under a door. A creeping stench punched his nose almost matching the haymaker he had received eight hours earlier. As Dangerfield's head jerked back in revulsion, the light bulb above him flicked on, as if wired to a motion sensor. Leaping to his feet, he reached out for the nearest wall for balance. His fingers found shallow grooves in the cold, hard surface. If his Korean had been more advanced than a small collection of obscenities, he might have made out that these crude scratchings spelt 'forgive me'. Other messages were randomly daubed around the cell. The majority were at knee height. If not in their crimes, the writers were at least unified in their choice of ink colour. Brown.

Heavy footsteps broke the silence. More time to fully regain his senses would have been handy, but the slamming of bolts and the grate of a key signalled that someone else was in control. The steel door creaked open like Dracula's coffin, although the blood lust of the man about to enter would make vampires look vegan.

Instinctively, Dangerfield took a step back as the yelling began. Two soldiers burst in waving rifles at him and took up positions either side of the doorway. They gestured for him to raise his arms. Instead he folded them across his chest, closed his eyes and remembered.

He was twelve. His dad was teaching him how to shoot a wood pigeon. As he held the air pistol up, he felt his father's big hands close around his. *Listen, Charlie, hitting your target depends on three things. First. Control the gun at eye level. Second. Focus on the front sight. Third. Smooth on the trigger. Remember... Control. Focus. Smooth*. Dangerfield opened his eyes. And repeated the three words in his head.

A baggy suit stumbled through the doorway: a thin guy wearing thick spectacles, clearly stolen from his tailor. Someone had shoved him. Regaining his footing, the man scrambled behind one of the soldiers.

The foul smell, his naked state and the freezing concrete had vanished from Dangerfield's mind. Eyes now wide open, his entire focus was reserved for his fourth visitor in as many seconds.

Filling acres of green cloth, embellished with more gold braid than a belly dancer's tunic, Colonel Chong stepped into the cell. If GCHQ had conducted a psychological profile on *this* man, they would have concluded that Colonel Chong Hwa was a man who would sell his own grandmother. And a full historical analysis would have revealed that Chong actually had. Thirty years previously, as a teenage member of the Korean People's Army, he had caught his grandmother stealing food to feed him and his sister. He had reported her to the State Security Department and then watched as officers from the feared SSD had dragged her out of bed and shot her six times. They had hung her dripping body by its feet from the willow tree that stood outside the village school; the same school that had taught both grandmother and grandson about loyalty. She would have died for her family; Chong's loyalty had only ever been to the Fatherland. To demonstrate publicly his hatred of his grandmother for stealing the fruits of her own back-breaking toil, food that was destined for the SSD, the nineteen year old Chong had run at her dangling corpse. Gripping the barrel end of his rifle in both hands he had swung at her as if trialling for the New York Yankees. If it had not still been attached to her neck, her head might have left the stadium. And thirty years on, Chong still failed to understand, that however many examples he had made of the ungrateful pigs that dishonoured their Supreme Leader, Kim Jong, there were still a few that had the audacity not to bow in reverence every time they passed one of his many giant portraits.

Dangerfield had never bowed to anyone. Not even the Queen. And wasn't planning to start anytime soon, despite both soldiers pointing their rifles directly at his chest. They glanced nervously at the Colonel and then back at Dangerfield, desperate not to miss even the slightest hint of an order. Chong looked Dangerfield's naked frame up and down. The man was clearly seething when he entered the cell, jealousy only adding to his anger. He started yelling, and gesturing furiously at the thin man, Chong's moves ludicrously animated for an obese monster; Gangnam, but without the Style. Leaping from his hiding place, the skinny translator stood beside Chong, who pointed his revolver at Dangerfield. Chong then bellowed. His side-kick translated at half-volume, “Where are the two computer scientists?”

Dad was whispering in his ear. *Control. Focus. Smooth.* Returning the Colonel’s stare, Dangerfield slowly unfolded his arms and made a gesture that required both hands. “They’re fucking your wife.”

Chapter Thirty Seven

The skinny translator began to shake inside his ill-fitting suit. He knew exactly what the prisoner had just said, but shock and disbelief froze his tongue. *What the hell was this naked lunatic thinking*? Civilians were always cowed in the Colonel's presence. Prisoners either fell to their knees, begging pathetically or impersonating statues, given away only by the piss running down their legs. Colonel Chong turned to him, his look of rage demanding a response. The translator's continued silence and profuse sweating was not the one required. The Colonel's fist made a cracking sound against the man's jaw. The translator's tongue must have defrosted because he could taste blood and feel two loose teeth. Jamming his Ruger101 pistol against the man's cheek, Chong grunted in his ear. And as the translation stuttered its way out, the bullet went in.

To Dangerfield the gunfire was the crack of a starting pistol. Launching himself forward, every sinew straining, his right hand lunged for Chong's wrist, twisting the revolver towards one of the guards. The neurons in the Colonel's brain had already fired. A small metal gift ripped through the guard's right eye and, without a word of thanks, the ingrate fell to the ground, writhing violently.

Reaching up with his left, Dangerfield snatched at the light bulb, the sudden darkness granting privacy to the guard's death throes. As Dangerfield grappled for Chong's pistol, he felt Chong's other arm close around his neck.

The second guard was in a straitjacket of confusion. In the near-darkness, the two combatants were visually inseparable. He waved the rifle at the combined dark blob that twisted and turned in front of him, unable to decipher when to pull on the trigger.

The Colonel pulled on Dangerfield's head like an alcoholic trying to open a whiskey bottle. For three or four seconds the impasse continued as they struggled to secure last place in 'Strictly Come Dancing'.

Fuck. Bored of this. Have it your way. Dangerfield jammed his head up sharply in the same direction Chong was pulling. The head-butt was intense. Two craniums in a head-on. Clattering across the concrete floor, the pistol disappeared into the gloom. Shaking with anger, and with adrenaline screaming through his veins, Chong roared and used his sheer bulk to shove Dangerfield to the ground. Wrenching the rifle out of the second guard's hands, the Colonel's thick fingers closed around the barrel and trigger.

Stumbling in the direction in which the pistol had fallen, Dangerfield remained low, frantically searching for it in the dark.

Waving the rifle wildly in Dangerfield's direction, Chong yanked furiously on the trigger. All six bullets sprayed aimlessly through the darkness. Only one hit flesh.

The synthetic green uniform offered little protection as the bullet penetrated the second guard's chest. Chong pulled on the now redundant trigger four more times before the futility of an empty chamber sank into his overloaded brain.

Dangerfield's hand found the discarded pistol as the Colonel scrambled towards the doorway.

The only source of light was in the corridor, now directly behind the Colonel's head. Chong had become a silhouette, like a black target board at a military shooting range.

Dangerfield raised the Ruger101. "Control, focus…"

The translator's corpse caused the khaki bulk to trip. Scrabbling backwards on his arse, still trying to exit the prison cell, Chong stared up into Dangerfield's eyes. Sweat washed his pleading face.

"Sorry, Colonel: Government diktat. All prisoners must complete their sentence." Dangerfield shrugged, "…and smooth on the trigger."

Undressing the translator's warm body took only seconds. The jacket of the baggy suit felt tight across Dangerfield's shoulders, and the trousers reached only halfway down his calves. Looking at his bare feet, he pictured an overgrown hobbit. Once again in solitude, in this stinking cell, now knee-deep in fresh meat, Dangerfield couldn't help himself. He held the pistol up to the light coming from the hallway.

"My precious!"

He slipped the gun into his breast pocket, climbed over Chong's body, and stepped out of the cell and into the light. He smiled to himself. The psychologists at MI6 would have a field day.

And if any of the corpses were listening from beyond the grave, they would be equally as confused by Dangerfield's Punch and Judy impression. Looking back from the corridor and staring directly at Chong's body, he screeched like a jackdaw. "That's the way to do it!"

Sometimes, he scared himself.

Chapter Thirty Eight

Dangerfield started to climb the stairs of the crude prison complex, his adrenaline coursing. His bare feet were cold but they felt on fire against the freezing concrete. He edged his way up two flights to the ground floor, pausing at the top step, his fingers tightening on the trigger of the pistol. Breathing deeply he noticed the air seemed fresher. Peering around the corner he could see down a dark corridor that ended in a thick steel door with a small square window. Natural light. He crept silently to the door, crouched below its window and pressed his ear to the cold metal. He could make out two men in lively conversation. A second later one burst into laughter. Dangerfield realised this deep dense bunker of a building must have swallowed the sound of gunfire that had come from deep within its bowels. Through the glass, he clocked an office with four desks, three of which were vacant, and at the far side, windows looking out onto a busy street. In a tiny adjoining office that looked more like a sealed glass cubicle, he spotted an SSD guard wearing headphones, facing away, head down. At the nearest desk were two more police guards. One had Dangerfield's ripped mask over his face and was gibbering away, shaking his head wildly. The other was keeled over next to him, laughing uncontrollably.

Opportunity screamed in Dangerfield's mind, a million neurons firing. Twisting its handle, he kicked the door open, throwing himself into the room. Before either guard could comprehend the violent intrusion, Dangerfield grabbed the comedian's rubbery head and slammed it against his colleague's. Their skulls cracked together like a pair of dried coconuts. Laughing boy slumped instantly, blood haemorrhaging from both ears. The comedian let out an endless yell. The thud of the pistol butt to the nape of his neck quelled his pain.

The man wearing headphones hadn't stirred. Inside his cubicle, still with his back to Dangerfield, he was engrossed in a computer screen. Reaching down, Dangerfield pulled the torn mask from the guard's dead head. It came off easily, stretched beyond use. Tossing it to the floor, he stepped over the bodies, jumped the desk and ducked below the level of the windows. Slowly raising his head, he peered out. A black Mercedes was glinting under the mid-morning sun. Must be Chong's. Had to be. Its driver leant against it, a Kalashnikov slung across his back. Two other guards flanked the police station door. Standing to attention, these living statues stared directly ahead, their rifles clasped across their chests. Dangerfield scanned the street. Pedestrians, heads down, walked briskly by, as bicycles and three-wheeled tuk-tuks, kicking up dust, criss-crossed each other.

Over the droning buzz of the tuk-tuks, Dangerfield could hear something much louder flooding the airspace outside. It took a moment to sink in that the pervasive sound filling his ears was one of the Government's daily propaganda broadcasts, pumping out from a network of suspended aerial loudspeakers. Yeah, worship your leader and forget you're fucking starving! He glanced again at the armed men outside, his finger tensing instinctively on the trigger of the pistol with its one remaining bullet.

"Fuck it!"

He ducked below the window, slumping to the floor, his back to the wall. Scanning the office, Dangerfield noticed that from this angle he had a better view of the man inside the glass cubicle, who was staring at the large text on his computer screen whilst talking into a microphone. As he watched the man, Dangerfield caught his breath. The man's lips were moving in sync with the raucous screeching voice that filled the streets, rang inside buildings and permeated the head of every citizen.

Chapter Thirty Nine

Dangerfield pounced the moment the man paused from reciting Government propaganda. He was scrolling to the next page of text when Dangerfield burst into the cubicle and slammed his head against its thick glass wall. Blood immediately seeped from the newsreader's ears, his body gently twitching on the cubicle floor.

Fuck... Fuck... Fuck! Dangerfield flicked the microphone's switch off. Through the office windows he could see that the guards outside hadn't flinched, and beyond them, the flow of pedestrians appeared unfazed by the lengthening silence from the public address system.

He threw himself into the broadcaster's chair, a screen full of Korean text staring at him. Heart pounding, his hand reached to the microphone again.

"What… the… fuck am I doing?" His finger hovered over the switch. With his brain on overdrive, thoughts and images flew through his mind. H.G.Wells' 'War of the Worlds' flashed up. The 1938 radio broadcast caused mass hysteria across America. Over a million Yanks had panicked, believing Martians were really attacking Earth.

What if...

Suddenly the alien text on the screen in front of him stuck its tongue out at him, jarring him back to reality. He only knew how to say 'fuck you' and 'fuck off' in Korean. However appropriate a parting shot, it wouldn't get him past armed guards, a city full of government slaves, and the one hundred miles back to the Chinese border.

"FUCKING HELL!" Dangerfield thumped the desk. He felt the blinding light of revelation flooding his mind. He was the atheist at his point of conversion, the delusional misanthrope at the moment of rapture, when the theory of life, the universe and everything reveals itself.

Dangerfield knew exactly what he was going to do. A growing smile turned into a maniacal laugh. He *was* going to communicate with thousands of Koreans. In Korean! And in Serbian! And Polish! He could communicate in every language known to man. Even Welsh. Who knows, possibly even Venusian.

He got off the chair, slipped to the front door of the office, fastened the bolts and returned to the cubicle. Crouched on the floor with his knees under his chin, he was out of sight from any police or soldiers who chose to look in. As Dangerfield reached up, he could feel the warmth of the dead body pressed against his lower back. His focus slipped for a moment. Doubts started to sneak in. *They're only theories. It's all fucking theory! Liz was right... I'm such a cunt.* He let out a massive sigh. *At least I got James out.* He stared at his bare feet. *Fuck this!* Beads of sweat started running down his face.

"Now, you cunt! Do it! Now!"

Hand shaking, he switched the microphone on.

Chapter Forty

As Liz idly stirred the froth on her cappuccino she weighed up her idea of calling Rufus Pole at the BBC. They'd collaborated before on a military budget scam. She couldn't understand her reluctance to call, as Rufus had admitted he owed the success of the case and his heightened celebrity to Liz's obsessive research. And it wasn't exactly a favour she wanted so much as advice. She'd hit a brick wall as far as the Roxburgh Institute went. And if the mountain wouldn't come to Mohammed…

Glancing around the café, at her fellow caffeine addicts, Liz picked her phone off the table. As she scrolled down her contacts to 'R', the screen switched to incoming. Number withheld.

This phone call didn't come out of the blue. It came out of every goddamn colour of the rainbow.

"Liz?"

Her phone was playing an evil joke. Had to be.

The joker tried again.

"Liz?"

How simple can a question be? She couldn't even confirm her own name.

"Hello? Liz?" There was an urgency in the voice now.

Liz's heart rate surged, her breathing deepening instantly, her brain a thick soup of confusion.

"James?"

"Yes. Listen. I need—"

"JAMES!"

Liz's shriek was so loud that every head in the coffee shop jerked in her direction. So loud that one old man yanked his hearing aid out. So loud that the newbie barista filled a cup, and then its saucer. And so joyfully loud that an office temp hit 'send' on an inappropriate message to her boss.

As the smiles and tuts filled the café in equal measure, Liz pressed her phone hard to her ear.

"I need—"

"Where are you ?" Liz demanded.

"Somewhere in the South China Sea. Listen—"

"But… but…" Three years hard labour at Cambridge and here she was, struggling to form sentences.

"I need you to go and see the Assistant Director General at MI6. Immediately. I mean right this minute. Her name's Sarah Watling."

"But where are you?" Liz's eyes flashed around the café, taking in nothing.

"I'm with the US Navy—"

Liz heard another man's voice in the background.

"OK. I'm not allowed to say any more on my location, but I'm safe and at sea."

"When are you coming back?"

Liz's question was ignored.

"Tell Watling everything's gone mental. Instead of wipeout, the North Koreans capability has been enhanced. Their missiles now have both range and guidance."

"Is that where you've been? North Korea?"

Again, James ignored her question. "They've the potential to reach the whole planet. Are you getting this? Charlie told me you were in the loop."

"How?"

"How what?"

"How did you speak to him? If you've been in North Korea and he's not even answering his phone. I've been trying it for days."

Liz noticed the delay in her brother's reply.

Eventually he spoke, his voice hesitant. "He visited me."

"In North Korea?"

"I've got to go. Remember. Sarah Watling. Urgent."

"James?" Liz looked at her phone screen. Gone.

She didn't know whether to laugh or cry. Glancing around the café she noticed a couple of still-curious customers avert their eyes. For a moment she questioned whether she'd imagined the phone call. She couldn't help checking her call record. There it was. Incoming. One minute twelve seconds. She shook her head. *In the loop, my arse!*

Liz texted Amy two words, 'HE'S SAFE!' before grabbing her iPad from her satchel. Tapping on the Reuters' icon she scanned through the headlines. She struggled to find any genuine news. As she scrolled to the bottom of the page, the words '*BREAKING NEWS*' flashed across the screen; '*Release of spoof movie sequel, 'Kim Jong's ill' enrages North Korean Leader'*.

Liz shoved her iPad back in her bag. *Why the hell would anyone do something so provocative?* As she made for the door, her smile returned instantly. *Great timing! He's outta there! Now, what was her name? Watling... Sarah Watling.*

The headquarters of MI5 was no stranger to Liz. She knew the building well. She'd often jostled with the paps outside and signed entry clearance a number of times. But MI6? That would be a first.

Eight years in the capital and the London Underground map was virtually engraved on her memory. As Liz stepped out of the cafe, her head was so full she didn't realise she was thinking aloud. "Okay. King’s Cross to Victoria. Victoria to Pimlico. Five minute walk. Go!”

Heading down York Way at almost a jog, Liz constantly scanned the road for taxicabs. There seemed to be hundreds. All taken. As she approached the huge pedestrianised space outside King's Cross Station, any thoughts of ringing Rufus Pole had evaporated. Her mind was racing. And in an entirely different direction. Charlie Bloody Dangerfield. This Sarah woman must be his boss. Surely she's in contact with him. If he’d visited her brother in North Korea, where the hell was Charlie now? Why wasn’t he answering his phone?

The queue at the taxi rank was ridiculous and her experiences with Uber so mixed that it would have to be the Tube. Traversing King’s Cross's vast open frontage, Liz slipped between clusters of tourists and passed benches of fat beggars and rake-thin druggies. Questions and thoughts constantly ran through her head. What if this Watling woman's out? What if the tube’s trains are screwed? What if I can’t get a phone signal underground?

Liz found the quietest spot immediately beside the Tube

Station's entrance, retrieved her phone and Googled MI6. Clicking on 'contact us' she leant against the wall and waited.

"MI6. How can I help?

Liz couldn't help noting that even the switchboard operator sounded as though she'd attended Cheltenham Ladies' College.

"Hello. Can I speak to Sarah Watling, please?"

"May I ask who's calling and what it's concerning?"

"Yes. It's Liz Green from The Guardian News." *Surely that's enough?*

There was a moment's pause before, "Ah, I see. MI6 does not have a Press Office. All media enquiries should be made through the FCO Press Office. Would you like their contact details?"

"The Foreign Office? No, I have their number, thanks. It's specifically Miss Watling that I need to speak to. Thank you." Liz sensed that persistence was going to be the order of the day. *Bring it on.*

"May I ask what it's regarding, please?"

The woman's 'Received Pronunciation' seemed exaggerated. And irritating. So Liz threw it back at her. "Well, no. I'm afraid one cannot. It's entirely confidential… and altogether urgent."

Another pause.

"I'm sorry, but I do need to know what it concerns. There are many different departments within MI6."

"Listen. This is Elizabeth Green from The Guardian News Corporation. This is a Category Seven, Grade One call for your Assistant Director General, Sarah Watling. I suggest you put me through immediately. If for some good reason Miss Watling is not available, then standard protocol requires you to transfer me to an appropriate colleague. And if the latter is the case then I suggest you try Mr Charles Dangerfield."

Liz stared up at the fat white clouds floating high over London. She pictured Amy reading the text she'd sent her. Amy knew her so well. So often her friend had introduced her at parties as 'Bullshitter Extraordinaire'. Well, it seemed to be working today, because the switchboard girl seemed lost for words. Liz took another deep breath and continued.

"I presume you've covered Category Seven calls in your training? In case you haven't, Category Seven stands for National Security Breach!"

"One moment."

Twelve moments of recorded orchestral music grated at Liz's will to live, before a new voice came on the line. But even 'Die Another Day' droning in E Flat Major couldn't dampen her spirits today. James was safe!

Chapter Forty One

The Public Address system in Kusong City had been silent for two very long minutes. Residents were finding it disturbing. Why had the Government's daily broadcast stopped mid-flow? In the streets, strangers exchanged nervous glances. In the factories, workers focused harder, their heads lower. Everyone knew the routine. It was ground into them. These speeches, commanding loyalty and respect to the Nation's leader, were always twenty minutes long. Always. They might not consciously hear every word, but subconsciously their brains logged the rhythm and progress of the effervescent reader. He can't have completed even half of it. Ten minutes max. This was the best gauged twenty minute period in the whole day. It was when mothers grabbed the opportunity to cook their scant supply of vegetables. Because, when the Government was using the Public Address system, it was the one time they could guarantee there'd be no power cut.

The loud speakers had been dead for three minutes now. The armed statues flanking the police station door came alive, shifting their weight. They looked nervously at each other. Something was wrong. The whole city felt it. The silence was screaming at them.

Sitting on the floor of the broadcaster's cubicle, Dangerfield crossed his legs and gripped the microphone. His mind had been racing. He'd covered the theory in seconds. And now he had a plan. One fucking crazy plan. The control of people had always fascinated him. In history lessons as a teenager, he'd been mystified how Hitler mesmerised a nation into blindly following his evil beliefs. He'd read with disbelief about the rise of cults across America, the followers of Jim Jones in Guyana, the Moonies from South Korea. How come people were so gullible? So pliable? After school, he would sit in Malvern Library and study it. Social Theory, Systems Theory, Durkheim, Kelsen, the Brown Experiment. He'd been to enough football matches to see herd psychology at its best. One gets up, the whole stadium gets up. At the Royal Albert Hall, if one starts clapping, the whole audience feels compelled to follow. Time to test the theory.

Dangerfield closed his eyes. *Let's get this fucking party started.* He let his thoughts drift to some of the darkest places he could think of. He thought about his close colleague Hassan, who'd been undercover in Iraq. Caught, held and tortured. They'd done a Duke of Gloucester on him, 'Out vile jelly!' He'd never see his children's faces again. Ever. He'd visited him on his return to London. The poor bloke was inconsolable. As he dwelled on Hassan's permanent blindness, Dangerfield could feel a pressure building behind his eyes. *Getting there…*

He thought back to the school trip to Auschwitz. The museum had been a window on hell itself. From the off, the whole class had been emotional, but when they got to Block 4… fucking hell… the curators had pulled all the stops out there. The mountains of children's shoes, the tangled ocean of human hair, the piles of empty cans of Cyclone B, each a wrecking ball to every visitor's heart strings. Coltrane, the school rugby captain had been the first to blub. This had triggered the whole class. Within seconds there wasn't a dry eye in the place, everyone overwhelmed by what they saw. Briefly Dangerfield had held it together, fascinated by the sudden group meltdown, but when he'd seen the enormous heap of artificial limbs, it was his turn to implode. Hadn't these people suffered enough? Blighted through their lives with parts of their bodies missing, and then herded like cattle into a gas chamber. Dangerfield pulled the microphone to his mouth. As he tried to imagine how utterly helpless they must have felt, his eyes began welling up. As the first tear broke rank, and raced to his chin, he let the wave of sadness wash over him. The sobs that followed were loud and heart-wrenching. *They should give me a fucking Oscar for this.*

Throughout the city the loudspeaker system suddenly burst back into life. And then someone pressed 'pause' on the whole street-scene. All pedestrians stopped abruptly in their tracks. No one was moving except for the sea of turning heads. Mouths gaped everywhere. Tuk-tuks screeched to a halt as drivers realised something momentous was happening. Engines stilled, they too heard the Government's sobs of despair, resounding through the airwaves, ringing down every street, sending them also into shock. If their exalted leaders couldn't hold it together, then what hope remained for them in their own lives? This was unprecedented. This was uncharted territory. This was God falling to Earth with a great wet slap, bursting into tears, and crying out, "I can't do this anymore." To the North

Koreans it might as well have been a Martian invasion, given the disbelief and fear growing in their minds. They'd never had to think for themselves before. The Government told them what to think, what to do. Obey your wonderful leader and all will be well. Don't evaluate. Don't question. All answers were given on a plate. And then force-fed.

The sobbing was getting louder, echoing through the streets. People looked to the loud-speakers and then back to each other. A few started to cry. Chong's driver began visibly shaking. One of the police guards stepped towards him and then stepped straight back.

As mass confusion erupted outside, hidden on the floor of a sound-proof cubicle, Dangerfield was a million miles from the madding crowd. He was in his own little world, in a different time and place. And focused. He knew these people were at permanent tipping point, teetering at the cliff edge. They just needed one little push. However threadbare, however moth-eaten, however blood-stained their carpet, he was going to yank it from under their feet, and they were going to fall. If they thought their leaders had thrown the towel in, then there was nothing to hold onto. No plan B. Just an overwhelming sense of loss, of their one and only shitty little option on existence.

Keep going... keep it fucking going... Dangerfield focused on his elderly neighbour, Mrs Hodgkins, who used to cook him tea when he was a teenager. When he left for college, he knew her visitors would be few and far between. In his first term at Cambridge, she'd made headlines in the Malvern Gazette. He pictured her excitedly hobbling to answer the front door on her eightieth birthday. She hadn't spoken to anyone for over a week. Her daughter and son-in-law were already an hour late for their annual visit, but she was just happy they'd made it. The expressions on the police women's faces carried the news. Both passengers were write-offs. Dangerfield pictured the poor woman stagger, her closed eyes seeing only loneliness in front of her. Why did shit happen to nice people? With a vice-like grip on the microphone, Dangerfield's shoulders shook with each sob, his heart bleeding for the poor woman. He'd studied the mood experiments of Dr Mengele and Facebook's experiments on emotional contagion. *Well, catch this!* He gasped loudly, catching his breath between sobs.

As the loud speakers continued generating despair in the streets, Dangerfield couldn't see the tears streaming down Chong's driver's face. Neither could he see the old man who'd been pushing a barrow of cabbages, drop to his knees, his face impersonating Edvard Munch's 'The Scream'. What Dangerfield *could* see was Liz crying. It was the final day of their first term at college. When all the other students were excited about heading home for the Christmas break after their longest ever period away from their parents, the two of them had had a heart to heart. For twelve years she'd suppressed all memories of her parents' tragic deaths, but for some reason, on that dark winter's evening, the flashbacks began. She'd bawled like a baby and he'd held her in his arms until exhaustion had eased her to sleep. He remembered wanting to hold her forever. Dangerfield imagined the distraught, tear-stained face of a nine year old Liz shaking her dead mother's body as it sat slumped in the front seat of a car. His sobs turned to a tragic wailing that reverberated in the streets. If only he could initiate emotional contagion and then crank it up to mass hysteria. He knew he had to dig deep if he were to have any chance of creating total pandemonium outside the police station. There was only one place to go in his head if he was to convince these institutionalised denizens of a Brave New Wasteland that the dim flicker of light at the end of their shit-lined tunnel had just gone out. And it was a place that he'd never had the courage to go to before.

Chapter Forty Two

Sitting cross-legged on the floor, Dangerfield suddenly realised he was mirroring the schoolboy he was about to become. *Fuck it! Let's get this over with.* He pictured a lone birthday card on a mantelpiece. It was from his dad who'd been stationed overseas for months. *Happy Eleventh, Charlie!* it read. *Look after your Mother.* Except that he hadn't seen her for three days. That wasn't so unusual. But this time she wouldn't be coming back. The two women from Social Services had wanted him to go with them, and at first he'd lied, telling them she was asleep upstairs. When they gently explained that she had died, he'd sworn and shouted at them to leave. He was in the school playground when he learnt the truth. Gossiping parents must have been overheard, because a classmate taunted him, "Your mum killed herself." Dangerfield yelled at him, "No she didn't. She didn't!" He'd chased the boy. "Don't… you… ever…" A single punch and the little shit was out for the count, sprawled on the grass. The questions in his head wouldn't leave him alone. What had he done to upset her so much? Didn't she love him? Had she hated him? Questions, questions, questions. They wouldn't go away. To cope, he'd boxed everything up and hidden it behind the Great Wall of China. Out of sight, out of mind. He'd had no Mother. She'd never existed. Gone.

Dangerfield stared at the microphone, now clasped

more loosely in his hand. He realised that for the last eighteen years he'd been the little boy with his finger in the dam. And now was the time to pull it out. If her dead body was in front of him now, he'd punch it back to life and demand to know what he'd done wrong, She'd left him with a dark curse. The curse of feeling unloved. Unlovable. He'd never know the truth. She'd left him dangling… still dangling. *Why did you leave me?* Questions, questions, never to be answered. As loneliness slipped its cold arms around him, the dam burst. Shaking uncontrollably, Dangerfield's sobs entered the microphone, became magnified and echoed through the streets of Kusong. His sobbing rose and fell and rose again, each wave of guttural cries more terrible, sorrowful and uncontrollable than the last.

As the loudspeakers screeched God's terrifying lament across the city, announcing the end of the world, primal instinct drew people into clusters seeking some kind of comfort. Among these downtrodden crowds, tears fell like rain, but it was generations too late for these dried twigs. Snap! An old lady started screaming, pointing to the sky above the police station. People nearby followed her lead, tearing at their hair and pointing at the same nothing. One of the armed guards, terror strapped to his face, hair-triggered bullets in their direction. He could have been a doctor. His metal anti-stress tablets worked wonders. Sufferers lay on the ground, motionless, every muscle relaxing. Snap! A tuk-tuk driver started his engine and drove straight into a group of pedestrians transfixed in the middle of the road. Although thrown from the vehicle, his right hand remained super-glued to the accelerator handle. His weight yanked it onto two wheels and as the tuk-tuk squealed around and around, spewing black fumes, the man's trailing legs engraved a circular rut in the dusty road. Snap! The second guard, smiling insanely, took three steps towards his partner, shot him in the face and then charged at the Police Station door. His vertical face-plant shook the bolts inside. The loud bang burst through Dangerfield's thick wall of concentration.

MOVE! Dangerfield flicked the microphone off and heaved himself off the floor. He could feel his eyes burning. Kicking the cubicle door off its hinges, he leapt to the front door. Through the Police Station windows he could see carnage and confusion everywhere. Bodies lying on the ground. People hugging each other. People crouching, heads in hands. A few were braying like animals. He could also make out a madly spinning tuk-tuk, weirdly, dragging a man beside it. And there, only ten metres away, was Colonel Chong's black Mercedes, its driver frantically dry-humping a headlight.

Ripping the bolts, Dangerfield yanked the door open.

Directly in front of him stood a man in uniform. And despite blood streaming from his forehead and nose, he was grinning and pointing a gun in Dangerfield's face. Dangerfield returned the guards stare, but in his peripheral vision noticed tuk-tuk man finally relinquish his grasp and slump into his self-ploughed rut. The guard, wavering on his feet, grasped his gun more tightly.

Forcing himself to maintain direct eye contact, over the guard's right shoulder, Dangerfield could just make out that the tuk-tuk was back on three wheels with its accelerator clearly jammed on. Screaming and jolting, it flew the few metres across the police station yard until its front wheel slammed against a low wall. Its back end took off, rotating around its front wheel and suddenly the vehicle was airborne. The guard's finger tensed on the trigger as his whole body was thrown into shadow. Dangerfield smiled at the man. A warm, gentle smile, that told him there was nothing to worry about. Told him that he was only imagining the demonic whirring sound closing in on him. Told him that a quarter ton of juddering metal was not about to crush his skull.

As the stretched elastic band of time retracted at Mach10, Dangerfield threw himself to the floor. Splitting the wooden doorframe and the guard's bones in one foul swoop, the flying tuk-tuk smashed itself to pieces.

Chapter Forty Three

Dangerfield leapt over the remains of the smoking tuk-tuk and raced to Chong's Mercedes. The driver had finished humping it and was slumped over the front wing.

Ripping him from the headlight, Dangerfield punched him to the ground and jumped into the driver's seat. As he pressed the start button he growled at him, "Say goodbye to your girlfriend," and accelerated down the street, swerving between small groups of pedestrians huddling together for comfort. The sky was overcast, the muted sun barely locatable. Estimating its position, Dangerfield took every road that led roughly west, weaving his way out of the city.

The reach of the tannoy system was impressive, because only when Dangerfield drove through the very outskirts of Kusong did residents appear undisturbed. Here huge concrete accommodation blocks gave way to shabby single storey homes and any isolated pedestrians he now passed were simply deferential in response to a fancy black car making a rare appearance in these poorest parts of the neighbourhood.

Scrabbling in the glove compartment, Dangerfield's fingers closed around an old-style phone. He flicked it open. The seventy percent battery and a time of three pm were obvious, but everything else on the screen was gobbledegook. Feeling sure all overseas calls would be routinely blocked, he still couldn't resist ringing the switchboard at GCHQ. *Incoming from North Korea. That'll wake someone up.* The phone buzzed continuously in his ear. Tossing it onto the back seat, he continued delving in the glove compartment. Dangerfield tore the bag of Korean potato chips open, tipping half its contents into his mouth. They came out at twice the speed they went in.

"Fuck! That's got to be dog flavour."

A final delve produced Chinese chocolate and as Dangerfield devoured it, he felt as though he was driving the only vehicle in the universe, overtaking few bicycles and only the occasional vegetable-laden tuk-tuk buzzing along.

The landscape became wholly rural with vast fields and woods to either side of the road. And pot holes were appearing constantly. As the adrenalin subsided, Dangerfield's head began to hurt. He could feel a pronounced bump at the back of his head that throbbed madly. This wasn't helped by the start of flashbacks, the most disturbing being the sensation of drone fuel splashing up his thighs.

The dashboard clock read fifteen-forty and darkness had begun lowering its black cloak. Concussion, exhaustion and hunger conspired to make Dangerfield's mind play tricks on him. Occasionally he'd pass a lone pedestrian, often with a small sack of farm produce slewn over their shoulders. Several times he thought they were hitchhikers. Worse, he'd imagined one of them was James, and found himself slowing down before a worried face had turned and then bowed towards him.

Startled by the Mercedes' headlights flashing on as they responded automatically to the low level of ambient light, Dangerfield thumped the steering wheel.

"Wake up, you twat!"

His concentration was divided between dodging the deepest potholes and trying to remember the Google map of this part of North Korea. He hadn't seen a single road sign but then remembered that even if there were any, he wouldn't be able to read them. *What the fuck. There are hardly any roads anyway.*

More than once Dangerfield was jarred awake by the car's suspension system thumping the heavy vehicle back out of potholes he'd failed to notice.

And darkness was getting closer. The monotony of the same road, with no streetlights and no road markings, was taking its toll. The twenty metre triangle of light that the headlights threw forward provided little visual stimulation and after two hours sitting in solitary behind the steering wheel, to Dangerfield the sound of the Mercedes' engine had become white noise.

Erupting from nowhere, a horrendous grinding noise caused Dangerfield to swerve the car. The sound split the air and seemed to be coming from behind him. What disturbed him more were the wing mirrors and rear view mirror all remaining entirely black. His breathing and heart rate skyrocketed as Dangerfield waited forever for his electric window to open far enough to stick his head out. Before he was able to, the entire car began vibrating, shuddering to the beat of an intense external force. And suddenly, the road ahead, and to the sides and behind, were bathed in light. For a split second Dangerfield imagined some divine intervention banishing all darkness, but as he found himself driving within a moving pyramid of light, that precisely tracked his progress, he knew exactly what was happening. Before his options even had a chance to fly through his mind, a different sound began to compete for his attention.

And the source of this sound was sitting on the back seat of the car.

It was flashing at him, its buzz insistent.

Chapter Forty Four

The helicopter veered to Dangerfield's left, dropping almost level with the Merc. Hurtling six feet above the deforested strip bordering the road, the copter's internal lights revealed a pilot and two uniformed passengers.

Dangerfield pressed his foot to the floor, the headlights from both vehicles illuminating any bends in their shared path. At around 80mph, he knew he had the Merc way beyond its comfort zone, the car crumping heavily at every pothole. As Dangerfield's focus flicked between road and helicopter, his 'Identification Friend or Foe' training at Sandhurst kicked in. It was only a month since his IFF refresher session and the faint silhouette of the helicopter against the dark forest screamed the latest Russian Black Shark model.

How the fuck did North Korea get hold of one of these babies?

The buzz from the phone on the backseat barely impacted on Dangerfield as he strained to keep the Merc on the narrow track. Its wheels clipped the road's crumbling edge each time his attention lingered a second too long on the helicopter. The consequent electricity flashing through his frontal lobes reignited the throbbing at the back of his head.

Ice patches were beginning to appear, and Dangerfield felt the car slide left or right as he hit the larger ones.

Slowing to around 70mph, the helicopter eased too, giving Dangerfield a better chance to observe it.

Shit! That's a Shark Ka-70 for sure. And modified by the looks of it.

A thin scattering of snow began to coat the road, enabling the Merc's headlights to penetrate further into the darkness. Initially it was this white strip contrasting with the darker verge that determined which way the road led. But as the snow thickened, and the rough verge increasingly matched the whiteness of the road, Dangerfield could rely only on smoothness of surface to guide him. A long straight section of road appeared, the dark line of trees to his right disappearing far into the distance. This gave Dangerfield his best opportunity yet to view the copter. In stark contrast to the black background, the Ka-70's internal lights now revealed its contents clearly.

"What the fuck?"

Dangerfield's brain took a second take as the homemade haircut and fat face of Kim Jong himself stared directly at him. He was holding a phone to his ear, his other hand imitating a knife cutting his throat.

"Love you too!" yelled Dangerfield.

Kim Jong waved the phone at him, pointing at it with his other hand. As the pilot tilted the Ka-70 thirty degrees to avoid a rogue tree, Dangerfield saw Kim Jong lurch forwards, his face squashed even fatter as it high-fived the cabin window. Another figure in the cabin leapt up to help peel him off and steady him. Lip-reading was unnecessary. Dangerfield could tell the animated lump was yelling at the pilot sitting in the Ka-70's nose.

With snow falling more heavily, Dangerfield turned the windscreen wipers on, the insistent buzz of Colonel Chong's phone sitting on the back seat, clashing with their regular slap. And then realization hit home. The Merc swerved left and right as Dangerfield contorted himself to reach his hand to the rear seats. The phone seemed louder, desperate to be answered.

Glancing back at the copter, Dangerfield could see Kim Jong back up against the cabin window, supporting himself with one hand, his other pressed to his ear.

Dangerfield flicked the Colonel's phone open and took the call.

"American bastard. Stop car!"

Looking across at the copter, Dangerfield yelled with an American accent, "Yeee…Haaa! Go screw yourself, cowboy!" *Kimbo studied in Switzerland. The twat must have basic English?*

The man's actions confirmed it. Shoving the phone at the soldier beside him, Kim Jong slumped to the floor and reached for the Ka-70's machine gun brace. Instead of gunfire, Dangerfield heard only screeching, as the man clearly failed to operate the sophisticated weaponry. As the soldier helped him back to his feet, Kim Jong snatched the phone back.

"You made me Pokemon monster! And more points than Hitler Pokemon! Shi-bal-nom-a!"

Dangerfield recognised the Korean phrase as one of the handful he'd learnt. *This guy's definitely pissed.*

Dangerfield heard a sudden rise in the copter's engine

note as it accelerated ahead. He had predicted this move and anticipated its turn. And as the copter now headed directly for him, its front spotlight became trained on his windscreen.

Wanna play chicken, huh? Dangerfield didn't need to dwell on the odds. There was only one gamble here. A no-brainer.

He pulled the car's sun visor down, sat tall in the seat and maintained his speed.

The copter skimmed the Merc's roof, its engine noise so intense, that Dangerfield felt the whole car vibrating as he yelled, "Fuck you!" at the top of his voice.

Veering again, the copter came around to fly parallel once more. *Yeah, he's pissed alright.*

Despite his focus continually switching between copter and road, Dangerfield was blind to the soldier beginning to crouch behind his leader and reach for the Shark's machine gun. Blind, because the internal lights in the helicopter's cabin suddenly revealed the most disturbing scene Dangerfield had ever witnessed. Hallucinatory drugs couldn't have bettered it. This heinous vision was captured in a moment, to become a permanent scar in Dangerfield's memory. Turning away from Dangerfield, Kim Jong bent over. In an instant the khaki trousers were down and bloated bare buttocks burnt themselves onto Dangerfield's retinas.

"Kimbo's mooned me! He's fucking mooned me!"

The visual attack caught Dangerfield right behind the eyes, a knock-out punch to his neo-cortex.

No-one will believe me! I don't believe me! How the hell do I unsee that?

Distracted by computational overload, Dangerfield felt the car shuddering as it strayed off the edge of the snow-hidden track. Dropping the phone, he snatched at the wheel with both hands and momentarily righted the car's path, but two tons of metal in motion weren't about to break the laws of physics. The disparate momentum of the Merc's front and rear ends, with minimal resistance from an icy road put it instantly into spin. As it slewed around, the four wheels threw up a circular curtain of snow and Dangerfield focused hard to see beyond it. He felt time slow down as the headlights provided a 360° panoramic scan of the road to nowhere.

Except that 'nowhere' suddenly began to look like an abandoned Welsh mining village, ripped up and thrown next to the North Korean-Chinese border.

"What the fuck?"

The car's headlights first blazed across what Dangerfield assumed was industrial drilling equipment, a black sixty-foot tall steel tripod poised like an alien from the film, 'War of the Worlds'. And continuing to spin, the headlights lit up two parked trucks, snow-chains glinting, their flat-beds loaded with huge carved ice blocks.

Dangerfield gripped the steering wheel, both feet off the pedals and focused on the position of the Merc as it continued rotating within its second spin, steeling himself to regain control at precisely the right moment. But before its second rotation was complete, the wave of bullets began. The first rounds pinged off the bodywork as Dangerfield threw himself sideways. With visibility gone he had to rely on blind guesswork as to the optimal moment to recover the spin. He yelled against the onslaught of the machine gun fire, jamming his foot back on the accelerator and yanking the wheel into the skid. He felt the rear-end jerk as the Merc powered out, regaining its footing.

About to snatch a look over the dashboard to check his exact path, Dangerfield's ears were instantly filled with a second round of gunfire and the sound of shattering windows. Shards of glass ripped through his stolen uniform, lacerating his skin. Instant pain, as if he'd plunged his shoulder into a wasp's nest, caused him to recoil, rotating his torso across the passenger seat. And looking out where the window used to be, he saw the copter veer suddenly upwards, twisting to avoid the huge alien tripod, now more clearly a crane.

Yelling through the pain, Dangerfield grabbed his chance, pushed himself vertical and pressed his foot to the floor. Deep ruts in the snow led from where the trucks were parked, and Dangerfield aimed for them, rubber once more gripping bare road. Sticking to the tracks, he accelerated over a short ridge and into the head of a valley. What sprang into view was so unexpected, so mental, his first thought was that the gunfire had actually killed him, and he'd been reincarnated as Alice in Winter Wonderland.

"What the fucking fuck?"

Chapter Forty Five

Dangerfield could swear he'd been catapulted onto the set of the animated film, 'Frozen'.

Kimbo moons me, and now this?

The forest ended abruptly and several acres of snow-covered fields stretched down towards a dark river. The Yalu river.

What freaked him was that beneath the black sky, these fields housed a floodlit miniature city. Made entirely of ice. Part Disneyland. Part Aleppo.

Ice castles were roofless. Translucent towers lay in pieces. And dotted amongst them, workers, fully in the throes of demolition. Dozens of men in thick, black puffer jackets were attacking ice columns with chain saws and separating huge ice building blocks from each other.

The wheels of the Merc kept clipping the steep kerbs of hardened snow, as Dangerfield struggled to take everything in. To his left he could see Kim Jong's helicopter circling wide to avoid the nearest of several overhead lighting gantries that, with the nascent moon, lit the eeriest of scenes.

This city's residents were snow giants. Aerial and ground floodlights illuminated the torso of a fifty foot Chinese warrior. It lay flat on its back, beside the remnants of a copycat of a building that Dangerfield recognised instantly. The Space Tower. Shanghai's tallest building. At least it had been momentarily, until he'd recently blown its top off. The irony of the spent, yet still frozen-hard phallus of a building wasn't wasted on Dangerfield, as Julie Hong's face flashed across his mind. She'd been the most effective agent he'd ever recruited. He knew the image of her pale innocent face would probably haunt him forever.

Dangerfield felt as though his brain was about to burst as he tried to process everything that had sprung into view. A crane was lifting a huge, bald and smiling head, from the icy shoulders of a man sitting on the floor. His legs were crossed beneath a massively distended belly. *Fuck, even Buddha's falling apart.*

Sticking to the deep tracks that led directly into this crumbling fairy-tale, Dangerfield found it impossible to keep his eye on the circling copter, his attention now stolen by the only building that appeared to be complete. Its huge clock faces were transparent and glass-like, compared to the cloudy translucence of its tower. Normally he could see it from his office window in London, proud and erect. Big Ben. And then it dawned on him. Big Ben was the giveaway. This had to be some kind of training or test facility for the Harbin Ice Festival in China, the most mind-blowing winter show on earth. Made sense, with labour even cheaper here than in China and another source of income for Kimbo.

His old mate with the CIA, Finkel, had invited him to Harbin to see the real thing, except his boss, Sarah Watling had had other plans for him. Dangerfield remembered the BBC reporting on it. Big Ben. Made of solid ice. A Chinese tribute to the growing international trade between themselves and post-Brexit Britain.

He tried to absorb the whole frantic half-kilometer that remained between him and China. The copter appeared to have halted, hovering beyond the nearest lighting gantry. *Is it waiting for me?*

Dangerfield knew the Shark Ka-70 was equipped to carry Hellfire missiles. *But surely within his own country Kimbo would have no such need?*

These bad boys were heat-seekers, and in this frozen wasteland, the Merc's hot engine was a juicy rabbit waving at a starving eagle. A roaring brazier to a freezing tramp.

Dangerfield's thoughts leapt from option to option. *And what the fuck does Kimbo want with me anyway? We've just handed him everything on a nuclear fucking plate!*

Fifty miles-per-hour was about the max the Merc could manage. The lorries had dug such deep furrows with their dead-weight ice loads that the frozen bank of dirty snow between the ruts scraped at the Merc's undercarriage. Every few seconds, the car was raised so high that the left or right wheels lost all traction. The car slewed right and left, striking the outer kerbs of rock-hard snow, shaking Dangerfield violently. As he fought to keep control, he noticed a long ramp approaching. It looked like a remnant of a demolished Forbidden Palace, its icy slope rising up and disappearing into the night sky. Suspended above the ramp, hung a bright searchlight. *Why the fuck is it quivering?* Dangerfield glanced around him. *And where the fuck's that helicopter?* The telltale red light of a laser suddenly hitting the Merc's windscreen answered his question. He watched the laser's red spot move and then diffuse as it crossed the part-shattered screen. The copter's Hellfire missiles used a laser guidance system, and with their top speed of around 1000mph Dangerfield felt like a granny sitting in a wheelchair crossing the path of the 7:20 Express from Paddington.

Dangerfield hit the pedal to the floor. 60mph… 70mph… Then he hit the ramp. Yelling as the Merc surged upwards, he waited. And waited. Time stretched weirdly. The instant he saw the ignition flames of a missile burst from beneath the Shark he yanked the wheel left and immediately right, the Merc's tyres squealing millimetres from the edge of the ramp. He ducked across the passenger seat. For a nanosecond the driver's side door window became a glass mosaic. The pressure of the missile streaking down the side of the Merc then punched a hundred beads of glass into the car, showering Dangerfield's body.

Dangerfield was eight years old. He'd won the jackpot on a slot machine at Butlin's holiday resort. Glass pennies rattled and jingled around the front of the Merc as they bounced off the steering wheel, headrests and dashboard. And then he was deaf. The only thing he could hear was a continuous whistling coming from inside his own head. As he looked over the dashboard into the silent dark sky he saw the helicopter was gaining height, rising beyond a huge gantry that straddled the ramp. Dangerfield's foot was still jammed on the accelerator. If he pressed any harder he could picture his foot punching a hole through the footwell.

Fuck! If Bruce Willis can shoot a helicopter down with a car, so can… But he could feel the Merc slowing, losing momentum as gravity pulled on it, the wheels getting minimal traction on the hard icy ramp.

In the car's mirror, something bright grabbed his attention. The Hellfire missile had turned, hungry for heat, and was again screaming towards him. Dangerfield willed the car up the ramp but it felt so heavy, so slow. As he passed beneath the gantry, its floodlights blazed on the ramp's final few metres. Beyond the end of the ramp he could see the copter still rising. And Dangerfield realised he was going to pass below it, completely missing his target.

The rear view mirror had become a blinding light as it reflected the propulsion flames of the surging rocket in its final seconds.

Fuck this! Your whole life's supposed to flash before your eyes and all I got was some fat bastard's naked arse!

Dangerfield watched as the copter turned. Its interior lights showed Kim Jong's greasy grin stretching from ear to ear. The Merc had reached the end of the ramp and as it launched into the sky, Dangerfield closed his eyes.

The Hellfire missile exploding was the loudest thing Dangerfield had ever heard, even with his damaged eardrums. He felt the Merc surge even faster through the air as the intense pressure of the explosion violently shoved every single particle in its wake.

The rocket had buried itself in the steel girders of the gantry that now stood directly between itself and the Merc, the gantry's baking hot spotlights irresistible to the heat-seeking missile. The combined force of impact and explosion tore the whole steel structure out of the ground, its concrete boots remaining embedded in the earth. For a moment, the whole arena lit up like a spectacular firework display. But as the site's network of electrical cabling was stretched, snapped and short-circuited, darkness fell abruptly on the whole scene.

Dangerfield had forgotten to breathe. He could feel his heart banging in his chest as the Merc sailed through the air. In panic and with zero understanding of why, he snatched the engine and headlights off. And in that final instant, before the parallel beams of light were extinguished forever, before darkness swallowed everything, he caught a glimpse, a flash, of the river zooming towards him.

He finally gasped for air, as if instinctively preparing for submersion. And then he was falling. Falling towards the dashboard as the car's heavier front end tilted the vehicle forward. Falling through blackness and into blackness as he braced himself for the impending splash.

The anorexic sliver of crescent moon had slipped behind a cloud, as if to avert its eyes, when the heavy Merc hit the frozen river. The car bounced only once, the front tyres bursting on impact, the chassis twisting cruelly and noisily. The exhaust system and all remaining glass abandoned ship. And upside down the Merc skated across the frozen Yalu river. Pirouetting elegantly on its roof, it crossed the border into China, coming to rest beneath the low overhanging branches of a thick forest pine.

Chapter Forty Six

Sarah Watling sat beside Professor Hammond and watched his wrinkled hands skate over the keyboard. She'd counted the liver spots on the back of them and was upset to have discovered three on her own before he eventually spoke.

"So, here's Wednesday the twelfth… and you want to listen from 12.30pm through to…?"

"Oh, just leave it open, Stan. I'll whizz through it. Probably wasting my time."

"Well, I hope you find what you're looking for… sorry, listening for." He stood up, gripping the table with one hand. "Let me know when you're done and I'll pop straight back."

"Thanks, but this could take a while. Really, don't worry. I know how to close it down."

Hammond pushed his chair in and headed across the office.

"Of course you do. I'll… er… be in my lab if you need me."

Reaching inside her navy jacket Watling pulled out earphones. She inserted them and was about to plug the jack into the side of her laptop when she looked up. Hammond, pausing at the door, had turned back to face her and was smiling.

"You know, I did actually find a needle in a haystack once."

Watling returned a thin smile and waited for the door to close behind him. Pushing the jack home, she made herself more comfortable in the chair. She breathed in deeply, picked up her biro, and twiddling it in one hand, clicked the touch pad.

Chapter Forty Seven

Watling sat with her head in her hands. She couldn't believe what she had just listened to. Her pulse was up, her thoughts running riot, although a tiny part of her felt vindication. If Blake had known how much her wrist watch idea had cost the taxpayer, he'd have immediately instigated an internal inquiry. And if he'd known of its intended target, he'd have gone ballistic. Thank God there was no money trail as far as MI6's expenditure went. It had felt prankish to have her own Prime Minister wired without his knowledge. More than once she'd suffered moments of self-doubt about the project. What the hell was she thinking, hiding it under cover of a gift presentation to the whole Government Cabinet. How could they have been so gullible? Surely they were primed to avoid free meals? To refuse gifts? Especially in politics. But when her duty agent reported from the post-election celebrations of its blinding success, she'd punched the air like Emma Raducanu after winning the US Open, at having pulled off the ultimate covert op.

Of the four Prime Ministers her career had out-lived, Blake had always appeared the most credible and consistent. Sure, she'd seen him bend a few rules in his previous term, but never break any. Until today. Less than a minute ago. In this recording of his meeting at the Roxburgh Institute, she'd listened to him nuke the whole rule book.

Watling found herself wringing her hands as she tried to take in all that she'd just heard. Shaking her head, she kept thinking the same thing, over and over again. *Impossible... Impossible.*

At the recent election she'd been as shocked as everyone that Blake had won. Every pollster had claimed the opposition were dead certs. They were about to yell 'Checkmate!' when Blake kicked their queen in the nuts. Or rather the media had. Every news channel in the country reported on a nameless witness to the opposition party's leader having sex with a bishop on Clapham Common. This had consigned the man's political career to history and launched a triumphant Blake into his second term as P.M. Like half the population, she'd questioned the timing of this media revelation. It had seemed way too much of a coincidence. To Watling's mind this had completed a double whammy. The world was still stupefied from a similar electoral twist only four months earlier with the U.S. Presidential Election.

Watling had completed a PhD in Mass Communications thirty years ago at the London School of Economics. Even before the days of Twitter, Facebook, and WhatsApp and the endless stream of other vehicles of mass communication that surfaced, the media seemed too connected for her liking. The irony wasn't wasted on her when a new broadsheet launched, calling itself 'The Independent'. Her dissertation had confronted media ownership, with a compare and contrast of media tycoons. Her succinct conclusion had been that despite there being plenty of eggs in the world of communications their origins all lay in the same basket.

Watling stood up quickly, almost knocking her chair over. She walked to the window, and with her arms folded, looked across the MOD campus. Nothing caught her eye. Because nothing was moving. All activity here took place buried inside secure buildings, behind thick security doors. Fresh air. That's what she craved. Her thoughts were racing. She knew she had to act quickly. But how? And do what? Protocols? What sodding protocols? They'd all been shredded two minutes ago by what she'd heard Blake discussing in the U.S.

Who the hell could she talk to? What were her instincts telling her?

Zilch… Nada… Blanko!

She'd ensured Bulstrode knew nothing of Blake being wired. He'd have instantly put the kibosh on it. She didn't know whether it had been experience or intuition but something had compelled her to go it alone on instigating the 'Blake Watch Project'. Suddenly she felt claustrophobic. *Sod this!* She needed to get outside, let the cold air fill her lungs.

Watling returned to the desk and double-checked she'd closed the audio program. And then she was through the door, laptop under her arm. As she marched quickly down the corridor, it suddenly dawned on her that she'd unknowingly bought herself a window of time, and she sighed deeply. Train time. Great Malvern to Paddington. Two and a half hours. Perfect. Time to absorb. Time to think. Friday, but in the opposite direction to any commuters. Not solitude, but a relatively quiet opportunity to get her head round the unimaginable, the impossible. As she reached the lobby her phone started ringing, the tone yelling ‘office’. Her eyes narrowed momentarily. She took the call. After what her ears had just witnessed, nothing could surprise her now. Nothing.

Chapter Forty Eight

The sounds seemed to be coming from somewhere near his feet. Two male voices gibbering in Mandarin. Slowly opening his eyes, Dangerfield saw only white. White ceiling. White walls. And as he looked towards the foot of the bed, men in white coats.

Dangerfield's whole body was aching. He tried wiggling his toes. No problem. Clenching his fists. Fine. But as he went to sit up, he thought he'd burst into flames. Dangerfield let out a loud groan and when he re-opened his eyes, a Chinese man was at his side adjusting what he assumed was a morphine drip. The other man was standing over him.

"Good morning!"

The man's arms were folded, black suit sleeves protruding way beyond those of the white coat. A curly mop of ginger hair attempting a 'coup d'etat' on a grinning face.

"How are you feeling?"

The tone was far too cheerful for Dangerfield's liking. He stayed silent, his eyes narrowing.

Finkel's eyebrows furrowed as his face moved closer, his words staggered,

"Doctor… Chen… here… removed… glass… from… your… inner… ear."

Dangerfield didn't respond. Finkel exaggerated his lip

movements even further, emphasising each syllable. "Hell… o… Can… you… hear… me?"

"Unfortunately, yes!" Dangerfield rolled his eyes, "Where the fuck am I?"

Finkel paused for a moment before replying. "My heart says punch you in the face, but my head says…"

Dangerfield finished the man's sentence, "Yeah, yeah, but your head says no."

"My head says… later!"

Dangerfield couldn't help smiling, regretting it instantly as pain surged across his face.

"Although, even if I did punch the crap out of you, it wouldn't show. Your face is already busted to hell." Finkel started chuckling. "Shame you lost that mask."

Dangerfield's heart plummeted as his short-term memory was triggered. *The mask... James... the drone... the leaking fuel!*

A prickling sensation rippled across his forehead.

"Cut to the quick. Tell me." *Finkel must know. Surely Wei would have told him.*

"Ah, okay, here it is. Are you sitting comfortably?" Finkel gave a wry smile. "Oh, sorry, probably not!"

Dangerfield could feel his heart beating as he tried to stay calm. *Why the fuck is he so buoyant? Gotta be good news.* He stared at the man's mouth, willing the words from it… '*Your friend is safe.*'

"You've cracked three ribs."

Dangerfield's brain floundered momentarily, until realisation dawned. He closed his eyes for a moment, breathing deeply.

"You were so goddamn lucky. If those Chinese woodsmen hadn't discovered you in that wreck on that frozen river…"

The word 'wreck' triggered an explosion in Dangerfield's head. He shot upright in the bed, the tight bindings pulling at his midriff, the increased morphine doing its job.

"The drone, you fucking idiot! What the fuck happened to the drone? For fucksake!"

Finkel turned to the Chinese doctor and patting his arm, spoke to him in Mandarin, the man heading straight for the door.

"Okay. Okay. Calm down. I was coming to that. Apparently your boss hit the roof."

"I'll deal with her. Tell me!"

"Her? She's called Edward Bulstrode?"

"FUCK HIM! FUCK HER! FUCK YOU! WHAT HAPPENED?"

Dangerfield started to growl.

"The drone's at the bottom of the East China Sea…"

Dangerfield slumped back in the bed as if his heart had seized and his lungs expelled their final breath. And as his fists clenched and the roar began, Finkel cut in, blurting out his words "…and your friend was picked up by the U.S Navy."

"BASTARD! How come it took you so long to spit that out?"

Finkel pulled his phone from his pocket and held it up, "Listen, you little ingrate. This is virtually burnt out! I've practically lost my fricking voice from talking to Langley all fricking night! If my boss hasn't already cleared my desk, then my career with the CIA is definitely on the goddam line!" Finkel started jabbing his finger in Dangerfield's face. "And why? Because of you and your goddamn private jolly! Thanks Finkel! Thanks very fricking much!"

Dangerfield stayed schtum, as he let the news sink in. The ecstasy of relief washing over him he found staggering. He could feel his eyes begin to well up. James was alive. Job done.

Finkel was still talking as he left the room. But Dangerfield barely took a word in. He caught something about 'back in forty-eight hours if I've still got a job' and what sounded like, 'a fricking travel pack under the pillow'.

Dangerfield reached for the morphine drip, opening the tap as far as it would go. And as he unwrapped the bandage around his head he thought about Bulstrode. *So he swapped the fucking chip…* He was picturing Bulstrode's face, and then the mask he'd nicked from Professor Hammond's 'cabinet of curiosities'. He could see Bulstrode's crumpled face folded in a drawer in the kitchen of his flat in Whitechapel.

Chapter Forty Nine

Sarah Watling held her phone to her ear.

"Sarah, it's Katie at switchboard. I have a journalist asking for you. I've tried to direct her to the FCO, but she's insisting it's a Grade Seven, Category One call."

Watling looked up at the ceiling and sighed. "Katie. How long have you been with us?"

"Six weeks."

"Ok. We don't have a grading system for incoming calls. Forward the call recording to Sheila, head of training, immediately. And now I'm going to hang up. I've got a train to catch."

"Oh no, sorry, but she sounded pukka. Said she was from The Guardian newspaper."

Something triggered in Watling's brain. "Did she give a name?"

"Yes. Elizabeth Green."

Watling crossed the lobby, nodding towards the security desk and slipped through the doors of the MOD research centre.

"Hello?… Hello?"

"Ok, Katie. Put the call through."

Chapter Fifty

Even though she'd closed the door, Liz could still hear The Spinster from her office, bellowing orders, his broad repertoire of management skills ranging from yells to threats. But she couldn't stop smiling. Her brother was safe, and presumably on his way home. She couldn't wait to see him. James and his smiley face. Her twin. The one and only constant in her life.

Simon's voice was getting louder, closer. She quickly placed the framed photo of herself and James down as her door sprang open, and covered the W.H.O. logo at the head of a report that she'd been reading. And, although her laptop screen could only be seen from where she sat, she still instinctively clicked on the previous tab in case Smith somehow spotted The Roxburgh Institute's name.

Smith started to address her, but suddenly turned and yelled back down the corridor, "Have I got to spell it out? I want it on my desk in thirty minutes."

Liz recognised the two familiar voices trying to protest. Smith cut across them, "I don't give a shit! In that case, on my desk, twenty minutes."

Liz remembered the first time he'd barked at *her*. It was week three into the job, five unbelievably long years ago. After she'd patiently waited for him to complete his enraged monologue, completely unfazed, she'd replied calmly, 'Simon…' and looking directly into his eyes, 'it's

OK… I was bullied as a child too.' He'd faltered and frozen, his carpet yanked. And when he'd attempted to speak, she'd said, 'You cannot bully *me*, Simon. There are two exits from that dark tunnel, you become a bully yourself, or you stand tall and head for the light.' He'd continued to stare, mouth agape. And then he'd welled up. Outed. Exposed. And for five years they'd maintained this unspoken understanding, of this shared experience. A virtual bond. Smith had treated it almost as their private joke. It was a rare occurrence with Liz, but whenever Smith did raise his voice to her, she'd roll her eyes, and his retort was always, 'Ah, got your bully-proof vest on, I see.'

"Hey, thought I'd have a quick catch up." Smith threw himself in the swivel chair in front of Liz's desk, and went with its spin.

"Sorry, Simon. Got a meeting in West London at eleven. About to head off."

"Anyone exciting?" Smith grinned, but Liz clocked the veiled interrogation, the prying behind his expression.

"Sadly not. But need validation on something."

"Fact-checking, huh?" Smith's nodding was exaggerated. "So, Liz…" Smith's grin reappeared. "…there's a rumour going around the office that you've met someone at last."

"OK… that's a bit left field. Maybe you'd better do a bit of fact-checking yourself."

"That's my Liz. Forever elusive." Smith began to spin in the chair like a child. "So how about the fact…" teased Smith, continuing to spin, "…that the collective take is that you visited the Lost and Found Office yesterday."

"Eh?" Liz shook her head and gestured for him to hurry up. "I'm going to be late, Simon."

"To collect your smile."

"Aha! Funny. No, some good news came in yesterday. That's all." Liz stood up to leave. "But on a darker note, I gather several South American countries are refusing to play ball with the IPCC if the Amazon wild fires return this year and I'm—"

Smith immediately cut across her, "I've got Williams looking into that. Anything fresh on Greta Thunberg? I'd like you to focus—"

"I'm on it," Liz lied. "Sorry, but as I said, I'm going to be late." She closed her laptop, grabbed the papers off her desk, and headed past him. Smith was still spinning in the chair. Liz turned and grinned as she stepped through the door. "You just sit there and have fun. There're some balloons in the top drawer. Help yourself! Oh, and if you don't mind, lock up after, would you. There's a good boy." She winked, and hit the corridor.

Chapter Fifty One

Sarah Watling pulled her front door shut more firmly than usual, took comfort from the harsh click of double Chubb locks, and set off at pace for the Underground Station.

Fifty metres from her, his focus on a shop window display, an agent turned his phone's Track App on, which instantly triggered the live-link to Bulstrode's computer.

Bulstrode had been anticipating this for the two hours he had been sitting at his desk, but the reality of the Track icon springing onto his screen caused a wave of electricity to streak across his forehead. All other tasks yelling for his attention suddenly faded into the background. Despite reading unrelated messages that continually flashed onto his computer screen, he absorbed little. His attention was continually broken by irregular updates through his left earpiece, as the agent pursuing Watling detailed her journey across London, her exit from Ladbroke Grove Underground Station and then her progress up Portobello Road past the street market's bustling stalls. From new tat, to hot food, to fruit and veg, and finally old tat.

Bulstrode had given his secretary strict instructions. No phone calls. No visitors. No coffee. And yet he had never felt so on edge. How the hell had Watling prised this one open? This project had been ring-fenced as Inner Sanctum Only.

The agent's deep monotonous voice could have put a

night owl to sleep, but when Bulstrode heard him say, "Target entering the Blue Door café," Bulstrode felt as if someone had tasered his brain. He attempted to manipulate his own thoughts. Justification mode. Watling was going to embarrass him. Roxburgh mustn't find out. Wipe the slate. No choice.

*

Relieved to be out of the heaving London Underground, Liz flashed her debit card to open the barrier at Notting Hill Gate Station. As she climbed the stairs, she checked her watch. Late. A little.

Sarah Watling had chosen the venue, having refused to talk over the phone. Perfect. That suited her too. She could have conveyed her brother's message there and then, but the relief of knowing he was safe had taken the edge off any urgency she felt.

Besides, like every other journo, she always preferred face-to-face. Far more productive.

Even by the age of six, Liz's mother had predicted she'd become a journalist. 'My little nosey angel,' Liz remembered her Mum affectionately calling her. Always asking questions. And never '*Are we there yet?*' This morning, she had a million questions. Her journalist's hat was pulled firmly on and meeting in the flesh gave her the opportunity to analyse Watling's body language and facial expressions. Like an inbuilt lie detector, a litmus test of truth.

A hundred yards down Pembridge Road she turned left

into Portobello Road. Mid-morning on a Saturday and the street market was fit to burst; tourists from all corners of the earth crammed together taking selfies and group photos at every opportunity.

Watling had said eleven o'clock at the noisy, bustling Blue Door cafe. Sit as near to the centre as possible, so that their voices would be lost in the melee.

On any other day it would be a simple ten-minute walk, but market day meant crowd-dodging. Weaving in and out, Liz avoided the tourists as deftly as she could, ducking and diving to avoid photo-bombing anyone.

As she approached the crossroads with Westbourne Grove, the pedestrian crossing turned red. Keeping interviewees waiting wasn't her style, so she darted between two slow-moving black cabs. The pavement behind the street stalls presented the path of least resistance, and so Liz stuck to it, imagining Watling would already be there.

She had honed her key questions for Watling on the Tube journey over here and was running through them in her head when her phone buzzed. Pulling it from her pocket, she read the text, *'Orange beret. Window seat, on right. It's heaving!'*

*

Looking across at the only other passenger in this section of the airplane, Dangerfield saw an Egyptian mummy. The guy was out-of-it. Motionless. Wired up. And completely bandaged.

Dangerfield tried to sit upright in his galley bed, without disturbing the support bandages gripping his rib cage. Good. No serious pain. He only felt a twinge as he reached for his buzzing phone.

"Where the hell are you?" Watling demanded.

Even with seeing her face, he wasn't clear if she was angry or relieved.

"This is a first. You never do FaceTime."

"Double-checking it's really you. GCHQ said you'd snuffed it."

"Not yet."

"Well, your location chip definitely died."

Dangerfield noticed Watling was only glancing at his image on her phone's screen, her attention clearly elsewhere.

"Where are you?" Watling pressed. "You've been off grid for days. I thought we had an agreement?"

"Yeah. We did." Dangerfield clocked the stewardess heading towards him. "I mean, we have."

"For fuck's sake Charlie." Watling shook her head, her sigh audible. "I hear Green's out."

"Really? Who told you that?"

"His sister. I'm seeing her any minute."

"He probably got bored of eating dog meat."

"Stop shitting me, Charles. Your chip died in northern China. In Dandong. That's on the border with North Korea."

"Okay. Okay. No more shit." Dangerfield nodded. "I hope you're sitting down… cos I've got big news."

"Go on."

"The missile guidance chip that Green uploaded? Someone swapped it. There *was* no ground zero. In fact the opposite. It's given Kimbo's missiles a kick up the arse. If push comes to shove, he could probably nuke a billion people."

"I see."

"Are you getting this? Someone swapped the chip."

"Yes, I get it."

"Sounds crazy but…" *Why the hell isn't she surprised*? "Well, get this, the finger's pointing at Bulstrode."

"Right."

"Where's the shock and awe?" Dangerfield gave a brief thumbs-up to the stewardess, and when she had passed, looked back at his phone. Watlings' face was closer to her screen.

"You know I never gamble Charles, but, I'll see your big news, and raise you by six billion."

*

The latest alert to hit Bulstrode's screen made his heart-rate jump. He turned the volume down on his left earpiece as the new incoming fed into his right. As the agents' now-dimmed monotone voice quietly detailed Watling taking the window seat in the Blue Door café, the louder feed caused Bulstrode's breathing to quicken.

Dangerfield? The bastard's supposed to be dead! And Watling… the bloody bitch! Thinks she can use my agents against me?

Bulstrode glanced again at the location dot on his screen

and as he listened in to Watling's and Dangerfield's conversation he twiddled his thumbs, and they rotated faster and faster until he heard Watling use the words *six billion*.

*

Liz's progress along the pavement came almost to a standstill, so she slipped between two street stalls and into the road. Looking across, over the heads of the crowds, there it was: the Blue Door cafe.

The signage above the cafe's door was in the style of shabby chic, the paintwork on the frontage, de rigueur.

Charming, Liz thought. Inviting.

*

"Six billion?" asked Dangerfield. "What are you talking about? Pounds? Euros? Dollars?"

He waited for Watling's reply. Despite the hum of the aircraft, he thought he could hear his heart beating.

"You're very feint. You on a plane?"

"You got it."

"To London?"

"Yes."

"Charles, I need to meet you."

"How about HQ in two hours?"

"No. Bulstrode thinks you're dead. Let's keep it that way."

"With you on that. So where are you now? There's a lot

of noise."

"Your favourite coffee shop."

"You're in Portobello?"

"Hang on. Think that's her outside. Yes. Green's sister's here."

*

Bulstrode's left ear picked up '*device hidden in café toilet*' and '*good to go.*' His right ear heard '*Green's sister's here.*'

He closed his eyes. His heart was pounding. *Two birds with one stone*. He could feel a vein throbbing in his neck, his pulse raging.

*

Dangerfield gripped his phone and stared at Watling's face. "So what's this earth-shattering news of yours?"

Watling ignored him, talking quickly. "I need to see the PM urgently. And I need *you* there. As a witness."

"Witness to what?"

"Our diamond watch investment. It's just paid dividends. In diarrhoea."

"Don't tell me Bulstrode saw the bill?"

"No. You know I kept him outside the loop on that one. But fuck it, Charles, we're all about to be shat on."

"The whole department?"

"The whole planet!"

*

The market stall that stood between Liz and the Blue Door cafe was engulfed in tourists, fascinated by the display of religious icons on sale. Buddha looked quite content, Liz thought, sitting next to Jesus, pinned to a gold painted wooden cross, with a Star of David hanging above his head.

Bulked up by thick winter coats, the crowd prevented her from slipping through the gap between stalls, to access the cafe.

A bright blue sky had been stretched over London since seven o'clock that morning, punctured by a white piercing sun. But the temperature, even four hours later, was near freezing.

Liz could make out a woman wearing a bright orange beret in the window seat of the café, talking on her phone. Pulling her coat collar up, Liz tried edging past her first obstacle, a morbidly obese man in a duffle coat. "Excuse me," Liz said cheerfully, placing her hand on the fat man's shoulder as he reached for a large silver crucifix. "Coming through."

*

Bulstrode repeated Watling's words in his head, 'The whole planet.' He had heard her words so clearly. There was no doubt. She knew everything.

"Now," said Bulstrode quietly. His eyes stayed closed as he increased the volume to his left earpiece. He could feel sweat beads forming across his forehead. “NOW!”

Momentarily both links were lost, the silence lasting forever, until he heard the agent’s words “Fucking hell! Thought this was supposed to be a controlled device?”

Bulstrode turned off both links. Several more seconds passed before he opened his eyes. And when he did, he gasped for breath. And began to shake.

*

“What do you mean, ‘the whole planet’? You’re not making any sense.” Dangerfield’s screen went blank. “Hello?… Hello?” He pressed re-call several times, but *Call Failed* kept appearing. So settling back in the galley bed, he listened to the hum of the aircraft and waited for Watling to call back.

*

Liz didn’t understand the fat man’s attempt to reply. She was unable to comprehend anything. Her brain burst at the same time as her body jolted violently backwards.

The organic wall that stood between Liz and the bomb shoved everything in its wake. As her head flew backwards her field of vision consisted of glittering fragments of the cafe’s window exploding into the street. Catapulted through the air with bodies spinning around her, she couldn’t feel anything. Not the tarmac scraping at her knees, nor the glass embedded in her arm.

The fat man she’d been trying to squeeze past had his

hand on her shoulder now. Shuddering two metres behind her was the rest of his body, propped up against a parked car, his torso half embedded in the driver's door. His mouth was opening and closing. But no words came out. And no air went in. In minutes, his lungs, crushed by the blast wave, would be the death of him, as air bubbles from disrupted alveoli entered his vascular system.

The thunderous crack of the explosion drifted quickly away but thick clouds of light grey smoke continued to billow upwards from the cafe's open frontage. The bomb had thrown bodies like rag dolls into the air. Liz's had been dumped in the centre of the road, landing in the foetal position.

As the seconds dragged their heels, a jumble of thoughts began racing through her mind, competing for attention. Her brain was on overload, failing to process anything. She pictured God throwing his toys out of the pram. A carved wooden Buddha sat next to her head, partially blocking her view. Other religious icons lay broken amongst fragments of coffee cups. And limbs.

Liz's focus fell on people who had been further from the café. They were running, limping and crawling, their mouths opening and closing. And yet all were silent. Everything was silent.

Trying to get on all fours, Liz felt like she was choking. Reaching inside her mouth her fingers scrabbled around but she couldn't find anything solid to pull from her airway. Panic sparking, she began to raise herself up, until a hand fell from her shoulder and slapped the road, a stub of bloody bone poking from its wrist. She stared at it.

Transfixed. And then heaved. Wave after juddering wave of vomit hurled over the Buddha's head.

Panting for breath, Liz stayed on her hands and knees with her eyes closed, heart pumping wildly. A stench, a creeping stench, was entering her nostrils. Despite the smell of vomit barely a foot away, an even stronger chemical smell dominated. Evil and pernicious, it took a foothold on her senses. This was her trigger. Fight or flight.

Liz climbed to her feet, her eyes opening to total carnage. A woman was crawling out of the cafe where the door used to be. She edged across the pavement towards Liz on hands and knees. Her vast shoe collection, neatly displayed in her bedroom in Italy, would no longer be of use to her. One side of her head, a perfectly controlled blonde bob, the other a red matted mess.

Liz looked up and down the road. In every direction, the crowds were no longer a single endless cluster, but hundreds of fragmented individuals bumping into each other, pushing and shoving. Others were hugging friends and family members, their arms wrapped around them, trying to guide them away from hell on earth. Liz could feel a weird pressure coming from inside her head. Why was everything still silent? She pushed a finger in each ear and a muted mesh of yells and wailing began to break through. Her thoughts were refusing to focus, but her body was telling her to move up the road, back the way she had come. As she made her first steps Liz scanned herself. Her jeans had become fashionable with splits at the knees, except for the red seeping through the blue. *Fuck. My favourite trousers*. Both arms felt intact, although her thick plum puffer jacket was ripped and blood-spattered. She had to get away. Keep moving.

As Liz headed up Portobello Road, numerous sirens wailed out of sync, their mash-up adding to the frenetic atmosphere. Horrified faces confronted Liz wherever she looked; some sobbing uncontrollably, others more resolute, determined to lead people away from the source of evil. Some shopkeepers and stallholders were desperately trying to direct the crowds out of the roads and onto the pavements as emergency vehicles attempted to navigate their way to the source of the vast plume of smoke contaminating the innocent blue sky.

Reaching the junction with Westbourne Grove, Liz realised her hearing was beginning to recover. Local police were yelling at vehicles to keep moving as drivers rubbernecked left and right, sensing a calamitous event from the faces and unnatural grouping of the crowds. Suddenly something pulsed against Liz's upper thigh. A minute earlier and she wouldn't have noticed. She instinctively reached for the source and felt the familiar shape of her phone in her pocket.

Chapter Fifty Two

"You okay, Love?"

"Hey, George. Yes. Thanks." Liz made straight for the escalator and as she stepped onto it she heard the scrape of a chair behind her. Turning, and travelling backwards, she called down, "Really, George, I'm okay."

George was on his feet and reaching for his walking stick.

"I may be old but I'm not blind."

"George. Really. I'm fine. I'll come and see you in a bit."

Liz turned her back on him and climbed with the escalator. Near the top, she could hear raised voices. The usually quiet corridor was alive with activity; journalists and support staff were dipping in and out of open glass offices, a loud hubbub of energy in the air.

"Did the Spinster call you back in? Thought you had a meeting somewhere?"

"Tom, you know I don't hang about. Box ticked. Done and dusted." Liz noticed he was staring at her knees. Although the blood peeping through her ripped jeans had dried, the trail down her shins was stark against the light denim. "Tripped over in the bloody underground."

"Hurt?"

"Looks worse than it is." Liz started down the corridor with Tom on her heels.

"Guess you heard about the terrorist attack in Portobello. Less than an hour ago. Bastards!" exclaimed Tom.

Liz felt a shudder down her spine and swallowing hard, tried to focus.

"Is that what this is all about?" She gestured to the sources of frenetic activity as she made for Smith's office.

"You'd think, but God no. The Spinster's spoken. Hard to believe, but something even bigger's going down."

"What's that then?"

"It's weird. One minute he's screaming for copy for Online, the next he's on lockdown. Disappeared into his office and now nobody can get through to him. I mean no-one. Not even Mann. Crazy or what?"

"But what sort of copy is he chasing?" pressed Liz.

"Stuff about North Korea. Said he wants a headline about Kim Jong being dick-less."

"What?"

"I know! Wants him portrayed as a frightened child. No balls to retaliate if the U.S do a first strike."

"Why the hell the provocation?" Liz went to head off, then suddenly changed her mind. "Anything else?"

"Apparently Reuters are claiming he speaks fluent English. Reckon as a teenager he attended a private school in Switzerland under a pseudonym…" Tom looked left and right, and lowered his voice, "and on the back of that, somebody with BrightLight Agency has dug up a Swiss prostitute, surprise-surprise. And sixteen years after the event she is claiming Kim Jong's got a micro-penis."

Liz snorted, "At least the Spinster's got his headline."

"Ha! Oh yeah!"

"Thanks, Tom." Liz blew him a kiss and increased her pace. As she approached Smith's office his P.A.'s head popped up from behind his screen."

"Hey, Liz."

"Rupert." Liz nodded at Smith's door.

"Can't go in there."

"What do you mean?" Liz saw his cheeks instantly redden.

"He said nobody. Not even the Queen."

Liz threw him a look.

"He… he's serious. I think there's something wrong with him."

"You only just realised? Relax. It's only The Spinster for God's sake."

"He didn't only raise his voice. He… threatened me."

Liz took a deep breath. "Is there anybody with him?"

"No."

"No? Then he can be disturbed." Liz reached for the door handle.

Rupert yelped, "Please don't!"

Liz stopped abruptly and looked him straight in the eyes. "Hey, chill. I'll take any blame."

Rupert jumped to his feet, but Liz already had the door open. She closed it behind herself to the sound of Rupert's groan, and turning round, found herself in an empty office.

She skirted Smith's huge desk and tried the door to the adjoining boardroom. Locked.

"Simon?" Liz could swear she heard something. A rustling? A foot scrape? The source of the sound seemed so close. As she moved behind Smith's desk and reached for the handle of a plain white door, her focus fell on two open pill bottles and a half empty bottle of gin beside his computer keyboard.

"Simon?" Liz pushed the door open. Three feet from her sat The Spinster, slumped on his private toilet. The first thing she noticed was his eyes. They were huge. Staring. Demented.

"Fuck! Sorry!" Liz turned to dive back into Smith's office, but the words 'Help me' stalled her.

The turbulence in Smith's face, the panic in his eyes, froze Liz to the spot. As she took in the ghastly sight, Smith spoke again, his mouth dribbling, wet detritus hanging from his lips and chin. "Nobody mentions the diarrhoea, the vomiting and seizures."

The man started coughing, the detritus becoming airborne. "I was hoping to quietly drift away."

Barely an hour had passed since hell hit Portobello Road and yet, somehow, the shock Liz felt now was even more intense, more personal. She started to shake.

"They didn't tell me who she was meeting." Smith's eyes seemed to be getting even larger, his voice unrecognisable.

"Who's she? Who's they?" Liz reached out for the wall to steady herself.

"Mann. He told me Portobello was a terrorist attack, but it was the *crank* that had to dominate all headlines."

"The 'crank'? Simon, you're beginning to sound like one. What's the crank?" Liz raised her voice. "And what the hell tablets have you taken?"

The only response Liz got was the continuing look of shock in Smith's eyes.

"Fuck it. I'm calling an ambulance. Simon, listen, what tablets have you taken?"

This time, Smith's words were incoherent mumblings. Liz crashed back into the office and grabbed the nearest pill bottle. Empty. The label read Nembutal. Her advanced First Aid training said, 'Shit!' She reached for her phone and rang Emergency Services. As she waited for pick-up she could hear Smith continuing to ramble.

"Crank it. Crank it now. Bloody crank it."

What tripped the switch Liz wasn't sure but when her synapses connected she felt a wave of nausea wash over her, exactly as the operator picked up. She dived back in front of Smith.

"You thought I was dead! That's what you were on about. So I was a target and you thought I was fucking dead!"

"Hello? Emergency services. Which Service do you require?"

Liz ended the call. And roared, "You knew and you let me go!"

After retching fruitlessly, Smith started to whimper. "When Mann told me I'd need a new senior reporter… that you'd gone… I felt so lonely. You know, Liz, it *is* lonely at the top. So bloody lonely." His shoulders started to shake as the sobbing took hold. "You won't believe me, but you're the only person that's ever meant anything to me."

"Oh, I believe you." Liz shook her head. "Meant so much that you didn't warn me!"

"I did try," said Smith quietly. He was looking down, his gaze on the soiled underwear around his ankles. "I didn't want to lose everything I've fought for. My status, my entire career… and you see… they threatened to take it all away."

Without a thought, Liz's journalistic instincts pressed the record button on her phone.

"They've hacked my computers… and phones… for years. Private stuff. Everything. The good, the bad and the really ugly."

Liz let Smith talk; several times having to bite her tongue, fighting not to interrupt the man's shocking monologue. *What the fuck could he be talking about? 'Population realignment'?* The only breaks in Smith's spilling of his guts, were his failed retch attempts. And as the man continued to off-load, tension and anger grew inside her, her hands clenching tighter and tighter. When Smith eventually went quiet, Liz watched him struggle to get to his feet until his left leg started shaking violently. He slumped back on the toilet seat, his foot now continuously slapping the floor. In slo-mo, Smith turned his head, and all Liz wanted to do was punch him.

"P… please…" Smith's voice wavered as he tried to reach for the toilet handle, but failed, his arm falling back in his lap. "Flush me… flush me away." Smith suddenly clutched his stomach with both hands. "Oh God! My guts!… Jeeze… hurts… so… bad."

Liz put her face in her hands. "I can't get my head round this. It's madness! How many billion?"

As Smith reached out towards her, one hand remaining

clamped to his stomach, Liz stepped back instinctively. And retrieving her phone, she pressed recall. "Ambulance."

Smith started chuckling inanely. "Crazy, huh? I can help cover up the impending murder of six billion people, but if it's one single person, you, I can't deal with it. What's that all about?"

"Overdose… Nembutal… Simon Smith… 90 York Way, Kings Cross, London… victims' on the first floor."

"You were my snapping point Liz. The bridge too far." Smith's breathing was raucous. "I can't go on. I don't want to go on."

Liz leaned forward and looked straight into Smith's yellowed eyes, regretting it instantly as his breath hit her nostrils. "You may not have a choice."

Smith missed the retort, his throat rattling as he spoke, his voice wavering in and out of coherence. "My dear Lizzie, you would not survive one minute in my head… no one could…" Smith again tried to raise himself from the toilet but slumped abruptly back. "…the monsters won't leave me alone."

"I told you to join a running group." Liz could feel a wave of tension flooding through her and kicked the toilet door, its 'bang' against the wall synchronizing exactly with her yell. "Fuck! I've got to get this out there." She pictured the faces of Rufus at the BBC and Reuters' Pete Campanelli.

"Not possible." Smith could only growl his words out. "Mann controls everything. CNN. Fox. BBC. Reuters. Facebook…" He began choking again. "Shit… this pain!"

Liz realised Smith was slipping forward a moment too

late. She guessed his lungs were collapsing, the rasping sounds alien as he fought for his final breath. Plunging forward, his face hit her Doc Marten's, his teeth grinding on her left toe-cap, white saliva flowing over black leather. Stepping back into Smith's office, Liz stood the two pill bottles back up. Both were empty. "Bye, Simon," she whispered. She made for the door, not waiting for a reply. She knew there wouldn't be one. As she pushed the door open, she stopped her phone recording, cleared her throat and flicked through her contacts list to 'D'.

Chapter Fifty Three

"How does that feel now?"

"Amazing."

"Really?"

Dangerfield could see disbelief in the woman's eyes.

"But then I am a masochist."

"What's a masso kiss?" A smile began to play on her lips. "Bet it's something rude."

"I'll show you next time."

Reaching for his trousers, Dangerfield swung his legs off the bed. The woman was nodding as she wrote on her clipboard.

"You're healing fast. Just try not to do anything too strenuous for a few more days."

"Yes, nurse." said Dangerfield. "By the way, I'm running low on morphine."

"I really think you'll be fine."

"It would help. Do your best," said Dangerfield, as he opened the door to leave. "I'll be here for a bit. Got a meeting downstairs in ten."

"Ok, I'll talk to the Doctor."

*

Sitting in the clinic's private lounge, adjacent to the entrance foyer, Dangerfield pulled his phone out and scrolled down his newsfeed.

Notting Hill Bomb…9 deaths…23 injured.

Prime Minister offers condolences to families.

Wildfires surge across Amazon Rainforest.

Taliban backtracks on promises to G7.

North Korea threatens revenge for US insults.

All the while he kept glancing through the one-way window onto the clinic's reception desk located at the rear of the foyer. Having been engrossed in their computer screens until this point, Dangerfield clocked the two male receptionists suddenly rise and, looking more like weightlifters, make straight for the clinic's entrance. He stepped into the foyer just as the two opened the clinic's door onto Wigmore Street and stood either side, like a pair of nightclub bouncers. Dangerfield realised that their screens must have been linked to street-cams because a minute later a black Jaguar XJ pulled up abruptly outside.

Stepping into the clinic, John Blake nodded at each bouncer before catching Dangerfield's eyes.

"Charles."

"Sir."

Dangerfield gestured for Blake to join him back in the lounge, and with the door closed, offered his hand. He noticed Blake's grip was excessive and the man didn't seem to want to let go.

"So," Blake paused, sighing deeply. "Sorry to hear about Sarah. Tragic. Nightmare."

Dangerfield held his tongue. He'd hardly slept. Anger had been brewing in him all night, and that morning, when he'd climbed out of bed, it had spewed out of him like a volcano. It was the second time in his life he'd lost all control. The second time that no-one was safe in his presence. He could replace his trashed kitchen, but Sarah? Who the hell could replace her? And he couldn't believe he'd cried. Cried? Fuck! That was rare.

He looked Blake in the eyes. "She was a good woman."

Blake nodded, remaining silent.

"I wasn't convinced you'd show," said Dangerfield.

"Really? Well, it appears a lot of shit's been going on behind my back."

"What do you mean?" said Dangerfield. *You and me the same, buddy.*

Blake snorted, "Over several years of meetings with your department, your name's cropped up a few times. And Sarah's used several adjectives to describe you. Perceptive, inventive and dedicated, I remember. I don't recall *stupid* being one of them."

Dangerfield shrugged. "Maybe your memory's going."

A weak smile flickered on Blake's face. "Let's cut to the nub." He gestured to the two nearest armchairs. "It appears there's a herd of elephants in the room. And whereas nobody's been talking about them, I couldn't even see them."

Dangerfield nodded, "And the nub?"

Another weak smile. "Ok." Blake paused for a moment. "The reason I agreed to meet you is that I got a call from Sarah, a few hours before..." Blake didn't finish his sentence but sighed deeply. "She told me things that she couldn't possibly have known. Unless of course your department has somehow had me tapped?"

Dangerfield pointed at his own wrist.

"What? Really?" Blake shook his head, pulling at his watch strap. "Was it just the two of you in on this?"

"Pretty much," said Dangerfield.

"And Bulstrode?"

"Err… no. I believe not."

Blake frowned.

Dangerfield continued, "Sarah and I go back a long way. We know things about each other."

"Meaning?"

"I've a…" Dangerfield coughed. "I have a problem with trust. But Sarah's one of the few people on the planet that I'd entrust with my life."

Blake leant back in his armchair, "You know, that's weird, but I had exactly the same feeling the first time I met her."

Dangerfield could sense a sea-change in Blake's demeanour, the look in his eyes wistful. He listened as Blake recounted the crux of the Roxburgh's plan. For several minutes he had to fight to remain silent as the unbelievable fell from Blake's mouth. And he remembered to nod like a journo every few seconds, the psychological lubricant to any interviewee's tongue.

As Blake bled, Dangerfield noticed the man's eyes beginning to water. And when Blake mentioned his daughter, Emily, he couldn't help but reach across and put a hand on the man's shoulder.

"Hey, we'll think of something."

Blake leapt from his armchair. "You think I haven't already wracked my brain for every possibility?"

Dangerfield knew to let the man rant.

"If I open my mouth, I'll be labelled a conspiracy theorist! They don't get much credibility, in case you hadn't noticed. I'd be portrayed as a nutcase. They'd probably do a David Icke on me. Or worse, a Princess Di! These guys control the world's mass communication systems. They can twist anything and everything. Fake News… Fuck News… Fucked!"

Blake began pacing up and down, his voice rising, "You'd think the Prime Minister of a country would have some fucking say in things. Some control. Some iota of power."

"John. Calm down. It's OK. We need some perspective here."

"Perspective?" Blake leaned against the lounge's door. "Here's some perspective. Who's to say that Earth and the planets are nothing more than specks of dust floating in space, atoms in an infinite Universe, that our tiny little minds can't even comprehend a fifth dimension let alone fifteen or maybe twenty dimensions? Maybe…" Blake paused for breath, his hands flying madly, "Maybe—"

"OK… OK." Dangerfield stood up and grabbed Blake's flailing arms. "You're losing it, mate. If we can just get back to our poxy little fragment of dust for a moment, and ask ourselves, what the fuck are we going to do?"

Chapter Fifty Four

Liz pulled Smith's office door closed behind her to be confronted by Tom and Rupert, standing like two obedient dogs that had awaited their master's return, and were now fully expectant of their reward, a doggy treat in the form of some juicy goss on their boss.

"Well?" said Tom.

"I've called an ambulance. Think it's too late though."

"WHAT?" the two screeched simultaneously.

"Overdose." Liz checked her phone again. *Fuck's sake! Come on, Charlie. Answer!*

"But… what should we do?" stammered Tom, the most animated of the two, his arms held out, imploring more information.

"You can't do anything for him." Liz looked from one to the other for a moment, her mind flicking through ideas. "OK. I'll tell you what to do."

The two nodded instantly, their eyes wide open.

Liz gave up on her phone call and was about to speak when she clocked a woman crossing the corridor, and before she could disappear into the opposing glass office yelled at her. "Jess!"

Liz focused again on the two guys. "Look. You were right Tom. Something big *is* going down. Something fucking huge. I want you to gather everyone in the conference room, right now. Every journalist, tech support, every editor. Actually, *especially* tech support."

"But… what about the Spinster?" Rupert whined.

"The Spinster's gone. I've called Emergency Services. There's nothing you or I can do now."

Rupert started for Smith's door but Liz held her hand up. "Rupert! The man's history." Liz raised her voice "In fact, we're all about to be fucking history if you don't jump to it."

Tom and Rupert looked at each other before being nudged apart, as Jess, the Online Editor, slid between them.

"Jess. Sorry, but I need an urgent word. Right now." Liz shooed Tom and Rupert in the direction of the glass offices, calling after them. "Everyone… Conference Room… Five minutes. Go, go, go!" And as the two headed off, their faces stricken, she yelled after them, "And don't forget tech support."

Liz sighed deeply, "OK. Jess. Here it is. This will—"

Jess interrupted. She was looking at Liz's shins. "Tripped and bumped your head?"

"No, seriously, Jess, I need you to listen. Look, I don't know how the fuck to put this, but there's a plot to depopulate the Earth. Sorry, not a plot… not a plot." Liz took a deep breath. "Fuck it… there's an actual programme that, as we speak, is being unleashed."

"Liz, I'm a little busy now. "Jess put her hand on Liz's arm. "Just need to see Simon."

"He's dead."

"What?"

"Look, Jess, I know we haven't always seen eye to eye, but, by God—"

"What do you mean, dead? I saw him first thing. He briefed the whole team."

Jess dived past Liz and yanked Smith's door open.

Liz called after her as the woman disappeared into Smith's office. "I've rung 999." Turning, she saw familiar faces heading towards her. "Hey, guys. Sorry but urgent shit happening. Straight into the Conference Room. Now, please."

"Like the old days!" one guy quipped.

Liz yelled out, "Take the far door. Simon's access is locked."

As more staff arrived, Liz ushered them along the corridor.

"Think I'm going to be sick!" exclaimed Jess, as she lurched out of Smith's office and then shuffled alongside Liz to avoid two paramedics hurtling towards them with George hobbling behind, his face creased in pain.

"In there! Through the white door on your left," Liz barked at them.

"How long since he overdosed?" demanded the first medic.

"No idea. An hour? Sorry, I don't know." Liz took Jess's arm. The woman was covering her mouth, but Liz could tell from her eyes alone that she was clearly in shock.

"Jess. Come with me." Liz headed off after the last of the staff, as they filtered through into the conference room. She was pulling Jess by her arm. "Listen, like I said, I know we haven't always seen eye to eye, but you *have* to hear this. I need you on board."

The conference room could seat twenty, but even with

everyone standing, it was packed. Liz pulled the nearest chair out and stood on it.

"OK, everyone. In a nutshell, Simon has taken his own life. But…"

A sea of exclamations filled the room.

"Listen… listen… listen." Liz waved her arms to try and quieten everyone. "Yes, it's a shock… BUT, what he revealed to me, just before passing, is that this latest inoculation campaign is part of a terrible, terrible plan to spread a brand-new man-made virus that's been designed to wipe eighty percent of humanity off the face of the earth."

The outcries of surprise were matched by those of mockery.

"Where's your tinfoil hat," yelled one guy.

"I've seen the movie!" yelled another.

"But we *survived* Covid!" called his neighbour. The three glanced at each other, grinning and shaking their heads.

Liz let out a sigh. "It's unbelievable, yes. It's crazy, yes. But…"

Peter Thornbright, an Associate Editor, had unlocked the door linking the conference room to Smith's office, and opening it, stood back to reveal one of the paramedics clutching his phone to his ear, his face flushed, sweat droplets across his forehead. The medic shook his head at them as he waited for connection. His colleague joined him, a defibrillator dangling from his hand. A multitude of gasps filled the room.

"Fucking hell!" exclaimed Thornbright. "I'm calling the

Home Office." He pulled his phone out. "Actually, bollocks to that, I'll get Clements. If the Defence Secretary isn't in the loop…"

Thornbright's reaction resonated across the room, faces becoming sterner, agitated.

Scanning the faces surrounding her, Liz's focus fell on the Online Editor standing beside Thornbright, Jess Maitlin. She was pulling her phone from her pocket.

Liz waved her arms for quiet again. "Listen. Everyone. Quiet a second. We have to get this online now! Jess, I need you to upload copy immediately. And directly. Not through Editorial Control though. Mann must be kept in the dark." Liz looked down at two young guys standing immediately in front of the chair she was perched on. "Can we do this? Can we sidestep E.C.?"

The techies shrugged, "Depends," said the skinnier of the two.

"You are kidding right?" rasped a voice from the far end of the conference table. "This is a wind-up, huh?"

Liz ignored the man and addressed the room. "The provocation of North Korea… of Kim Jong himself, is what these arrogant bastards want. They want him as a scapegoat. A cover. Simon's dying words referred to 'the crank'. His instructions from Mann were to crank up the humiliation of Kim Jong. Haven't you noticed a multitude of stories on Kim Jong dominating Facebook feeds this morning? You surely can't believe North Korea doesn't pick up on social media?"

"Who are these bastards?" called the guy at the back. "Not Dan Brown's bloody Illuminati again?"

"Who are these bastards?" repeated Liz. "Who controls the Banks? Who controls the Media? Who owns the Cloud?"

"Just because you're paranoid, doesn't mean people aren't out to get you," chirped Thornbright, holding his phone to his ear.

Liz looked expectantly at the two lads in front of her.

"Ahh… well… we've never tried uploading direct. In fact, I think our contracts state that all copy *has* to go through the Editorial Control Department."

Liz was about to speak when Thornbright, standing beside Jess, suddenly yelled.

"Are you talking to Mann?"

Jess Maitlin jumped as thirty pairs of eyes fixed on her.

Thornbright tried and failed to snatch her phone from her.

"Bloody idiots, the lot of you!" said Jess. "This is such crap! Liz Green's got you eating out of her hand."

As the volume in the room started to rise, Liz felt her temperature rise with it. Everyone began to throw their penny's worth in until Thornbright yelled out even louder.

"WHAT THE FUCK?" He was staring at his phone.

"Phone died?" said one of the tech boys.

"No internet whatsoever!"

"Mine's died too."

His colleague opened his iPad. "Weird. No internet at all. Nothing!"

Chapter Fifty Five

The roar from the Rolls Royce engines had reduced to white noise for Dangerfield and Blake as the RAF Airbus crossed the Pacific Ocean. The turbulence was occasional, the talking constant. They agreed that the first part of their plan was easy. To fly right into the belly of the beast. The second part, Dangerfield commented, also involved flying, "Entirely by the seat of our pants".

Dangerfield stood in the plane's toilet cubicle, staring at his reflection in the mirror. And then checked his watch. "Four minutes… not bad," he thought, out loud. A final smooth around his neck and he was back in the aisle. Blake's eyes met his. He stifled a smile as the man's forehead furrowed like a scrunched newspaper, his eyes attempting to pop out of their sockets.

"Bulstrode? What the…" Blake was stuttering, his head flicking left and right. "Where the hell…"

"Hey, John, chill. Just testing," said Dangerfield. Blake's mouth was agape. "Wanted to make sure it's convincing."

"SHIT! Bastard!" Blake held one hand to his chest. "Almost gave me a bloody heart attack."

"Don't die on me yet. We've a job to do," said Dangerfield as he settled into his seat, relieved to see how shaken Blake now looked.

"Makes me wonder who else I've spoken to in error,"

said Blake. "Where exactly does it stop? Not a full rubber bodysuit I presume?"

Dangerfield could see Blake scrutinising his neck, when his phone beeped.

"Oh, hang on, it's Liz Green. You know her? From the Guardian," said Dangerfield. Blake nodded.

It was Dangerfield's turn to frown as he listened to her. Blake tried to read his expressions, then gave up, gazing out of the plane's window as it skimmed above the cloud line.

"Sarah? Of course I've heard. Saw it on GCHQ's Intraweb… WHAT? You were there?... But you're OK?... Thank God!" Dangerfield then listened, biting his tongue, as Liz related the terrifying news she had just learnt from her boss in his final throes of death. "Why don't I sound surprised?" He caught Blake staring at him again, and rolled his eyes when Blake frowned aggressively at him with a finger to his lips. "No, you're not going mad… Yes, of course I believe you. I remember arguing with you at college that most conspiracy theories are usually based on *some* degree of logic." Dangerfield then returned Blake's frown. "No internet?... Most of Europe?... Fuck! Listen, Liz. Just spread the word, however you can." He watched Blake shaking his head. "Liz, I can't tell you where I am, but trust me, I'm on it!… Yes, yes and yes. Does that answer your question?"

Dangerfield ended the call and looked up at Blake.

"Superb bit of PR. She's confirmed exactly what you've shared with me. That the latest virus the W.H.O has been warning us about is actually man-made, and will be distributed via a counterattack to North Korean nukes. The

West comes out as heroes for appearing to defend the world, whereas North Korea takes the blame for 'the Mother of all Pandemics'."

"Oh yeah, it's clever stuff!" yelled Blake angrily. "Except the cost's coming in slightly over budget… at six billion lives!"

While the plane completed its journey, the two men grappled with different ideas, interrupted only by their encrypted phones beeping endlessly as U.S. media alerts sprang on their screens. As the plane began its descent, Dangerfield read the latest one.

"Fucking hell! Roxburgh's propaganda onslaught is relentless. Apparently the U.S. President's just called Kim Jong, a fat-faced blob of jelly!" Dangerfield shook his head. "Wow. So, obviously there can't be any mirrors in The White House."

"Except some of what the Roxburgh's are putting out there is true. Kim Jong's prison camps are hell on earth, and millions of his people *are* starving," said Blake.

Dangerfield shook his head, and then looking out of the window, noticed the iconic skyline of Boston coming into view.

During the plane's final descent, the two men were at last silent. Blake had his head in his hands while Dangerfield watched the storage facilities and aircraft hangers slipping silently behind them.

*

"Mr Blake!" The security guard stared through the

round greeting hole in the bullet-proof glass and then flashed a glance at his colleague. "We weren't expecting you, sir." He looked again at his colleague. "At least, I don't think so?" The guy focused on his computer screen for a second. "Nope. You're not on this morning's list."

"Jeez, Jed, it's the Prime Minister of Great Britain. Let the gentleman in." The other security guard reached over Jed's shoulder and pressed a button. "Sorry, sir."

The gates to the vehicle entrance remained closed, but a wide pedestrian entrance began to slowly slide open.

Dangerfield smoothed his hand under his chin, tightened his tie and stepped out of the cab.

"Mr Bulstrode! Sir. We weren't expecting—"

"Jeez, Jed! Is there an echo in here?"

Dangerfield joined Blake at the steel gate beside the security office, nodding at the men through the glass.

"Not listed on your system, did I hear?" said Dangerfield, impersonating Bulstrode's accent. He pursed his lips and slowly, solemnly, shook his head. "A rare blip indeed." He then threw a huge grin at them, "So I'll forgive you this time! How are you both?"

"Good, sir. Good."

Dangerfield winked at the camera trained on his face as he stepped through the gate. Blake had paused. He was gazing at the sign headed *The Roxburgh Institute*. Dangerfield thought he caught a wistful look in the man's eyes, whose focus seemed to be drawn to the last on the list of departments: *The Life Extension Clinic*. Reaching back, Dangerfield put his hand on Blake's shoulder and spoke under his breath. "Hey. Let's do this." And giving Blake a weak smile, "The security here is shocking."

"Like I said on the plane, that's only stage one," said Blake.

"I know, I know. Just keeping it light." Dangerfield shifted his grip to Blake's arm.

Again, Dangerfield could swear Blake had a faraway look in his eyes. A definite look of detachment.

"Confidence is key here. Confidence buys everyone," said Dangerfield firmly.

Blake raised his eyebrows, "You're preaching to the converted."

"OK, got it." Dangerfield nodded a smile. "You do your job, I'll do mine."

As they made their way down the short glass tunnel to the main entrance to the huge Roxburgh complex, Dangerfield pointed through the glass and across finely mowed lawns to an enormous bush in the shape of a question mark. "I'm no garden freak, but I do love a bit of topiary."

"Well, I'd settle for a close shave today," said Blake.

"Close shave? Just get me in front of them. I'm going to slit their throats."

Blake stopped momentarily. "Aren't you even slightly nervous?"

"Nope. Anyway, we discussed it. This is our best option."

"Only option," Blake whispered. "We're not even in the building yet."

"Like I said: confidence. If a politician of your calibre can't blag his way into a building…" Dangerfield again put his hand on Blake's shoulder. "How many TV interviews have you blagged your way through?"

Blake smiled, "True."

Double doors slid swiftly open to the sound of a robotic upbeat. 'Welcome!'

Dangerfield strode in, nodding to the security guards that stood either end of a wide desk. He threw a greeting to the three front-of-house girls. "Behaving yourselves?"

"Yes, Mr Bulstrode. Of course, sir," chirped the central girl.

Dangerfield clocked her name badge as all three attempted to blind him with clinically white smiles.

"Who are you here to see today, sir?"

"The usual crew, Candy… the usual crew."

"Oh, I'm afraid Mr Roxburgh is in a private meeting."

"Don't we know! We're supposed to be in it. Over twenty minutes ago." Dangerfield shook his head. "But your guys weren't at the airport to collect us."

"Oh, I'm so sorry, sir." The girl looked distraught. "I'll look straight into that…" She glanced at her colleague who immediately reached for the phone.

"Jed's already onto it," said Blake quickly.

"Ah… right. Okay. I do apologise Mr Blake, sir," said Candy, her colleague's hand wavering momentarily before returning the handset to its cradle. "I'll let Mr Roxburgh know that you've arrived."

"Robert already knows. Just messaged him." Blake made a point of looking at his watch and then at Dangerfield, "We'd better go straight through." And then grinning at Candy, "We don't want the wrath of the Rox, do we?"

"No, sir," said Candy, her smile beginning to return.

Blake pulled his phone out and thrust it at her. "Log these in and we'll head straight over. Life Extension Building, right? Level Four again?"

"Yes, sir."

As Candy's colleague pulled a small lockable tray from beneath the desk, Dangerfield retrieved his phone from his pocket. He was about to pass it over, when he felt it vibrate. The text from James burnt into his retinas. He read it again.

Dangerfield turned his phone off and handed it over, whispering to Blake

"We're too late…"

Chapter Fifty Six

Robert Roxburgh was floating. Transcendental. It was a state he often sought. And more recently craved. His mind would focus on whiteness, blankness and then nothing. And in this state he felt detached. Not a true Out of Body Experience but an O.B.E. that he manufactured. He'd named the process Hyperfocusing. He not only felt detached from his body, but from the world. Looking at the Earth from afar he became the man in the moon, gazing back at it hovering in the vast blackness of the universe. It was his way of getting into role when big decisions were expected of him. If anyone asked, he referred to it simply as 'getting a perspective'. His father had introduced the notion to him, 'You'll only be able to see the whole picture, Robert, if you stand back'. He'd loved his father. Always fascinated by the fantastical yarns that he'd shared. 'Look after the planet after I've gone,' he'd heard him say innumerable times towards the end of his life. To be entrusted by his father to manage humanity, to guide and encourage the human race on an upward trajectory, was an honour.

But of late, these past two or three decades, things had been getting out of hand. Scientists from multiple disciplines agreed that humanity was in serious trouble. Some claimed the situation irredeemable. What had been an honour had become an onerous duty. A poisoned chalice. A pressure on him that was growing. And multiplying like a cancer.

The argument for biting the bullet had grown steadily stronger and stronger. Turning a blind eye or treading water were no longer options. An absolute and literal deadline had arrived. Right here. Right now.

Earths ecological system and energy resources could no longer sustain humanity's bloated population. And worse, this over-population was the fundamental cause behind the impending climate disaster. Impending? The disaster was already here. Standing on everyone's doorstep. Banging and thumping on every door. Shouting, 'I'M HERE!'

So, what did we do?

We opened the fucking door.

His own Institute had concluded that desperate times would demand desperate measures. The Extinction Rebellion crowds were sure to concur. But their angry demonstrations proved insufficient. So, we gave Extinction Rebellion a 'motivational' kick up the arse, by starting wild fires across the globe, and claiming that it was purely the horrendous results of the greenhouse effect. Karl Lynx had suggested Australia, Singh had insisted on California. Whereas Mann had demanded both… 'and let's throw in Turkey and Greece'. A regrettable mistake, although done with the best of intentions.

Roxburgh felt so guilty for not acting earlier. He hadn't exactly had his head in the sand, but he'd only been nibbling at the problem, not confronting it head on, as his father would have done, 'Forgive me father, for I have sinned.'

Roxburghs' colleagues occasionally referred to him as 'Procrastinator in Chief.' And he couldn't argue with that. Inaction had exacerbated the situation. In fifty short years the World's population had tripled. Tripled! Why the hell hadn't he acted earlier, to stem the tide of births that was now drowning humanity's progress?

'Survival of the fittest? Bullshit!' his father had told him. 'The dinosaurs were the most powerful creatures on Earth. So where are they now? Left to itself, Nature would screw things up. Kick Nature in the balls, son. Show it who's boss. Nature has no brain, no logic. Nature doesn't care about anyone or anything. Nature's just another word for fate.'

Robert Roxburgh had lived his 'three score and ten' years. And the rest. His father's parting words before his final breath were, 'See you later, son.'

Now he was going to press the button. He had to press the button. And hopefully, in the nick of time.

As Roxburgh opened his eyes, his father's voice echoed in his ears, *Cometh the hour, cometh the man.*

"Robert. We were about to wake you," said Mann, smiling.

"I wasn't sleeping," said Roxburgh looking at his disciples sitting around his boardroom table.

"Shortest power nap ever!" called Stepanov from the opposite end of the table.

The gentle thrum of gases pumping into the glass-walled boardroom was piped music to Roxburgh's ears. An elixir of life. Optimised levels of oxygen and nitrogen, without all the impurities, delivered at a controlled pressure, for well-being and enhanced brain function.

"The Crank was successful!" said Mann excitedly, "Kim Jong's exploded in the last few minutes. Perfect timing. I knew I had him on the cusp. The Defense Chief says multiple launch plumes have been detected. Nuclear warheads attached. Even he was shocked at the number of missiles launched." Mann looked around as he thumped the table. "Power of the Media huh! Our algorithms' gone and done it again! Information management at its best."

The response he received was muted. Only Paul Keats, the U.S. President nodded.

Solemn faces stared into the grain of the mahogany table. Except for Ashram Singh's. He'd barely looked up from his laptop since he'd stepped into Roxburgh's transparent boardroom.

"Robert," Singh called out, his eyes not leaving his screen. "Our pre-programmed Worldwide News Bulletin has just hit all channels. Announcing North Korea's nuclear attack. Nothing more for forty eight hours." Singh looked up for a second. "Total blanket until the new pandemic's done its job."

Keats opened his mouth to speak but Singh raised his hand. "And I confirm…" Singh's fingers raced over his keyboard as he spoke, "…that as of this second, the rest of the World now joins… Europe, in a complete… global… internet…" He slammed his laptop closed. "…shutdown!"

Reactions around the table varied. Some glanced at each other before folding their arms, their stares returning to the polished tabletop. Others sat back in their chairs, crossed their hands behind their heads and stared up through the transparent ceiling. George Ascot, the centenarian, jolted awake momentarily before continuing his gentle snore.

"Totally down?" asked Roxburgh.

"Yes. Totally."

Roxburgh began to speak, "Gentlemen—"

"Well… virtually."

Roxburgh felt a flash of exasperation. "Please don't confuse us, Ash."

"Well, everywhere except China. Their national intraweb's proved to be a bigger Russian doll than we thought. Looks like they've got a security wall hidden within a security wall within a security wall." Singh started shaking his head. "I don't get it. We were sure we'd circumvented every layer."

Mann interrupted, "Don't worry about it. Who the hell speaks Mandarin outside China?"

Vadim Stepanov chipped in. "The time is now, Robert. The Defense Chief's waiting for your go-ahead. Only you can give it."

Keats shifted in his chair. "Look. Do we really have to go through with this? Maybe we could just nuke North Korea. You know, take Kim Jong out of the equation. We'd wipe him away in a second."

Mann leapt to his feet and yelled at Keats. "Have you been paying fucking attention? We've created a situation here. A window. A fucking window of opportunity to kick the human race into the future. Grow some balls, Keats. Grasp the fucking nettle with the rest of us."

Keats also stood up. "Calm down, buddy. I get it. I do get it. It's now or never."

"What? It's not now or never!" said Mann, spittle flying from his mouth. He walked up to Keats "It's NOW. Got it? It's fucking now! *Never* is when I put you in office again."

"Hang on, the voters—"

Mann raised both his arms in exasperation. "THE VOTERS?" He swung round, gesturing at everyone in the room, "WE put you in power. Your career was over. Ashram here rigged the vote in your favour. I, personally, brought you back from the dead. My social media platforms breathed life back into your rotting, bloated carcass."

Keats started to speak but Mann exploded again. "Oh fuck!… you believe it was you, don't you? You, who won the people's hearts. You, who actually won the vote. You're the man, right?" Mann laughed. "I could make you the man… the man all Americans would kick into deep space in a nanosecond." Mann shoved his finger in Keats's face. "I could do worse than have you killed. How about a quarter of a billion Americans seeing you as the Devil? A paedophile? A necrophile? A tax dodging racist? Take your pick." Mann turned to Roxburgh and lowered his voice. "A little bit of news can go a very, very long way."

Roxburgh looked around the table. All eyes were on him now. His chair scraped loudly as he stood and, reaching for Keats' arm, he addressed him directly. His voice was calm but firm, "Paul. How many times have I run through this with you? *Not* pressing the button will lead to far more suffering in the world. Climate change will affect food production. There'll be starvation on an unprecedented scale. Constant and widespread border disputes. More refugees. And when—"

"But I'm not happy with this option."

Roxburgh let go of Keats' arm, and with exasperation edging his tone, said "Obviously none of us are *happy* with the situation, but…" Roxburgh let out a huge sigh. "How can I put it more simply?" He glanced at the ceiling. "Try looking at it this way. A bit of a positive spin if you like." Roxburgh patted Keats' stomach. "Humanity itself is morbidly obese. We're bursting at the seams."

"But—"

"Listen!" Roxburgh held his hand up. "We're going to be leaner, and therefore stronger. Fit to face the future. To Build Back Better!" Roxburgh gestured to Keats to return to his seat. "Paul. Remember why we're here. We are leaders. The ones with the strength to make decisions. Others have the freedom to go about their daily lives, blinkers on. We have the bigger picture in our sight. We *are* the bigger picture."

Another scrape of a chair and Stepanov was also on his feet. "The geographic distribution of the virus is all mapped out. The research for that alone took over a year. The selective immunisation campaign took nearly two years and the development of our single-blow virus has taken our microbiologists a lifetime to perfect. I repeat, the time is now." Stepanov glanced at his neighbours, "We are all agreed. There *is* no discussion anymore. Its distribution *must* go hidden under cover of our retaliatory strikes. North Korea's attack and our 'defence' *must* coincide if we're to place the blame on Kim Jong." Stepanov leaned across the boardroom table and pushed the internal phone towards Roxburgh. "Robert, save your breath, the train's leaving the station."

"We're committed now, Robert," said Mann. "We've successfully provoked North Korea. Their nukes are about to kill hundreds of thousands anyway."

Roxburgh took a deep breath and, looking around the room, met each man's eyes. '*Cometh the hour, cometh the man.*' He gestured for those standing to sit, and picked up the telephone. "Gentlemen, to each and every one of you sitting around this table, I congratulate you. For your fortitude… you have my gratitude."

Roxburgh held the receiver to his ear, "To the future of Mankind."

Chapter Fifty Seven

An unnatural silence accompanied the two men as they crossed the lawns to the white cube-shaped buildings of the Life Extension Clinic. Dangerfield looked across at Blake, who appeared disturbingly calm. His eyes were closed.

"FUCK!" The word exploded from Blake's mouth. "Hundreds of thousands dead. Possibly millions!"

"My sentiment exactly, but what's done is done," Dangerfield said. "We can't go back in time, mate."

Blake looked at him, but stayed silent.

"We're into damage limitation now. It's the 'response'… the virus distribution that we need to try to avert."

Blake let out a huge sigh as they stepped up to the mirrored entrance door, "Fuck it!"

The incongruous smile that sprang onto Blake's face told Dangerfield only one thing. Dangerfield smiled too and the two men grinned at their reflections. And waited for the mirrored door to open. About two nanoseconds.

"Thank—" Blake's greeting to the guard was cut short.

The guard was reaching for the internal phone when Dangerfield head-butted him. As the guard crumpled backwards, groaning loudly, the phone flew from his hand, clattering behind him. He was scrabbling to his feet when Dangerfield booted his head like a soccer ball, his groan fading to silence as unconsciousness kicked in.

"Sometimes I hate this job," said Dangerfield looking across at Blake. "Poor fucker's only doing his job."

"So how do you cope?"

"I do *my* job."

"Think of the bigger picture," Blake reminded himself, wistfully. "There's always a bigger picture."

As they passed the elevator doors, Dangerfield rubbed his forehead. "How's the mask looking?"

Blake didn't answer.

Half way up the first flight of stairs Dangerfield started punching the air.

"What the hell are you doing?"

"Picturing some of the evil fuckers from my past."

Dangerfield clocked the concern on Blake's face.

"Preparing myself. Getting myself angry. Sympathetic nervous system. Adrenaline's an instant pain killer."

"For physical pain, maybe. Anything for emotional?" Blake said, looking away.

"Focus, John. We're here to cut the snake's head off. We'll let the rest of the planet worry about its writhing carcass."

As the two men climbed the third flight of stairs, the building felt deserted to Dangerfield. Ghostly, clinically clean, the air sterile. And until they reached the end of the corridor on the fourth floor, they hadn't seen a soul, other than their own reflections that now stared back at them from a second mirrored door.

A loud click initiated its opening.

"Jesus Christ," said Blake, staring into a room within a room. "Looks like The Last Supper."

Dangerfield scowled, “Except there are twelve Judases.”

Chapter Fifty Eight

George Ascot, comfortably into his second year as a centenarian, woke up. He opened his eyes, blinked repeatedly, rubbed them and blinked again. As he acclimatised to his surroundings, remembering who he was and where he was, he looked around the glass boardroom. Something caught his eye. His bumbling voice seized the attention of every man in the room.

"Hello? It's B… B… Blake," Ascot pointed between Singh and Keats, his finger wavering as he spoke. "Wh… why's he crying?"

Of Ascot's audience of eleven, Mann's head swivelled the quickest. "What the hell?"

Blake, his face alight with tears, pulled on the handle of the glass door. Locked. "It's Emily. My daughter. They've given her forty-eight hours. You promised you could help."

Dangerfield couldn't believe his ears. He put his hand on Blake's shoulder and whispered, "You fucking genius!"

Blake banged on the glass door with both fists.

"Try yelling," said Dangerfield. "Maybe they can't hear you."

"Emily needs your help. I need your help. She can't wait another minute."

Dangerfield scanned the men inside the glass chamber. The only one standing, looked shocked, his mouth open, arms limp at his sides. The telephone in his hand grabbed

Dangerfield's attention. A tall guy with bleached blond hair, leapt to his feet and started looking wildly around at his colleagues, gesturing furiously at them. The two nearest men, seated with their backs to Dangerfield, were a man in a turquoise turban and, turning as he stood, a man whose profile Dangerfield recognised instantly. The US President.

As Dangerfield glanced to his left, at a steel rack of gently vibrating equipment, Blake yelled again, his wet face pressed up against the glass door.

"Please! Some of you have children."

"Ignore him, Robert! First things first…" Mann pointed at the phone still in Roxburgh's hand, "…the Defense Chief?"

Roxburgh nodded, his tongue playing against his lower lip.

From the far end of the table came the deep, firm voice of Karl Lynx, who'd sat quietly since the beginning of the meeting. "Timing is everything, Robert. We *cannot* afford to miss this opportunity. You've always insisted that this is *our* decision, that we're a collective…" Lynx gestured to Roxburgh to use the phone. "…and we'll still have over a billion people left to manage. In forty eight hours, these surviving remnants will need someone to blame for their anguish, and North Korea's their perfect go-to, somewhere to direct their anger. It's key to their healing process. We've gone through this a thousand times."

"Of course. Yes." Roxburgh's voice was quiet and calm. "But what's Bulstrode doing here? I didn't invite him."

"No idea!" said Mann. "Probably thinks he's on the

team. Or wants a ringside seat at the main event." Mann's laughter was harsh. "Ignore him. He's not important now."

Roxburgh began to raise the phone to his ear. "But we *do* need Blake. He's vital to us, to the aftermath. Do not let any of us underestimate for one second the horrendous aftermath."

"The storm before the calm," threw in Singh.

Roxburgh ignored him. "The masses that remain, our survivors in Europe, will need a figurehead. A leader. Someone that appears stoic, empathetic."

"If the remnants of Europe need a leader with empathy then it's simple," said Mann. "Let his daughter die."

The bangs on the glass were constant and loud, the voice quieter but clear. "Please help my Emily. You promised."

Keats looked out at Blake. Blake was on his knees, his hands held up in pitiful prayer. "She's only got a few hours to live. I'm begging you!"

Keats made for the door.

"Sit down, Keats. Your career's over. You're finished," Mann said.

"Really? In that case, I've nothing to lose." Keats's fist clubbed the side of Mann's face so hard the man fell to his knees, hovered momentarily, and then keeled backwards at Keats's feet. Keats yelled as he stamped on Mann's crotch. "That's for Democracy!" And, against the turmoil of chairs scraping and the mass of exclamations, screwed his heel around. "No more nepotism from you!" Keats hit the emergency door release.

Dangerfield kicked the door open, barged past Keats and sprang at Roxburgh. Throwing him to the floor,

Dangerfield ripped the phone from the man's hand and pinned him down with a knee on his neck.

Roxburgh tried pulling and pushing at Dangerfield's thigh, spluttering and croaking, his arms now flailing in desperation.

As Dangerfield went to stand, he felt two hands around his own neck.

"Bulstrode!" Ashram Singh's scrawny fingers clawed at Dangerfield's face. "What the hell are you doing?"

Flying backwards, Singh collided with two of his colleagues. And as he looked at what lay in his hands, let out a high-pitched scream.

Mask ripped off, face stinging, and with anger rising, Dangerfield punched Roxburgh, the man's expensive teeth rattling in their hardware.

"That's for Sarah!"

He punched again and again, separating porcelain from titanium. "That's for the billions of innocent people you were about to murder. You arrogant… fucking… bastard!"

Roxburgh gasped for breath, his bleeding, toothless mouth gaping. Dangerfield smashed the phone against the transparent wall and thrust its broken carcass down Roxburgh's throat. "Choke on it, bitch!"

The volume rose in the glass boardroom as a shouting match ensued. Against a herd of yelling men, Keats and Blake held their own until a splintering crash stopped play. Fragments of wood flew in every direction as Dangerfield smashed a chair over the boardroom table. He pulled Blake, with Keats following, out of the room and slamming the thick glass door shut, rammed a chair leg through the door handle, wedging it hard against the glass wall.

Dangerfield yelled, "Fuck you, you fucking fuckers!" throwing a double V-sign at the men.

"Nicely said," Keats nodded in agreement.

"Couldn't have put it better myself," added Blake.

"Saw it on a T-shirt," said Dangerfield as he studied the machinery vibrating beside the door. He turned the oxygen tap down and the nitrogen tap to max, "Oops!"

Heading down the corridor to the stairwell, the sound of fists pounding on glass faded into the distance.

"Are we just going to leave them to die?" asked Keats.

"Paul, from one puppet to another, cut your strings. It's your country, your laws, you decide," said Blake, quickening his pace. "Gotta go. Needed elsewhere."

Dangerfield crouched to wipe his bloodied hand on the elevator carpet and looked up at Blake. "When your days as a politician are over, I guarantee you've another career waiting for you."

"Really?"

"God, yes. On the stage. That performance! Your acting was a masterclass."

As Dangerfield stood up, Blake sighed deeply. His shoulders began to shudder, his voice breaking.

"I wasn't acting."

Chapter Fifty Nine

"Bit chilly, huh?"

Without turning to look at the woman, Dangerfield nodded, "Love it."

She stamped her feet, the grass dampening the sound. "Well, I suppose it can make you feel more alive."

On the far side of the graveyard, beyond the pall-bearers, beyond the tight cluster of mourners, a row of hawthorn trees were in blossom and fit to burst. Beside them a yew tree stood, its gnarled trunk firmly planted, its territorial claim eternal.

This time Dangerfield looked at her. "Would you excuse me?"

A man had appeared beside the ancient yew, low hairline, high frizz factor. And a quizzical expression.

Carefully picking his path between gravestones, Dangerfield skirted the ceremony, pausing momentarily when a contrail caught his attention, its chalky white line tracking across the broad blue sky.

He nodded at two undercover security staff as he passed the wooden gated entrance and climbed the grassy bank to the yew.

"Of all the graveyards, in all the world, he has to walk into—"

"Shut up, Finkel." Smiling, Dangerfield shook his hand. "Missed you too. How're the ribs?"

"Marinating nicely."

Dangerfield stood beside Finkel, and the two men continued watching the proceedings from afar, talking quietly.

White surplice making him stand out from the crowd, the vicar's voice fell in and out of earshot, the only other sounds, the random trill of a thrush and the distant thrum of a jet plane. Dangerfield looked up at the sky again. The contrail led directly towards the sun.

"I love this," said Finkel, his voice muted, almost a whisper.

"Love?" said Dangerfield.

"Oh, don't get me wrong. Obviously sad as hell. Jeez, she's only a little child, but… I dunno, I mean, it seems so right, you know… personal. No paparazzi, no bigwigs, just family and a few—"

"No bigwigs? Don't you recognize your own President and his wife standing over there?"

"OK. Well… OK. But Keats's wife's behind that. She's met Sandra and…"

"Emily."

"Yep, Emily… more than once. Has quite a bond, which you can understand given…" Finkel cleared his throat. "Anyway, Keats's over here for the Emergency Agenda Meetings. China's Premier flies in this eve—"

Dangerfield interrupted, "Really?"

"Sorry," Finkel threw a weak smile, "Jetlag."

"I imagine the world'll be kissing China's feet now."

"For intercepting Kimbo's Nukes?" Finkel nodded. "No doubt."

"They were hardly gonna take their eyes off their neighbour from hell, were they?" said Dangerfield. "So is it Keats or the Chinese Premier that explains your presence in the U.K.?"

Finkel shrugged. Dangerfield looked at him and waited.

"There's something I want to run by you," said Finkel hesitantly. "Anyone at MI6 fluent in Swahili?"

"The CIA's got its own agents in Africa," said Dangerfield under his breath, "Anyway, I'm kinda grounded until the fan stops spinning."

"Fan?"

"There's shit everywhere. Your Federal Bank's being taken into public ownership. That's fucking massive. The W.H.O's under investigation. And tomorrow's Global Emergency Meeting in London, as you'll know, has a worldwide one-child-only policy at the top of its agenda."

Finkel nodded. "The elephant in the room finally kicked the drinks cabinet over."

"More like a great woolly mammoth stamped on the giant Internet Hub."

Finkel looked at Dangerfield, "It's total chaos out there."

"I like a bit of chaos," said Dangerfield. "People wake up, man-up and say what they really mean."

"In that case…" Finkel smirked, whispering, "you're the most…"

The vicar stopped talking and the whole graveyard became silent. Not an eerie silence Dangerfield thought, but as if nature had held its finger to its lips; a 'shush' to leaf flutter, to birdsong, to the breeze.

Across the graveyard, the pall-bearers were lowering Emily in her tiny coffin. Everyone was staring at their feet. Except Dangerfield. He was looking up. Focusing on his breath, as it entered and left his body. The blue sky had another guest. Not a contrail this time, but a cloud. A small white cloud. Its shape reminded him of something. Was it a four-leafed clover? He watched as it slowly morphed. Nope. It was definitely more like a teddy bear. But with only one leg.

Thank you, readers!

I hope you enjoyed reading DEADLINE as much as I enjoyed writing it.
If you would like to write a review on Amazon, that would be absolutely wonderful! Please use the appropriate link:

In the UK:
https://www.amazon.co.uk/dp/1739923405/

In the US:
https://www.amazon.com/dp/1739923405/

Sneak-Peak!
Jon Gray's next novel, coming 2022:

LIFE LINE

Prologue

Charlie Dangerfield pressed his phone to his ear. And waited. From his balcony he noticed a seagull, eight storeys below, take flight from a warehouse roof and head west towards Whitechapel.

"Hey, Stupid, the sea's the other way."

"I'll hang up then."

Dangerfield laughed, "Liz! Sorry, I was talking to a bird."

"You might need to revise your chat-up lines."

"Funny. Listen, I've a job for you."

"Really? You screwed up again?"

"Ha ha! Come on, give me a break." Dangerfield watched the seagull fly out of focus. "How about The Flower Market, eight o'clock?"

"Columbia Road? Ok, make it eight-fifteen. I'll jog there. Meet you at the Ravenscroft end."

"Sure. I know a great bakery nearby."

"Good. I'll be starving. So what's this about?"

"Can only tell you details face-to-face. But journalists are being bumped off. And it's about as dark a story as you could imagine."

Chapter One

Jimmy Schneider's expression flicked to 'earnest' as he stared at his reflection in the camera lens. "How's this?"

"That's perfect. Hold it. Counting in. Three… Two… Shit! Hang on, Spider. Moped alert."

The camerawoman stepped from behind the tripod and covered the lens. The bike screamed past, the sound raucous and mechanical, a swirling tail of dust lingering long after it had disappeared from view.

"For God's sake, Emma. We're in the middle of nowhere. That's the third one!"

Emma shrugged, "They're like buses."

"Take Eighty-Three?" said Schneider, smiling.

"Ha ha," Emma held her hand up, "Take Three. Come on Spider. We can do this."

Anyone with spindly limbs might have taken offence, but Jimmy Schneider embraced his nickname. He'd always liked spiders, had loved the film 'Charlotte's Web', and now, having established a career within the BBC as an investigative reporter, thought that 'Spider' reflected exactly the tenacity he had demonstrated in getting to where he was today. Most investigative reporters remained behind their desks. He had managed to forge a career in front of the camera.

This was against all the odds. Media channels liked safe bets, using tried and tested presenters of popular game shows to move into travel shows. Celebrities loved it. Paid-for 'jollies' around the world? Easy peasy, lemon squeezy.

But Schneider knew the score. Suggest a bit of danger, a little risk, unsafe hot-spots in the world and the celebrities' agents wouldn't even pick up the phone. Endanger their fees? I don't think so!

Anger had helped fuel Schneider's motivation to succeed. At every big media event when subjects-studied or colleges-attended arose, and it invariably did, Politics or Classics at Oxford or Cambridge were the common denominators. Schneider's Sociology from Surrey University only got derision. Once, an arrogant arse had publicly joked that above every toilet roll dispenser on the Surrey campus were the words 'Sociology Degrees. Please take one!'

Yeah. He'd take 'Spider'. Ten years on and he'd built himself one powerful web of contacts.

"Three… Two… One… Rolling!" Emma gave the thumbs up.

"Today, I'm thirty miles from Georgetown, the capital of Guyana. And feeling a little tense. This is the area that became known as Jonestown, after James Warren Jones moved here. Jones was an American religious cult leader, responsible for the mass suicide of…" Schneider let out a short, pre-planned sigh, "...almost one thousand people in a single day." And then, gesturing around him, "Yet the people who live here today…"

Emma knew the script. The poignancy of the intro's final line needed a close-up. Schneider's facial expressions were renowned, so revealing, so powerfully engaging for the viewers that they felt compelled to watch on. It was the documentary's money-shot. Schneider had had a specialist drama tutor to hone his range of facial poses. Adjusting her camera, Emma zoomed in.

From behind a second lens, some fifty metres away, another woman played with its zoom feature. Schneider's face filled the frame. She could see his lips moving but was too far away to hear a word he spoke. Zooming again, she captured his left eye. Azure blue against bright white. Beautiful. But orders were orders. Compressing her shoulder firmly against the palm tree, she held her breath. And pulled on the trigger.

About the author

Jon Gray's final school report read: 'Gray's too preoccupied with existential questions.'

True. Questions about life and love. And outer space. So he climbed on trains, planes, and bicycles and escaped to the brightest jungles in Malaysia and the darkest recesses of China. And somewhere that he never, ever wants to go to again.

Now a Post-Graduate in Conflict Resolution from the University of London and having worked with refugees from across the planet, some of the dirtiest windows on the world have opened, fuelling the imagination every writer thrives on.

Based in rural England, Gray pictures the best, fears the worst, and hopes for revelation.

Website: www.jongrayauthor.com

Printed in Great Britain
by Amazon

73750705R00215